PRAISE FOR

Love, Suburban Style

"A highly enjoyable and uplifting love story, just made for summertime reading."

—**RomRevToday.com**

"Great read. Suddenly home-sweet-home just got more interesting."

—*Quick & Simple* **magazine**

"Rita Award–winning author Markham . . . provides a fast-moving, ultralight take on single parenthood, suburban sex, and keeping up with the soccer moms that should please chick-lit fans."

—*Publishers Weekly*

Bride Needs Groom

"A passionate story."

—**RomanceReviews.com**

"TOP PICK! Markham once again brings you laughter and tears in a wonderfully heartwarming romance."

—*Romantic Times BOOKreviews Magazine*

more . . .

"Contemporary fans will love this."
—Rendezvous

"Romance fans will enjoy this lighthearted romp."
—Affaire de Coeur

"A heartfelt love story . . . sexy and funny."
—TheRomanceReadersConnection.com

"A fun romp."
—HarrietKlausner.wwwi.com

Hello, It's Me

"A sweet romance for hopeless romantics."
—Booklist

"Touching and humorous . . . Markham's novel will keep you glued to the page."
—Romantic Times BOOKreviews Magazine

Once Upon a Blind Date

"Breezy, sumptuous fun."
—Booklist

"Humorous . . . lighthearted . . . an altogether fun, fast read."

—*Romantic Times BOOKreviews Magazine*

The Nine Month Plan

"A wonderfully touching romance with a good sense of humor."

—*Romantic Times BOOKreviews Magazine*

"Exhilarating . . . Markham sends Cupid's arrow straight to the bull's-eye with this sparkling tale."

—*BookPage*

"Markham spins a sweet . . . surprisingly bold story . . . a total fun and delightful read!"

—**RoadtoRomance.com**

Other books by Wendy Markham

The Nine Month Plan
Once Upon a Blind Date
Hello, It's Me
Bride Needs Groom
Love, Suburban Style

ATTENTION CORPORATIONS AND ORGANIZATIONS:
Most HACHETTE BOOK GROUP USA books are available
at quantity discounts with bulk purchase for educational,
business, or sales promotional use. For information,
please call or write:

Special Markets Department, Hachette Book Group USA
237 Park Avenue, New York, NY 10017
Telephone: 1-800-222-6747   Fax: 1-800-477-5925

That's Amore

WENDY MARKHAM

FOREVER

NEW YORK   BOSTON

Copyright © 2008 by Wendy Corsi Staub
All rights reserved. Except as permitted under the U.S. Copyright Act of 1976, no part of this publication may be reproduced, distributed, or transmitted in any form or by any means, or stored in a database or retrieval system, without the prior written permission of the publisher.

Cover design by Diane Luger
Cover photography by Herman Estevez
Handlettering by Ron Zinn

Forever
Hachette Book Group USA
237 Park Avenue
New York, NY 10017
Visit our Web site at www.HachetteBookGroupUSA.com

Printed in the United States of America

Forever is an imprint of Grand Central Publishing. The Forever name and logo is a trademark of Hachette Book Group USA, Inc.

First Printing: July 2008

10 9 8 7 6 5 4 3 2 1

For my friend Kathy Genett,
who knows all about loving, and losing, and
braciole . . .
For my guys, Mark, Morgan, and Brody . . .
And for Auld Lang Syne.

In loving memory of my Grandma, Antonia "Della"
Piazza Corsi,
who made pounds and pounds of fresh pasta for
countless New Year's Day dinners,
all of us crowded in the dining room with
the extra leaves in the table.
The old house is long gone, but you—and the
memories—will live on in my heart forever.

Acknowledgments

With gratitude to my editor, Karen Kosztolnyik, and Celia Johnson, Beth de Guzman, and staff at Grand Central Publishing; my agents, Laura Blake Peterson, Holly Frederick, Tracey Marchini, and staff at Curtis Brown, Ltd.; my publicists, Nancy Berland and Elizabeth Middaugh and staff at Nancy Berland Public Relations; Pam Nelson and staff at Levy Home Entertainment; Patty and Rick Donovan and Phil Pelleter at the Book Nook in Dunkirk, NY; and to my grandparents, Pasquale and Antonia "Della" (Piazza) Corsi and Samuel and Sara (Tampio) Ricotta, for the loving foundation and inspiration.

That's Amore

Prologue

What's next for Daria Marshall, then?"

"Hmm?" Daria's attention is focused not on her dining companion, George, but on the opposite end of the busy Tex-Mex restaurant, where an eighteenth-century Native American maiden is serenely sitting, cross-legged, on the terra-cotta tile amid the lunch hour throng.

She's been there since they walked into the dining room fifteen minutes ago, and hasn't moved a muscle.

"You're not really going back to LA now that you've finally made it to Arizona, are you?"

"Excuse me?" Daria shifts her gaze to her fabulous friend, who is regarding her from across the table in a typically fabulous outfit, clean-shaven cheek balanced on professionally manicured hand.

"You just finished telling me that you can't handle the traffic or the smog or the fear of earthquakes—"

"It's not *fear*," she cuts in defensively. "It's just that I was checking out paint colors on the wall of a nineteenth-floor penthouse when that last one hit a few weeks ago, and it freaked me out a little."

"Did you spill the paint?"

"Yes, and it spattered on my client's Prada pumps."

"A few drops of turpentine and Ms. Diva will never be the wiser," George says airily. As if he wouldn't go out of his well-coiffed head if anyone dripped a drop on his own designer loafers.

"Did I mention Ms. Diva happened to be in the pumps at the time?" Wincing at the memory, Daria dredges a tortilla chip through the fresh guacamole they're sharing.

"Well, no one ever said life as Interior Designer to the Stars was going to be a bowl of cherries."

"Not 'stars,' George. Star. Falling star, for that matter."

Her client, an erstwhile A-list bombshell, hasn't had top billing—or any billing to speak of—in two decades. Having exhausted her personal makeover options and face-lifted herself into a freakish perpetual wide-eyed expression, the Hollywood has-been has thrown herself into fanatically redoing her home instead.

Daria soon learned why she—a newcomer in the LA design world—landed what seemed like a plum client. Everyone else in town had either steered clear of the notorious Ms. Diva, or already been hired—and fired—by her.

Daria joined the latter list, and admits as much to George.

"I'm sure it's for the best," he says.

"Excuse me, are you ready to order?" asks the waitress, a pretty, sunburned blonde.

"Not just yet." Daria reaches for her untouched menu.

"Can I get you another round of margaritas while you decide?"

"Absolutely." George drains the few drops left in his glass.

"Not for me, I'm still working on this one."

"Come on, drink up and live a little. Bring two, please," George tells the waitress, who disappears before Daria can protest.

"Are you trying to get me drunk?" she asks George.

"You bet," he replies cheerfully. "You've been stressed from the moment you got off the plane this morning."

"I was even more stressed before I got on the plane, actually. The freeway traffic to LAX was awful."

"How long have you been in Los Angeles now?" He has to raise his voice as the mariachi band approaches their table, playing the "Mexican Hat Dance."

"Four months."

"I think it's time to move on."

"I think you're probably right, but I should—"

"Good. Be quiet and listen," he practically shouts over the music. "I have a proposition for you."

Daria sips the tequila-laced salty lime slush, shaking her head.

"What?" he asks. "You don't even know what I'm going to say."

"Yes, I do."

He sighs dramatically and waits a moment for the band to move on before saying, "It's not easy having a psychic best friend."

"I don't know because I'm psychic, I know because

you're predictable. And because this isn't the first time you've propositioned me."

"Then say yes this time, and I won't bug you about it again."

She shrugs. "Yes."

"Yes?"

"Yes!"

"Are you serious? You'll move here?"

"Dead serious." She flicks another glance at the maiden. Still there, but starting to look a little filmy.

George mentioned that this Tex-Mex restaurant borders the vast Navajo reservation. Daria wonders if there's a burial ground nearby. There's a palpable aura of sorrow about the meditating maiden, incongruous with the boisterous restaurant crowd and the maraca-shaking mariachi.

"So you're actually going to move in with me and work in my new business?" George is asking.

"Which isn't exactly up and running . . ."

"I'm working on it," says George, who is renovating an old adobe building and opening an interior design firm in the heart of Phoenix. "I should be ready to open the doors in another month if construction goes as planned. We're going to be a great team. We'll meld my southwestern flair with your eclectic design style, and—"

"I'm sure you mean eclectic as the utmost compliment."

"I'm sure I do. When can you move?"

"I think I just did," she says wryly. "I'm here now. I'll just stay. I can call Chelsea"—her roommate in LA—"and have her ship my stuff here. Most of it is still in storage anyway—the place was tiny. I can leave it there for a while."

"So you don't need to go back at all? Isn't there anyone you need to give notice to, or say goodbye to?"

Daria just looks at him.

"Oh, right, I forgot. You don't like strings, and you don't do long goodbyes."

"I don't do goodbyes at all," she reminds him, to borrow a line from her gypsy mother.

Whenever it's time to move on—and it frequently is—Daria has always gone with as little fanfare—and as few possessions—as possible. It's family tradition.

"Okay, then . . . my futon is all yours, for as long as you can stay." He pauses. "How long do you think that'll be?"

"As long as you need me—or as long as I can, anyway."

"Yeah, yeah, until the wind blows you in a different direction. I know your deal."

"And I know yours. You'll miss me when I'm gone, but you'll recover, just like always."

"And sooner or later you'll pop back into my life." He smiles. "Roommates again—it'll be just like old times."

They met a decade ago, in a New England college town as art majors, and struck up a fast friendship. Those four years—sans summer breaks—were the longest Daria ever lived in one place, making George the most steadfast friend in her vagabond life.

They've been roommates twice since graduation. The first time, she was living in Boston and took in George after he'd come out to his conservative parents only to find himself instantly disowned and homeless. The second time, he was doing grad studies in Paris and she flew over for a visit and parked herself in his flat for the semester.

"Only this time," George adds, smile fading to a warning scowl, "I hope you won't bring any of your 'friends' along."

"You know I can't promise that." She casts another glance toward the Native American maiden, but the spirit has dissolved.

"Well, as long as they're harmless spooks this time around. I can't handle the ones who get their kicks moving my stuff around."

"Don't call them spooks—it's disrespectful—and that only happened once." In Paris, the pesky spirit of a nineteenth-century dandy liked to hide George's socks and pilfer his designer cologne. "And anyway, Jean-Claude stopped bothering you when I told him to cut it out."

"You had to tell him a few times, and I still never found the other half of that black cashmere pair," George grumbles.

"Maybe I shouldn't come after all," Daria suggests. "I mean, I don't want to disrupt your life, and anyway, you don't need a third wheel around now that you're in a relationship . . ."

"I never worried about being the third wheel in yours," George points out.

True.

But he never really got much of a chance. Her marriage to Alan lasted only six months, after a whirlwind courtship.

"Here you go," the waitress says cheerfully, setting down two more margaritas. "Ready to order?"

"We haven't actually looked at the menus yet," Daria

says apologetically. "We haven't seen each other in a year, so we're trying to catch up."

"Two years," George amends.

"Has it been that long?"

"No worries," the waitress interjects, "I'll be back."

"Listen, Daria, you've got to get out of LA before a building tumbles on you or some hysterical washed-up diva shoves you from a high floor. And if you don't come here, where else are you gonna go?"

"New York," she muses, thinking of her older sister. "I haven't visited Tammy in ages. Or my parents, either, for that matter."

"Do you even know where they are?"

"Of course I do." She hesitates. "I think. I mean, I know my father's still in Italy, and I'm pretty sure my mother's in Wisconsin, although her phone is disconnected, so I could be wrong. Either she's moved, or she couldn't pay the bill again. She'll turn up."

"Well, when she does, if she needs a place to stay, she's always welcome in my house," George says generously, long enamored of Daria's unconventional, liberal mother—especially in contrast to his own conservative one.

"I'll tell her. If she turns up," says Daria with an eye roll, far less enamored.

Lately, she's found herself wondering what it would have been like to have had a traditional upbringing, with parents who stayed married to each other and in one place.

Which is funny, because her family's gypsy lifestyle has always seemed to suit her, while her lone attempt at putting down roots—with Alan—proved disastrous.

Face it, Daria: some people just aren't suited to the whole home and hearth scene, and you happen to be one of them.

"So, darling . . ." George lifts his margarita glass in a toast. "Here's to your fresh start in Phoenix."

"Cheers." She clinks his glass.

"How many fresh starts does that make this year?"

"Three," she says with a shrug and a grin, "but who's counting?"

"Listen, you never know . . . maybe you'll love it here so much that you never want to leave."

"Nothing personal, but I doubt it."

"Nothing personal, but maybe you should be thinking about settling down at your age."

"I'm not even thirty yet!" she protests, though his words strike a chord within her.

"You can't wander around aimlessly forever, Daria."

"It's not aimless. And who says I can't? Look at my mother."

"Do you really want to become your mother? Think about it."

The thing is . . . she *has* been her.

She reflects mostly on her mother's multiple husbands and myriad occupations, and never having much of anything to call her own. Her address, her hair color, not even her name has ever stayed the same for long. Aurora Rivers—the Rivers courtesy of her fifth and most recent ex-husband—is a loving soul, and she adored her two daughters as well as all of her spouses, but she wasn't really there for them, and still isn't.

Just as she doesn't do goodbyes, Mom doesn't do family ties or strings attached. Apron included.

"Daria, you're doing the right thing, coming here to Phoenix to live. And I wouldn't be surprised if you decide to stay forever."

Forever.

There's that word again.

"Well, I'd be surprised," she tells George.

"Never say never, darling. I don't believe in it."

Daria smiles sweetly and shoots back, "Never say forever, darling. I don't believe in that, either."

Chapter
1

Well? What do you think?"

Sprawled on her sister's couch, Daria looks up from the obituary section of this morning's *New York Times* to see Tammy framed in the bedroom doorway.

She's wearing a flowing red dress that hugs her considerable curves, along with a pair of sequined pumps that look suitable for transforming a girl to Oz and back.

"Be honest," Tammy adds as she twirls around, modeling.

"Wow," Daria tells her sister. "You're gorgeous."

"You're just saying that." Tammy waves away the compliment, but a pleased smile touches her lipsticked lips. "Right?"

Daria shakes her head. "Wrong. You look great. There's something really exciting about a red dress . . ."

"I know. That's what I thought when I bought it."

Her sister's salt-and-pepper hair is caught back in its usual ponytail, though today it's held by a jeweled barrette instead of a plain old elastic band. Tammy's even wearing makeup for a change, and gold earrings that are almost as big as the shiny ornaments on the Christmas tree in the corner.

At forty-three, more than a decade older than Daria's thirty, Tammy was born during their mother's short-lived third marriage but was a biological souvenir of the second, as Mom likes to say. Daria is a product of the fourth.

As sisters go, they couldn't be more opposite.

Where Tammy is statuesque and full-figured, Daria is tiny—just over five feet—and narrow-hipped with a long, slim waist despite a fierce junk food habit. She wears her jet black hair short, sleek, and tucked behind her ears, with long bangs swept to the side. The gamine style compliments her olive skin and fine bone structure and brings out her startling aquamarine eyes, as do the smoky eyeliner and lush mascara she uses as regularly as she does her toothbrush.

Daria and Tammy might not look alike, but they do have more than just a maternal bloodline in common. They both know things they can't possibly know, see things nobody else can see, hear things nobody else can hear.

That inexplicable, so-called gift is the most striking similarity between them.

And how they've chosen to use it—or not—is perhaps their most striking difference of all.

"Are you sure this isn't all . . . too much?" Tammy asks, gesturing at herself, head to toe. "I mean, for me."

"No, you're gorgeous. Seriously," Daria assures her, and adds with a sly smile, "Gorgeous enough to go to the wedding of two total strangers, even."

"I keep telling you, they aren't total strangers. Well, the bride isn't, anyway. Mia came to me for a reading. It was the Fourth of July and—"

"And her friend saw your sign—" Familiar with the oft-repeated tale almost six months later, Daria gestures toward the window on the far wall, where neon letters announce, *Madame Tamar, Psychic and Spiritualist.*

"Right, and her friend—her name's Lenore—dragged her in off the street and—"

"And that pretty much makes Mia a total stranger. Like I said."

"Not anymore."

"You haven't even seen her since that one time."

"No, but her friend Lenore keeps coming back for readings and she keeps me updated." Tammy leans into the nearest mirror, festooned with a fresh holly garland.

Pursing her lips into an O, she dabs a fingertip at the corner of her mouth. "And anyway," she says, a little distorted by the O, "if it weren't for me, Mia and Dominic wouldn't be together in the first place."

"I don't know about that. People find each other and fall in love on their own all the time."

Not that Daria herself has ever experienced true love, despite a whirlwind marriage.

But still.

"Well, I'm taking credit for this Chickalini wedding," Tammy declares firmly. "I told Mia she was going to be married before the year was out. To a man whose name starts with a D and ends in a K sound. And even Lenore said that if it weren't for me, Mia wouldn't have been open to Dominic when they met."

"Maybe . . . maybe not."

"Come on, Daria. The woman sits next to some strange guy on an airplane—and the next thing you know, they're getting married in a Vegas?"

"She was wearing a wedding gown when she got on the plane," Daria points out, amused by the tale despite having heard it ad nauseam. "She was headed out there to get married as it was."

"Yeah, but not to Dominic. She was going to marry someone else, sight unseen. Listen, you can't argue with fact. I saw it, all of it, from the second I touched her hand back in July. When I'm right, I'm right."

Okay, Tammy does have a point there.

When she's right, she's right.

And when she's wrong . . .

She often finds herself in trouble. How many times in the past few months since she came to visit Tammy has Daria opened the door to find a tearful—or worse yet, furious—client demanding to know why Madame Tamar's prediction didn't come true?

People in that frame of mind aren't interested in understanding how these things work. They don't care about how challenging it is to interpret symbols and images and comprehend cryptic messages from the spirit world.

They just want to know why they haven't come into a big sum of money or landed a new job or fallen in love or whatever it was Madame Tamar foresaw in their future. Sometimes, they even demand their money back.

Sure, Tammy is making a decent living, and yes, she rolls with the punches . . . but is all that stress and responsibility really worthwhile? As far as Daria's concerned, Tammy would be better off keeping her paranormal gifts to herself.

Right. Just like I do.

Daria learned years ago—the hard way—that it's better not to meddle in other people's lives—no matter how much you know about them, or how sincere your intentions are. She vowed never again to let the spirit world steer her to alter a stranger's path. Too risky, no matter what her sister says.

We're just so different, Tammy and me. It's a wonder we get along as well as we do.

She's glad she came here for a visit—on a whim, of course—rather than hang around in Arizona twiddling her thumbs and waiting for George's business to open. Tammy welcomed her warmly and told her to stay as long as she wanted.

I'll bet she never thought she'd still be stuck with me three months later, Daria thinks wryly. Not that Tammy seems to mind. In fact, she gets wistful whenever Daria mentions going back out to Arizona, which she has to do sooner or later, since that's her new home.

"All I know," Tammy tells her, "is that I'm glad Mia and Dominic are having an official wedding so their families can share the joy. And I'm glad they invited me because I've been looking forward to it for weeks. I've got to get going if I'm going to make it out to Astoria on time."

"Have fun."

"I'm sure I will." Tammy turns away from the mirror and reaches for her warm winter coat, draped over a nearby chair. "Who doesn't love weddings?"

"*I* don't."

"Why not?"

"Sour grapes?" she asks, tongue in cheek.

"Oh, come on, Daria." Tammy shakes her head and looks like she wants to say something more.

This time, for a change, she leaves it at that.

At the door, she turns back. "Listen, if anyone drops in for a reading, feel free to pinch hit for me."

"Ha, not a chance."

"Yeah, I figured. But it never hurts to ask. Especially considering you're just hanging around, anyway, since you happen not to have plans on a Saturday night."

"Do I ever?"

"You could have a date every night if you didn't scare away every guy who shows interest."

"Right. I put on a rubber mask and say boo when I see them coming." Daria grins.

"You might as well."

She shrugs. Yes, she's been asked out by a few decent guys since she arrived in New York in October and hit on by countless others who might be more—well, indecent. She's just not interested in a fling—which is all a potential romance could ever be here, because she's not going to be sticking around much longer.

Which is exactly the excuse she used when she was living—albeit briefly, so far—out in Phoenix. And before that, in LA. Which was right after New Orleans, where she went for Mardis Gras and decided to live, staying until just after Easter, when the soggy heat set in.

"Anyway," she tells Tammy, "you should talk. I don't see you out there dating."

"You know I can't do that." Tammy hasn't dated since losing her husband, tragically, to cancer years ago.

"You *can*, but you won't."

"Because I can't," Tammy says simply, opening the door. "Have a cozy night, honey."

"Have a thrilling night, yourself."

Listening to her sister's ruby shoes creaking down the stairs, Daria heaves a sigh.

Alone at last. Privacy doesn't come easily when you're sharing a drab five-hundred-square-foot one-bedroom apartment on the second floor of an old building.

Though the place is looking pretty spectacular at the moment, if Daria does say so herself.

It wasn't easy to find fresh holiday greens in the heart of Manhattan, but she managed. Now the halls are decked with lush lengths of boxwood and holly, even sprigs of real mistletoe. Tiny white twinkle lights are strung from the crown moldings, and pots of poinsettias in shades of creamy pink and white are clustered on every possible surface.

Elegantly decorating Tammy's apartment for the holidays reminded Daria that while she doesn't long to return to the days of comparing paint samples with a washed-up Hollywood actress, she actually does miss being creative and productive.

But do you miss it enough to go back to Phoenix and a full-time job?

With a sigh, she decides some music is in order.

Something loud and mindless, good old-fashioned classic rock and roll.

She plugs herself into her iPod and scrolls until she gets to the Rolling Stones. Perfect. The Stones are her all-time favorite. You can't mope around when you're listening to Mick. She cranks the volume, kicks off her own sneakers, and stretches out on the couch.

It's not exactly the most comfortable piece of furniture in the world, and has doubled as her bed ever since she came to visit her sister a few months ago. It was supposed to be only temporary.

Like everything else in my life.

She'd become restless waiting around in Phoenix for George's contractor boyfriend to finish work on the new design studio, which was taking a lot longer than anyone expected.

Her plane had barely touched down at JFK when George's boyfriend flew the coop, leaving George to not only mend his broken heart, but begin the search for a new contractor. As of Thanksgiving, work was once again underway . . . but progressing painstakingly. Or maybe it just seems that way to Daria, cooling her heels here in New York . . . and now almost beginning to have doubts about the whole Phoenix thing.

She's really starting to wonder—as the Stones sing in her head about not always getting what you want—what it is that she *does* want.

Does she want to go back to Phoenix, or maybe make yet another Fresh Start someplace new?

Her life has been a series of Fresh Starts. She's always pretty much just drifted wherever the wind seemed to take her. But this time, the wind doesn't seem to be blowing in any particular direction . . . including west.

With the New Year already looming just a few days away, she'd better figure things out quickly. George is aiming to launch the business in early January, and he has no idea she's waffling.

I swear I'll figure this out, she tells herself. Then, for good measure, she turns off her iPod, unplugs her earphones, and repeats it aloud.

"I swear I'll figure out what to do with my life. Really. I mean it."

Her voice sounds hollow in the empty apartment, punctuated only by a steady dripping somewhere in the bathroom.

Shower or sink this time? She could—no, she *should*—go tighten the faucet—but that would probably be futile anyway. The plumbing in this building is always acting up.

Well, what do you expect for the ridiculously low rent Tammy is paying? She's been living here for years now, ever since she married the love of her life, Carlton.

I could do so much with this place, Daria thinks, casting her artist's eye beyond the holiday accoutrements at the beige Ikea-purchased furniture, blah window treatments, plain white paint. The un-embellished apartment is a designer's dream.

Only Tammy would absolutely freak if Daria so much as rearranged the furniture.

This was hers and Carlton's newlywed love nest, as Tammy likes to say, and she'll never change a thing. Nor will she ever move. Not when Tammy believes Carlton's comforting spirit is hanging around here—though neither she nor Daria have ever actually glimpsed him—and rent control keeps the place affordable in a neighborhood where real estate has sky-rocketed.

Daria wouldn't mind a little more action just beyond the building doorstep, though.

This midtown stretch of Lexington Avenue is always unsettlingly quiet on weekends, without the hordes of weekday office workers. You have to go across town—or downtown—to find any Manhattan excitement. But the city itself is even more subdued than usual in this blustery December dusk. Not much goes on here during holiday week; most people are busy with their families, or traveling.

Everyone has someplace to be but me.

Well, that's not exactly true.

Daria does have options. If she weren't here in New York with her sister, she'd be back in Phoenix with George, or in LA being Designer to the Fallen Stars, or down in Florida, where her vagabond mother finally surfaced to spend this winter, or even in Italy with her equally vagabond father, who ages ago went overseas on vacation and never came back.

He and Daria haven't seen each other in a few years now, and she's never even met his wife and stepchildren, so he's been pressing her to visit.

Visit . . . or stay.

"It's beautiful here," he told Daria. "And as an artist, you really belong in Florence."

Artist . . . flattering description, but not exactly accurate. True, she majored in art. But her father seems to have this misguided vision of her standing in front of an easel wearing a beret, in search of her muse.

Florence, Florida, Phoenix. . . .

She honestly doesn't feel any of those places beckoning her right now. Nor is she drawn anywhere else, for that matter.

Oh, well. No Strings Attached—that's her mother's life philosophy, and it might as well be Daria's.

Except, of course, for that brief period when she *was* attached, briefly, legally, to Alan.

Yeah, and look how that turned out.

So the youthful marriage was a stupid mistake.

So she's twenty-eight years old, and she technically doesn't have a life.

Not one that fits, anyway.

You can't change the past. You can only let go and move on. And moving on always was Daria's specialty, just the opposite of her sister's.

With her alimony savings running out, though, she'd better figure out where she wants to go next, and get there. She either needs to return to her job in Phoenix, or find another one—here, there, somewhere.

Where?

Frustrated with this train of thought, Daria goes back to the newspaper obituaries searching for . . . well, she'll know when she finds it. She always does.

She scans the photos, but not the names. The names usually don't mean a thing. She usually just gives them nicknames of her own, based on how they appear to her— Little Carrot Top Girl, Dapper Top Hat Man.

But today, as she's looking for Worried Middle-Aged Mom, she's got Yours Truly on her mind.

It's not easy never knowing quite where you belong until you get there.

Blame her chronic restlessness on gypsy blood—literally. She probably got Tammy's share, and then some.

But as much as she's moved around, this is the first time it's *bothered* Daria that she doesn't instinctively sense what to do next or where to go.

She absently turns a page and stares at the newspaper.

Maybe I should just forget Arizona and New York and

start over someplace else. Someplace I've never been. I just wish—

There! That's it! There she is.

Smiling out at her from a vintage black-and-white headshot, the woman has a beehive hairdo circa 1971-ish. Worried Middle-Aged Mom.

Dianne Freeman.

That's her name.

Why do families always provide such dated photos for their loved ones' obituaries?

Probably because they like to remember them in the prime of their lives.

Certainly Dianne Freeman looked older in person— well, not exactly *in person*—when Daria spotted her hovering around a brownstone near Washington Square Park yesterday afternoon. Older, and a little bewildered.

They usually do. Especially the ones who've recently crossed over.

Daria scans the obituary. Yup. Very recently, in this case. Dianne Freeman died suddenly at her Greenwich Village residence on Christmas Day. No cause of death given. Survived by a husband, two children, four small grandchildren.

Yes, and she wants to contact them through Daria.

But I'm not going to track them down and tell them that I have a message from you, Daria silently tells Dianne Freeman's picture. *I'm sorry. I just can't.*

Astoria, Queens

"Come dance with me, baby! They're playing the tarantella!"

Ralphie Chickalini looks up from a clump of sickening-sweet white wedding cake frosting to find his fiancée bearing down on him with outstretched arms.

Francesca's spike-heeled dyed red satin pumps have long since been discarded in some corner of the church hall, and her bare feet are already bopping in time to the jaunty orchestra music. Ralphie can't help but notice that her face is flushed—from too much wine or exertion, most likely both.

Earlier this afternoon, her hair was a gravity-defying, sprayed-stiff heap, save a duo of ringlets coiled against her rouged cheekbones like snails clinging to a stucco. A red silk poinsettia seemed to grow out of a crevice high atop the towering coiffure.

Now the flower is wilted (who knew it was possible for silk flowers to wilt?), the column of hair is listing dangerously to the east, and the snails have been joined by dozens of escaped serpentine wisps.

The elaborate style was crafted in the lone bathroom of the Chickalini house by his sister Rosalee's lifelong friend Bebe, formerly known as Bernadette Lapozzi. Unfortunately, a beauty school diploma didn't transform her into José Eber. And although she recently added the title Certified Fashion Stylist to her business card, a Parisian flair to her first name is pretty much the only trait Bebe shares with Coco Chanel.

Waiting impatiently outside the door with a full bladder and ten minutes to shower and get into his tux, Ralphie listened to Bebe and Francesca's nonstop chatter about Dominic and Mia's wedding today.

Weddings, weddings, weddings . . . that, as far as Ralphie can tell, is most women's favorite conversational topic. Married, single, engaged, they all love to talk about weddings.

As he waited and eavesdropped, he could only pray his fiancée wouldn't agree to Bebe's offer to do her hair when their own wedding rolls around next summer. And that was *before* he caught a glimpse of this particular 'do.

"Look at your future bride, Ralphie!" Bebe crowed when she opened the bathroom door with a grand flourish. "Isn't she just go-aw-jus?"

He didn't dare admit aloud that his formerly lovely future bride now bore a frightening resemblance to Frankenstein's.

Nor does he now dare to suggest that Francesca go into the ladies' room to unpin and comb out the entire leaning tower.

Like his sisters Rosalee and Nina, his wife-to-be is notoriously sensitive to criticisms of her hair. And her makeup. And her wardrobe. And her jewelry. After a year of dating and another eighteen months of engagement, Ralphie has learned to keep his opinions to himself.

"Baby!" Francesca grabs his arm. "Come on! Why do you have to be so blah?"

"I'm not blah. You just happen to be extra social. That makes me seem extra blah by comparison. Here, want some frosting?" He offers her a forkful.

"Mmm." She swallows, licks her lips, and promptly goes back to cajoling. "Everybody's out there, Ralphie. Come on."

"Later. You go."

She opens her mouth to protest, but he cuts her off. "I'm serious, babe, go ahead. I'll be right here having my cake and eating it too." He grins at her.

"Are you sure?"

"Yup." He pokes a hunk into his mouth, swallowing the sugar-grain-and-Crisco glob and saying "Mmm," as though it's the best thing since sliced Italian bread dipped into olive oil and grated Parmesan.

Francesca shrugs and turns back toward the dance floor.

Relieved, Ralphie watches his fiancée weave her way into the clapping, jigging, joyous crowd.

There, a barefoot, laughing Nina, clad in a red brides-maid's gown, faces the bride's octogenarian grandfather and clasps his outstretched hands high overhead, still bouncing to the jaunty beat. The rest of the crowd deftly partners up to follow suit and align with Nina and Grandpa Junie, the first link in the human tunnel. Even the gig-gling Chickalini grandkids are well versed in the intricate Italian folk dance, a beloved standard at family weddings and parties.

Watching one pair of dancers after another duck for-ward merrily to pass through the snaking line of arched arms, Ralphie can't help wishing some of that buoyancy would seep his way.

This is, after all, his big brother's wedding reception: a particularly momentous occasion for the Chickalini family, in part because nobody ever expected wayward middle son Dominic to give up his prized bachelorhood.

In typical ladies' man fashion, Dom, a slick ad sales-man, jetted off to Vegas for a long business weekend a few months ago, presumably leaving behind his usual string of would-be girlfriends, and probably having al-ready scheduled dates with all of them upon his return.

The next thing Ralphie knew, his brother was back

home with a gold ring on his finger and a beautiful stranger—Mia Calogera, also of Astoria, Queens—in tow.

Moments after the initial shock wore off, Pop pulled out a celebratory bottle of champagne and welcomed Mia to the family. But Nina and Rosalee—Dom and Ralphie's older sisters—weren't about to settle for an out-of-state elopement and a family toast at the dining room table.

So here they all are, some three months after the fact, in a church hall semi-transformed by dozens of flickering votives and tulle-wrapped pots of Mia's favorite orchids, dancing the night away with the bride and groom.

All, that is, except Ralphie.

And Pop.

That's the other reason this is a momentous occasion—and not in a good way.

This is the first official Chickalini celebration since the loss of their cherished patriarch over two months ago—aside from Thanksgiving, which wasn't much of a celebration without Pop.

How can Nino Chickalini not be here, at the wedding of his middle son?

Ralphie is incredulous anew at his father's jarring absence. It's all he can do not to break down in tears right here, missing his father desperately.

But Pop wouldn't want that.

It wasn't that he didn't believe men should cry—not at all. Nino Chickalini had shed plenty of tears in his adult life—tears of joy, but mostly tears of grief for his lost wife. But if he were here, he would remind Ralphie that a strong man bears his sorrows gracefully in public.

Of course if Pop were here, Ralphie wouldn't feel like crying in the first place.

If Pop were here, he'd be sitting in this vacant chair beside Ralphie, nodding in time to the Italian folk music. He'd be wearing one of his dark silk dress shirts, open-necked to reveal the gold cross Ralphie's mother gave him years ago, on their own wedding day. Of course he'd request that the band play Dean Martin's "That's Amore," the Chickalini family anthem.

When the moon hits your eye like a big pizza pie . . .

Big Pizza Pie. That's the name of Pop's restaurant.

What's going to happen to it now?

The ailing Nino Chickalini had been little more than a figurehead at his treasured Ditmars Boulevard pizzeria these last few years.

After he died, joint ownership passed on to his five children.

Nina's husband Joey, who gave up his lucrative Wall Street job years ago, pretty much runs the place, with Nina there as much as possible, and frequent help from the rest of the clan. Even the grandkids, right down to Rosalee and Tim's preschooler Adam, have rolled up their sleeves to sprinkle shredded mozzarella on oven-ready pies and refill napkin holders.

But it was always Pop's place. Pop's menu, using Pop's recipes and, in the summer, Pop's fresh basil, oregano, and tomatoes grown in Pop's tiny patch of garden behind the nearby Chickalini home.

Now the yard—as barren as Pop's chair at the head of the dining room table—is a frozen wasteland of muddy boot prints left by Nina and Joey's kids cutting through from their house next door.

Ralphie won't be living on Thirty-Third off Ditmars for long. He and Francesca, who accumulated a truckload of household stuff at the bridal shower his sisters threw for them last summer, will get a place of their own before their wedding.

She makes a decent salary as an executive assistant at a midtown marketing firm. The Buccigrossis are old-fashioned parents who are paying for the upcoming wedding, and who charge their only daughter nothing to live in their pink-aluminum-sided duplex over by the Neptune Diner on Astoria Boulevard.

As Francesca put it, where—besides Loehmann's and the salon—is she going to spend all that money? Over the years, she's socked away more than enough for a down payment on what she likes to call a "honeymoon love nest."

At first, Ralphie had her convinced that the two of them should buy out his sisters' and brothers' shares of the house Pop left them all, and live there.

Francesca didn't wholeheartedly embrace the idea from the start, but she didn't outright change her mind until just before Christmas, after a night out with the girls—including Bebe. Who just happened to know someone who knows someone who wants to sell their condo over on Steinway Street via word of mouth, no brokers.

"Let's at least go look at it after the holidays," Francesca persisted. "Don't you want a place that's all ours, baby?"

"This place would be all ours," he pointed out, looking around at the familiar, comforting surroundings.

"Not really. There's too much history here. And it's so . . . old."

As far as Ralphie's concerned, those are the very reasons the house is so appealing.

Now he's got to go look at some condo that's barely in the same neighborhood.

He doubts he'll like it, especially with the Bebe connection hovering around the place like a dark cloud, but what does it matter?

Francesca has her heart set on a fresh domestic start somewhere other than the house where Ralphie's lived all his life. The one connection to Pop, and the only one Ralphie ever had to his mother, who died giving birth to him.

None of his siblings seem to have a problem with the prospect of packing up and putting the house on the market now that Pop is gone. They all have homes and families of their own now—all except Ralphie. They agreed to hold off on dealing with the house until after Dom's wedding reception and the holidays, but the wedding is here and the holidays are drawing to a close.

Yup, things are changing fast.

Around the corner at Big Pizza Pie, Nina and Joey have already altered the menu, adding new toppings like goat cheese and alfalfa sprouts, and a vegetarian minestrone.

Vegetarian minestrone?

Pop vetoed that oft-presented idea repeatedly over the years, convinced that a proper minestrone begins with a ham bone simmered with herbs in a stock pot for a full day.

But Pop no longer has any say over the menu.

On a September night when autumn's first chill hung low with thousands of stars in the black sky, Nino Chickalini's old heart, broken when he was widowed in his midthirties and damaged in a near-fatal coronary a decade later, finally just gave out.

With Pop gone and Dominic married, Ralphie has become—almost overnight—the last remaining resident of the comfortably shabby house on Thirty-Third Street just off Ditmars Boulevard, where Pop raised five kids.

For all those years, the house was a hotbed of activity—people coming and going at all hours, phone ringing off the hook, dog barking, clutter, chatter, arguments, practical jokes. It was all punctuated by the constant arrivals and takeoffs of planes at neighboring La Guardia Airport.

Of course the family chaos was at its height when all five Chickalini children were living at home, and naturally it tapered off as his siblings moved out and got married.

At last the inevitable: only Ralphie is left.

Maybe he should have seen it coming from the start, but he was blindsided.

He's not ready for the final unavoidable step, either. Not just yet. But the end of an era is bearing down on him.

Looking at the empty chair beside him, he thinks, *No. It's already here.*

Chapter 2

The door buzzes just as Daria is settling herself back on the couch with popcorn and the television remote.

Her first instinct is to ignore it.

Her next is to answer it, because what if it's Tammy and she's forgotten her keys?

With a sigh, she deposits the bowl of popcorn and remote on the coffee table and pads in her sock feet over to the wall intercom.

"Yes?"

A pause.

Then a female voice asks, "Madame Tamar?"

Daria should have ignored her second instinct. After all, it's a Saturday night in the heart of the holiday season. What could be better for the psychic counseling industry?

"Sorry," Daria says into the intercom. "She's not in."

"Will she be back later? It's . . . kind of an emergency."

Yeah, it almost always is.

"Try her tomorrow," Daria says, and adds a decisive, "Goodnight."

Just in case she's tempted to take Tammy up on her offer to hold down the fort with readings in her absence.

Crossing to the window, Daria looks down on the street below. Within seconds, a woman emerges from the building's vestibule. She shuffles off down the street with her head hanging. She was just stood up by a date—that, or someone broke up with her.

That's almost always the case with Saturday night walk-ins. They show up here in search of answers when they can't get them from the men in their lives.

Daria turns away from the window with a twinge of guilt.

You did the right thing.

Her days of psychic meddling are long over, and it's for the best, considering what happened back in Boise with Emmy Biggs.

When Daria spotted the drab-looking middle-aged woman waiting her turn at the supermarket butcher, there was a rugged-looking spirit attached to her.

As the butcher went to work slicing her filet mignon, Daria found out the woman's name, and that the spirit was her late husband, Hank. He'd been killed a few years before in a mining accident, one that—thanks to a settlement and an insurance policy—had left his wife pretty well-off.

Now he needed Daria to convey a message for him—and he was pretty darned persistent.

Daria never did like bullies and tried to resist, but when Hank toppled a tower of soup cans just as she pushed her cart past, she knew he meant business.

What was there to do but follow his widow out to the parking lot?

"Excuse me . . . ma'am?" she reluctantly asked as Emmy loaded her bags into the back of a new SUV.

"Yes?"

Daria took a deep breath, knowing she could very well be met with skepticism. Occupational hazard.

"I'm a medium, and Hank is here, and he wants me to tell you something."

Shockingly, Emmy seemed to take that in stride.

"What is it?"

"I'm not quite sure, but I'll just tell you what I see. He keeps showing me Barbra Streisand in the movie *Hello, Dolly*. Does that mean anything to you?"

Emmy immediately grew misty. "That was our favorite movie! I was an extra in it when I was a kid—they filmed it near my hometown. And just the other day at the coffee shop, I mentioned to my friend Selma that I've been feeling like Dolly Levi, waiting for her dead husband to give her a sign that it's all right to move on and get remarried."

"I take it you have someone in mind?"

Emmy grinned and told her that she did. She'd been dating a cowboy named Billy Butts. She met him just before she was supposed to move back east to her hometown in Westchester County, New York, to be near her sister and mother.

"He's such an old-fashioned gentleman, really good-looking, and so charming," she gushed. "He just seems too good to be true! And now he wants me to stay out here and marry him, but I didn't want to say yes without some kind of sign from Hank. Just like Dolly and Ephraim."

"Well, Emmy, I'd say you just got your sign," Daria said, wishing her well and going her merry way. She

should have known the whole scene seemed a little too
pat for comfort.

It wasn't until months later that she heard from Emmy
again.

Rather, Emmy's lawyers.

It seemed she had gone ahead and married Billy Butts.
And Mr. Too-Good-to-Be-True really was. The honeymoon was barely over when he tried to bump off his bride
and claim her hefty bank account.

"If it weren't for you coming up to her out of the blue,
Ms. Biggs-Butts would never have married him."

And if Daria hadn't emitted an involuntary snorting
laugh at the bride's married name, they might have dis-
missed any hint at her involvement.

But laugh she did—and dismiss they did not.

Before the mess was sorted out in court, Daria—along
with Emmy's former friend Selma—had been accused of
cooking up a scheme with Billy Butts, who was no cowboy, but rather, a notorious con man from back east.

The press had a field day with headlines like *"Does
She See Dead People—Or Just Rob Live Ones?"* and
"So-Called Psychic Cheats Sad Sack Widow."

In the end, she managed to escape charges—and Boise.

She drove off into the sunset—literally—until she
could go no farther, and found herself in Seattle.

There, in the ultimate cliché, she quite literally bumped
into Alan Spencer on the street. He spilled his Starbucks
all over her T-shirt and when she wouldn't let him pay
her dry-cleaning bill—who dry cleans Gap T-shirts?—he
insisted on taking her to lunch.

Alan was so appealing that she—like Emmy Biggs-
Butts—felt as though he was the answer to a prayer.

She—like Emmy Biggs-Butts—should have known it was all too good to be true.

Intelligent, respectable, relatively good-looking, financially secure with a job at Microsoft, Alan seemed perfect for her. Perfect in general.

Most important: he was safe. Stolid. Solid.

There wasn't a whimsical bone in Alan's body, and he had no idea that—until he came along—there hadn't been a sensible bone in Daria's. She—who had spent her life wishing on falling stars and dandelion fluff when she wanted something to happen—decided it was time to take control of her destiny and mold herself into the woman she thought she had always wanted to be.

She got a secretarial job, let her hair grow into a boring ponytail, snuffed her supernatural skills. When spirits buzzed around her—and they did—she ignored them if Alan was around, shooed them away like pesky mosquitos if he wasn't.

After the Boise debacle, she welcomed the chance to live a so-called normal life at last. When Alan proposed, she listened not to her heart—which was always her fickle mother's mistake—nor to her mother, for that matter. It wasn't that Aurora didn't like the idea of Daria getting married after a whirlwind courtship, or that she wanted to meet her future son-in-law first. No, she had—as she put it—a negative vibe about the whole thing.

Daria ignored it. Nor did she listen to her sister—who did object to the whirlwind courtship—and certainly not to the spirits, who also seemed opposed to the match.

No, for once, Daria listened to her own common sense . . . at least, she thought that was what it was.

Turned out she was wrong.

It doesn't make sense to marry someone you don't love, just because their world represents the stability lacking in your own.

Unlike the hapless Emmy Biggs-Butts, Daria's marriage didn't crash and burn with a murder attempt and a courtroom drama.

Her union with Alan simply wilted, like a discarded dandelion that was supposed to be left growing in the meadow to ultimately yield a billowing cloud of wishes come true.

When it was over, she was stronger, wiser. Ready to resume the familiar rhythm of her vagabond life—if not ready to channel spirit messages for unsuspecting strangers.

Sorry, she silently tells the strange woman making her way down the block below, probably in search of some other psychic counselor—or maybe the nearest bar.

With another twinge of guilt, Daria turns away from the window.

And sees that she has company.

He's right there, a few feet away, not the least bit filmy the way apparitions sometimes are.

This guy is stout, with distinctly Mediterranean features and a thick patch of dark hair. Visible in the vee of his dark silk dress shirt is a gold cross, and he's wearing a gold wedding band on his left hand.

His big dark eyes connect with Daria's, and she sees the sorrow in them.

He needs something, Daria thinks wearily. *They all do.*

Yes, but she's not getting involved.

Never again.

She shakes her head at the spirit and grimly picks up

the popcorn and television remote again, determined to ignore him, just as she has all the others.

It's the only way.

"Uncle Ralphie?"

Startled, he finds his father's young namesake staring solemnly at him through wide-set brown eyes.

Looking at his nephew is like looking into a mirror. The resemblance is hardly a coincidence. Nino is Ralphie's birth son, the product of a tempestuous high school relationship that ended before his girlfriend found out she was pregnant. They rekindled the flame for a while, but of course it couldn't last. The odds were stacked against them.

Ralphie was the one who refused to accept that. There was a time when he nobly—and foolishly—thought they could raise the baby together. Thank God Camille's common sense prevailed. She said she couldn't bear the thought of their son becoming a casualty of a misguided youthful marriage and the product of a broken home.

Does she think about him, wherever she is now? Does she wonder if they made the right decision, allowing Ralphie's sister and brother-in-law to adopt the baby?

Probably.

Ralphie is lucky that he gets to watch Nino growing up. He'll never have to wonder whether they made the right decision back then. He knows they did.

"Uncle Ralphie?" Nino asks again.

"What's up, kiddo?" he asks in the well-practiced, jovial uncle tone that usually comes so easily with Nino and the other nephews, T. J. and Adam, and with his niece, Nino's sister Rose.

"Why aren't you dancing?" Nino asks.

"Because I'm eating cake," Ralphie replies. "Did you get a piece?"

"Three."

"You ate three pieces? Where the heck did you put all that?" Ralphie playfully pokes the boy in his midsection. Nino is skinny . . . just as Ralphie himself was at that age. Someday, he, too, might grow up to be a lanky six-foot-four.

His hair and eye coloring might be lighter than Ralphie's, and his features more classically handsome, but he's built the same way. Long and lean. He's a good basketball player, too. Lately, Ralphie has been giving him pointers on the court down at the Y, where he coaches on a youth league. Nino can't be on the team for a few more years, but he likes to help out, just as Ralphie once helped his oldest brother Pete when he was coaching.

"I could have eaten two more pieces of cake, even, after that—but Mom wouldn't let me," Nino informs him. "She said all that sugar would rot my teeth and they'd all fall out and I'd look like a hillbilly."

Ralphie, who spent many years on the receiving end of that particular line of Nina's, can't help but smile affectionately. Nina's a terrific mother—thanks in part to all the practice she got on her baby brother.

Growing up, Ralphie reportedly once told Nina he wished he had a million dollars. When she asked him why, he said he wanted to buy her a ticket around the world to pay her back for all she'd done for him.

"For a little kid, you were perceptive way beyond your years," Nina likes to remind him whenever she retells that story, which is often.

Yes, from an early age, he instinctively sensed his sister's restlessness; her wistful longing to leave Astoria and travel the globe. He understood that she'd sacrificed her dreams to stay home and raise him—just as their mother sacrificed her own life to bring him into the world.

Ralphie was perceptive well beyond his years, indeed.

It's taken him a lifetime to accept the burden of guilt that came with knowing that Rosemarie Chickalini would be here if he weren't.

It took him nearly as long to reward his selfless sister with something far more precious than a ticket around the world. By then, she had already realized that all she would ever need was right here in Astoria.

Ralphie knew it from the start, though. He has it all at his fingertips. His family, his fiancée, a home—for now— his health, a decent IT position across the Queensborough Bridge in midtown Manhattan.

Losing Pop was rough, that's all. Before it happened, Ralphie was more than content with his plans for the future.

But between his father's death and Dominic's sudden marriage, Ralphie had to put those plans on hold. Well, he didn't *have* to . . . he chose to. Francesca agreed that it would have felt rushed and chaotic to go ahead with their own midwinter wedding on the heels of Dominic and Mia's wedding, and Pop's funeral.

It's all been too much. Too much change. Too much—

"Uncle Ralphie?"

"Yeah, Nino?" He watches a dancing Francesca pat her hair to check for her drooping silk poinsettia—earlier referred to by Bebe as the "Piece Duh Resistance."

"You know that kite you got me for my birthday last fall?"

"Yeah?"

"You know how you said you'd take me to the beach and we could fly it?"

His heart sinks. "Yeah . . ."

"Well, remember how you were too busy with work in September . . . and then—well, you know."

And then Pop died.

"I'm sorry we never had a chance to go out to the beach, Nino," Ralphie says.

The beach has always been their thing. Nina and Joey aren't big on it, nor is Rose. But Ralphie has been taking his nephew down to the Rockaways since Nino was in diapers. He taught him to swim in the surf, skip stones, beachcomb for shells, and search for sea life in the tide pools.

"We'll go in the spring," he says now. "Definitely. I promise."

"Or maybe someday in January? If it warms up?"

"Uh, sure. Maybe."

"Are you okay?"

"Yup. Why?"

"You look like you're worried about something."

Sad, yes, but worried? Why should Ralphie worry? Everything in his life is settled. It will be again soon, anyway.

Come summer, I'm going to marry Francesca Marie Buccigrossi. And everything about her is right.

Fun-loving, Italian-Catholic, a great cook, she fits into the family. From the moment he brought her home a few years ago, she slipped as comfortably into the Chickalini household as yet another chair pulled up to the big old dining room table.

"This one's a keeper," was Pop's approving declaration when he took Ralphie aside after Francesca presented him with a jar of her homemade pesto as a nice-to-meet-you gift.

"You might not want to say that until you've tasted the pesto, Pop," Dominic advised, eavesdropping in the guise of big brotherly concern, as usual.

"If Pop tastes the pesto, he'll probably want to date her himself," Ralphie replied—then saw his father's expression and thought, *Oops.*

Pop never dated. *Never.*

If anybody even dared to suggest that he consider it, he was outraged. In all Ralphie's life, there was only one woman he had ever caught his father admiring in the many photos he kept around the house.

Yes, there was only one woman for Nino Chickalini. His wife Rose. *Mom.*

And now they're together—I know they are, Ralphie reminds himself, watching the dance floor clear as the beaming groom takes the glowing bride in his arms to slow dance to "Always and Forever."

Here comes Francesca, making her way toward him, stopping to chat along the way. She hugs the Chickalinis' longtime neighbors, Mr. and Mrs. Cebriones, then moves on to delightedly tickle Dom's friend Maggie's new baby boy, who happens to be wearing the blue and white bib Francesca cross-stitched for him.

Yes, she's indisputably part of the family. Maybe more so than Ralphie is tonight.

And yes, she makes a helluva pesto. Oh, and her meatballs are even better than Nina's, though Ralphie would never admit it to his sister.

Francesca will take good care of him, the way his sisters take care of their husbands. The way Mia and his other sister-in-law Debbie take care of Ralphie's brothers.

They'll walk down the aisle in June, and Francesca will become Mrs. Ralph Chickalini, and move into an uncluttered condo on Steinway Street or somewhere, and the family will be complete.

Well, not really.

It will never be complete again, with Pop missing.

Plus, the family is still expanding; there are bound to be more Chickalini children. Dom and Mia are planning to wait a few years, but Francesca is always saying she wants an early start on her planned brood of at least four. She doesn't like odd numbers, and two isn't enough.

"Four little Ralphies running around . . . doesn't that sound exciting, baby?" she likes to ask Ralphie.

Sure. He loves kids. He wants to raise one—or a few, maybe even four—someday. And Francesca will be a great mom.

"Uncle Ralphie?"

He finds Nino still hovering at his elbow. "What's up, kiddo?"

"You're not eating your cake."

"That's because there's nothing left but frosting."

"That's the best part."

"Here . . . knock yourself out." He slides the plate across the table toward the little boy.

"What about my mom?"

"I won't tell her if you don't," Ralphie says with a conspiratorial grin.

"Ralph! Come here, you have to meet someone!"

He looks up to see Lenore, Mia's best friend, beckoning him over to where she's sitting. Beside her is an unfamiliar woman in a red dress—middle-aged, with a graying ponytail. Must be one of Mia's relatives or something.

"Be right back," Ralphie tells his nephew, and unfolds his long legs to stride over to the next table.

"You look so handsome in that tuxedo," Lenore tells him—and her brown eyes are a little wistful behind her glasses. The victim of a bitter divorce, she's trying hard to get on with her life. A little too hard, maybe, Ralphie acknowledges, not letting his gaze linger on her unnatural blond hair—or, God forbid, her plunging cleavage.

"This is Madame Tamar," Lenore tells him, indicating the woman beside her—who has dark hair and no visible cleavage. "She's responsible for this." She waves a hand around the room.

"For what?"

"You know . . . for the wedding."

"You're the wedding planner?" Ralphie asks. "It was great. Really. My fiancée even said we should—"

"No, she's not the wedding planner," Lenore cuts in with a laugh. "She's the psychic."

"The . . . psychic?" Ralphie blinks.

Madame Tamar gives a little nod.

"She's the one who told Mia she was going to marry Dominic," Lenore explains, "and that was before they even knew each other."

Oh. Right. Mia said something about that, back when Ralphie assumed his new sister-in-law was a little ditzy.

She isn't . . . not really. Just exuberant, impulsive, a whole lot of fun . . .

And, apparently, pretty damned gullible, Ralphie decides, eyeing the so-called psychic.

"Madame Tamar keeps telling me I'm going to have a long and happy relationship with someone I already know . . . right?" Lenore looks at Madame Tamar, who nods. She's looking a little uncomfortable, Ralphie can't help but notice.

"Well . . . it's nice to meet you," he says politely, sticking out his hand to shake hers.

The woman grasps his hand, shakes it . . . and hangs on.

"What? What? Do you feel something?" Lenore asks excitedly. "Do you see something?"

"I see that you don't like change," Madame Tamar tells Ralphie. "That's what I see."

Ralphie raises an eyebrow. So he doesn't like change. Who does?

"Change," Madame Tamar goes on, "is inevitable. Right? You live. You die. In between, things are constantly in transition."

"That's so true!" Lenore says with a profound nod.

Ralphie frowns, looking from her back to Madame Tamar, whose gaze is transfixed on his face.

"You and I should talk," she tells him thoughtfully, releasing his hand at last. She reaches into a beaded purse and pulls out a business card. "Give me a call. Or just pop in."

He looks down at the card she thrusts into his hand.

Madame Tamar, Psychic and Spiritualist.

Sure.

And he's *Ralphie Chickalini, Star New York Knicks Forward.*

"Well, I've got to dance with my fiancée now." He rocks back on his heels. "I promised her I would."

He sees Madame Tamar's gaze flick in Francesca's direction, then back again. He doesn't like the look on her face.

Before she can say anything, Ralphie says, "Nice meeting you. And nice seeing you again, Lenore."

With that, he beats a hasty retreat to the dance floor, shoving the card into the pocket of his tux.

As if he's going to show up on some fortune-teller's doorstep.

Yeah, right.

Still . . .

He watches his brother Dominic whisper something in his bride's ear as they sway together on the dance floor, obviously oblivious to everything but each other.

Madame Tamar did make one prediction that was dead-on, when she saw them getting married long before Dominic would ever have considered it.

Even so, Ralphie doesn't need a stranger telling him what tomorrow holds for him. He already knows—and it isn't change. His future is mapped out neatly, and there's a level of comfort in knowing what to expect.

At least . . . there *was*.

Until tonight.

For some reason, his brother's wedding and his father's absence—not to mention that psychic's presence—have Ralphie feeling uneasy.

"Baby! There you are. Dance with me!"

As Francesca launches herself affectionately into his arms, Ralphie smiles. "Having fun?" he asks.

"The best time ever." She says that every time they're at a party. "What about you?"

"Sure."

This—she—is what Pop would have wanted for me. It's what I want.

So why is a nagging little voice asking, *Are you sure about that?*

Yes! I'm absolutely sure!

Ralphie holds tightly to Francesca, who snuggles and sways against him in time to the music, talking about the band they'll have at their own wedding.

". . . and I want to make sure they can play the long version of 'Shout,'" she decides. "Everyone loves to dance to 'Shout,' you know?"

Ralphie doesn't love to dance to "Shout." When it played a little while ago, he sat that one out.

Few others did. The dance floor was rocking. So she's probably right.

Francesca's definitely a part of this Chickalini world, he reminds himself yet again. She fits seamlessly into the family, the circle of friends, the neighborhood. With Francesca, it's easy. It's right.

She's one of us.

No denying that, or that everyone is crazy about her.

What about you, Ralphie? Are you crazy about her, too? that nagging little voice persists, and even Francesca's chatter can't quite drown it out.

Chapter
3

Happy New Year! What can I get for you?"

Daria tilts her head, considering. "Do you have a cabernet?"

The bartender—a balding middle-aged man in a size-too-small blue suit—nods. "Sure thing."

"And a pinot grigio too?"

"Chardonnay all right?"

Maybe not, but she shrugs and nods.

"Double fisted tonight, huh?" the bartender asks with a wink as he reaches for a bottle and uncorks it.

"The white's for my sister. The red's for me."

"Rose Red and Snow White, huh?"

Daria, who's wearing a red slip dress, smiles. "Something like that."

As he fills two clear plastic tumblers, she looks over her shoulder, her interior designer's eye surveying the gala scene here at Most Precious Mother Church Hall off Ditmars Boulevard.

Balloons, confetti, noisemakers. Crêpe paper streamers festoon the basketball hoops at either end of the floor. A train of steaming tinfoil trays crosses a buffet table, filling the air with the scent of garlic, tomatoes, sausage, gravy to mix with the faint aroma of wet wool, perfume, and gym sneakers. Multi-generational guests socialize in shiny jewel-toned cardboard hats and tiaras. A band—whose members have white hair, if any at all—is playing "Celebration" and there are people on the dance floor, mostly women.

It's as if she stepped onto the set of *My Cousin Vinnie*. Not in a bad way; not at all. It's just that she's never been to a party quite like this one, and she doesn't know a soul, and . . .

And, seriously, what am I doing here?

All right, she knows why she's here, technically speaking. Tammy's friend Lenore heard about it from the parish priest while they here for the Chickalini wedding the other night, and thought it sounded like fun.

Fun? Ha. *Last* New Year's Eve was fun. Daria was in Sydney, Australia, with a couple of friends. They had traveled Down Under after consulting a time zone map, aiming to be among the first around the globe to welcome the New Year.

No wonder it feels like it's been such a long year, Daria thinks wryly. *It has. Longer than usual.*

Last New Year's Eve at midnight, she decadently kissed a good-looking Aussie guy she'd met just hours earlier. As the sun rose over the southern Pacific Ocean on January first, the future seemed bright with promise.

Daria—still in her slinky black cocktail dress, sitting

on a sandy beach sipping champagne from the bottle—decided she'd return to the States only to get her stuff. She was going to give notice to her landlord and her boss, then return to Sydney. To live.

It wouldn't have been the first time she decided she belonged somewhere on a whim, then picked up and moved there. Daria's famous for Fresh Starts.

But Australia didn't happen.

Maybe because it was just the champagne talking. Maybe because she didn't buy the good-looking Aussie's line. Okay—she *didn't* buy it. Not at all. He was an obvious player.

But it wasn't about him, anyway.

It was about adventure. She craved it. Always has. Craved it, and lived it.

Lately, though . . .

Maybe it's time to grow up, figure out where she belongs, and settle down there.

That's what you thought you were doing when you moved to Arizona, she reminds herself.

But here she is in New York.

Just temporarily.

She thinks.

Well, anyway, you can't get more settled than spending New Year's Eve in a Queens church hall with your widowed sister and her divorced friend Lenore.

But is this where you belong? she asks herself dubiously, looking around at the roomful of strangers, none of whose lifestyles are likely to be remotely similar to hers.

With her self-imposed deadline looming, she has a couple of hours to figure out whether Arizona is going to be her last Fresh Start, or just another stepping stone on the path to God only knows where.

"That all?" the bartender asks, sliding the plastic tumblers toward Daria.

"For now." Maybe for good. She needs a clear head if she's going to figure out her life. "How much?"

"Oh, admission to the party covers your drinks. It's open bar till after midnight."

"Really? That could be dangerous."

"Not for me."

She smiles and drops a couple of ones into his tip basket.

Tammy is right where Daria left her, sitting on a folding wooden chair at a long table, munching from a white plastic bowl of chips.

"Where's Lenore?" Daria asks, setting down the wine and slipping into a chair.

"Not here yet, obviously." Tammy takes a huge gulp of her wine.

"Good thing I came."

"Yeah. Not because of me, though."

"Because . . . ?"

"Because you were going to sit home alone, and anything's better than that. Right? Ruffle?"

"Ruffle?" Daria echoes, confused, wondering if the wine could have gone to her sister's head that quickly.

Tammy slides the bowl of chips toward her. "Ruffles."

"Oh. No, thanks."

Tammy crunches into one. "I know, it's not caviar. And this place is no Ritz." She gestures at the table, covered with a red plastic tablecloth fastened to the underside every few inches with strips of masking tape. "Not your idea of a great New Year's Eve, but like I said, better than sitting home alone."

"Who said I want caviar and the Ritz?" *I just want to figure out my next move, like I told myself I would do by New Year's Day.*

"Maybe it's me. Maybe caviar and the Ritz are what I want." Tammy sounds a little wistful.

"Really?" Daria asks. "Because we could always—"

"No, not really." Tammy sighs. "It's just . . . what are we doing *here*?"

"I was just wondering that myself. We don't know a single soul."

Tammy answers her own question. "I know, but we're here because Lenore invited us—"

"Which is why it would be nice if she showed up," Daria cuts in. "And anyway, that's why *you're* here . . . but why am I?"

"Because, for one thing, the food smells great and there's nothing decent to eat at my place. And for another, it's better than—"

"Yeah, I know. Only sitting home doesn't sound so bad. I was planning on ordering a pizza, watching *Sleepless in Seattle* on cable for the hundredth time, and eating that whole box of truffles I got for Christmas."

"Then you shouldn't have said yes," Tammy snaps.

I did it for you, Daria wants to snap back. *I should really be home doing some good old-fashioned soul-searching.*

But, getting a closer look at her sister's face, she bites her tongue.

"Are you okay, Tam?"

"Not really. This song . . ." She points vaguely toward the band. "Hear it?"

Daria listens as the lead singer croons a midsong stanza opening, "*Hello . . . is it me you're lookin' for?*"

It takes her a moment to recognize the old Lionel Richie ballad. "Yes, I hear it," she tells her sister, knowing what's coming.

"Carlton is sending me this song."

Daria nods. Her sister believes that if you hear a meaningful song at a particular time in your life, it's no accident. Tammy is convinced that spirits use music to communicate with the living, and as far as she's concerned, this particular rendition of "Hello" is coming straight from her husband in heaven.

Maybe she's right. Maybe she's not, but if it brings her comfort, let her go on believing.

"I've been thinking . . ." Tammy shakes her head. "Never mind."

"What?"

"Just . . . the other night, I met this guy who—"

"Asked you out?" Daria perks up, wondering if Tammy has finally realized that if she started to date again, she wouldn't be cheating on a man who's been dead for years.

"No! Nothing like that. He's much younger than me, and anyway, you know I'm not interested in that. No, what I was going to say was that his aura was so oppressive . . . it was like he was literally carrying around this burden of heavy black grief, mired in the past, not letting himself let go. I could see so clearly what he needed to do, but it wasn't until later that I realized . . . I'm doing the same thing, in a way."

Daria just nods in silent agreement, not wanting to say it's about time her sister figured that out.

"So I was thinking this guy was being stubborn, because he hates change and can't let himself move on, and meanwhile . . . I'm the same way."

"It's hard, sweetie. I know."

"And the holidays . . ." Tammy shakes her head. "They're especially hard. You know?"

"I know."

"Even after all these years, New Year's Eve . . ." Tammy toys with another potato chip. "It's just like Valentine's Day, Halloween . . ."

"Halloween?"

"It was a romantic holiday for me and Carlton. Remember how we always used to dress up together? One year, we were Samson and Delilah, another year we were Bert and Ernie . . ."

"Bert and Ernie? That's romantic?"

Tammy cracks a smile. "Maybe not so much. But New Year's Eve . . . you're supposed to be in love, kissing someone at midnight, dancing cheek to cheek . . ." Tammy eats the potato chip in her hand, crunching joylessly.

Ruffles happen to be one of her weaknesses. Truffles are Daria's. Truffles, and Fresh Starts.

"Hey," she says to Tammy, "I'll dance with you."

Her sister lights up. "You will?"

"Sure. Just like when we were kids," Daria says and gestures at the band. "The next 'Beer Barrel Polka,' I'm all yours."

Tammy laughs and sticks out her hand. "Deal."

Daria shakes it. "And if we do get a 'Beer Barrel Polka,' I'm sure Mrs. Kowalski will be sending it."

Her sister grins fondly at the memory of their long-ago neighbor in Chicago.

Mrs. Kowalski taught the two of them to polka back when Tammy was in her midteens, Daria about five and up to her waist. They made an awkward pair, but it was fun, whirling around the old world apartment on the south side.

Mrs. Kowalski used to feed them homemade sausage and pirogi, too, and sew missing buttons on their clothes. They lived across the hall from her for less than a year, but the elderly woman did all the things she thought a mother should do. Things their own mother didn't do.

Not because Aurora didn't love them.

More because she simply didn't know how.

To polka, to cook and sew, to be a mom.

At least, the kind of mom Mrs. Kowalski—and a lot of other people—thought she should be.

Daria wrote to their old neighbor for a while after they moved away, to Indianapolis, to Fort Lauderdale, to Dallas.

Mrs. Kowalski wrote back a few times, newsy notes in spidery handwriting on stationery that smelled faintly of cabbage, cigarettes, and Jovan Musk perfume. Eventually, the notes stopped coming.

Maybe the forwarding addresses expired.

More likely, Mrs. Kowalski did.

It would be nice to see her again, wherever she is. Chicago, or the Great Beyond. So far, though, she hasn't popped up yet—in the flesh, or otherwise.

Speaking of which. . . .

There he is again.

The old Italian-looking guy, the one with the gold cross and the wedding band and the beseeching expression in his eyes. The same guy—*ghost*—Daria chose to ignore when he appeared the other day in Tammy's apartment.

He's hovering a few feet away, watching her.

Persistent, aren't you? What do you want from me? And what are you doing here?

For that matter, what is *she* doing here, really?

She's been wondering all night.

Yeah, well, now you know.

Okay, she doesn't really *know*, but she has some idea.

Her presence at Most Precious Mother tonight is no accident. She's here for a reason. One that has nothing to do with her sister or great-smelling food, and everything to do with the spirit, Sad Eyes . . . whoever he is.

Another New Year's Eve at Most Precious Mother Church Hall.

Ralphie has missed only one that he can remember—when he and his brothers and sisters all came down with a stomach bug on the thirtieth. It was either that, or Great Aunt Connie's leftover Christmas ham had gone bad in the fridge after a few days. Without a mom in the house to keep track of stuff like that, the Chickalini brood had endured their share of toxic leftovers over the years.

But other than that year, when he was still in grade school, Ralphie has always been right here to ring in the New Year.

The crowd has changed over the years, as has the neighborhood. Astoria used to be primarily Greek and Italian, but the last few decades have brought in a multi-cultural flair, along with an influx of upscale professionals and hipsters. Not that the hipsters are celebrating New Year's at the church hall.

The party definitely used to be more of a family affair. These days, most people leave the little ones at home. His sisters Nina and Rosalee are here with each other, rather than their husbands. Joey is on late duty at the pizzeria, Timmy at the firehouse.

In a couple of years, Ralphie supposes, he'll be doing the same thing—working all hours to support Francesca and their four little Ralphies. Working as the IT guy at a Manhattan accounting firm is a far cry from his dream career as star forward for the New York Knicks, but his job provides a good living and a nice benefits package for a family man. What more could a guy ask for?

That's what Francesca likes to say whenever he hints that he's not exactly thrilled with his position.

Anyway, what's he going to do? Quit?

You don't like change.

He half-smiles at the memory of Madame Tamar's profound comment.

Then, spotting Bebe making her way through the crowd, he abruptly tells his brother Dominic, "I'm going to the bar to get another beer."

"One for me, too!" Dominic calls as he heads for the bar, and Ralphie circles his thumb and forefinger to show that he heard.

Bebe is the last person he wants to see right now. She popped in yesterday for a holiday visit, arriving about five minutes after he returned from dropping his brother Pete and family at the airport for their flight back to Germany. He was looking forward to some peace and quiet, having the house to himself again, but no such luck.

Bebe brought with her a tin filled with unappetizing dark green and neon blue-frosted Christmas cookies and an ALOHA HONOLULU honeymoon brochure courtesy of her cousin Alma over at Liberty Travel.

Ralphie promised to show it to Francesca. Which he didn't do. Mostly because Francesca was home sick in bed all last night and all day today. Ralphie figured he would be forced to come solo tonight or sit at home, since she wouldn't even let him come over to see her, saying she didn't want him to catch it. Anyway, as usual, her mother was taking care of her.

Ralphie's future mother-in-law thrives on taking care of her daughter, her sons, her husband—and yes, Ralphie himself, when he lets her. Mrs. Buccigrossi doesn't speak much English, but he's learned to say things like "I'm perfectly capable of cutting my own meat" using hand gestures.

Francesca unexpectedly rebounded late today, and here she is, in a figure-hugging purple sequined dress and heels about as tall as the counter stools at Big Pizza Pie—as is the pile of hair on her head.

Ralphie—who is learning—told her she looks perfect.

Francesca isn't a hundred percent herself, though. He can tell. She's putting on a good show, but a couple of times, when she didn't know Ralphie was watching, he caught her looking . . . well, sick.

"Nina—" He finds his sister on the edge of the dance floor, watching, and taps her on the shoulder "—do you need a drink? I'm going to the bar."

"Oh—no, thanks, sweetie. I've got to be up early to make the pasta and I don't want to be all hung over."

Ralphie nods. Regular old spaghetti and meatballs are a Sunday staple in their family, but New Year's Day calls for the big guns. Instead of coming from boxes on the supermarket shelf, the noodles—enough for a dozen Chickalinis with big appetites—are traditionally made by hand, with a delicate egg dough that's rolled out, pains-takingly cut, and dried on special racks passed down by Ralphie's great-grandmother.

"Hey, Neens, are you okay?" He asks his sister, notic-ing that she seems a little lackluster.

"Sure. I just miss Joey. But it's okay." She shrugs. "It's the restaurant business. God knows we're used to it."

God knows they are. All of them. Ralphie spent much of his childhood helping Pop make and serve up pizzas to hordes of loyal customers. Big Pizza Pie is as much a Chickalini family tradition as New Year's Day dinner.

He promises Nina a dance later and leaves her by the dance floor, looking wistful.

"Hey, kid, good to see you! What'll it be?" Lou San-tarello, an old friend of Pop's, is bartending tonight. "The usual? A Bud?"

"Two Buds, a seltzer, and an orange juice."

"What, no champagne?"

"Not tonight." Ralphie shrugs.

The seltzer is for Mia, who said she's champagned out after her wedding reception. Francesca, on the other hand, has already downed a couple of glasses of cham-pagne. The orange juice is for her whether she wants it or not—and Ralphie figures she doesn't.

"Hey, Ed!" Lou calls. "Can you run out back and grab me another OJ?" To Ralphie, he adds, "Can you wait a few minutes for it?"

Ralphie shifts his gaze to see Bebe clinging to Domi-nic's arm, talking his ear off.

"I can wait as long as it takes," he tells Lou.

"Okay. What else did you need? Two Buds and a seltzer, right? Hey, look who's back," Lou exclaims cheerfully. "How's it going, Rose Red? Another chardonnay and cabernet for you and Snow White?"

"Another chardonnay," a female voice answers, "but this time I'll have some Irish Cream, if you've got it."

"I've got it. On the rocks?"

"Sure. I don't suppose you've got some whipped cream you can squirt on top?"

"Got it. What, are we making a dessert here?"

"Well, I was supposed to be home alone tonight eating pizza and an entire box of truffles, so I'm trying to make up for lost chocolate."

At that comment, Ralphie, who's been watching Francesca socialize and half-listening to Lou's banter with the female voice, turns his head.

He finds himself looking at the church organist Millicent Milagros's curly gray head, but she wasn't the one who was talking about chocolate. That voice was throaty, while Millicent speaks like she sings, in a high-pitched, trilling soprano.

Ralphie adjusts his gaze and realizes someone is standing at the bar between him and Millicent. Someone tiny, especially next to Ralphie's lanky frame.

Rose Red.

That's what Lou called her.

The first thing he notices is her mouth. She's smiling broadly. Her white, even teeth are like something out of a toothpaste commercial, the kind that advertises a kissable mouth—not that Ralphie's thinking about kissing her. Just noticing some nice orthodonture, he assures himself. That, and an attractive color of lipstick, exactly the shade of a luscious, ripe August tomato—not that Ralphie's any expert on makeup, or, for that matter, tomatoes.

Fashion, either, though he does note that she's wearing a red dress with spaghetti straps, made of some kind of soft fabric that falls in a graceful straight cut to a point about halfway between her hip and thigh. It looks like a 1920s flapper dress, Ralphie concludes, and can't help comparing it to the tight red number his fiancée was wearing the other night.

He likes this style better. A lot better, he notes, and pushes back a twinge of guilt as he finds himself comparing Rose Red's hair to Francesca's. They're both brunettes, but Rose Red's is almost black, cut very short and pushed back behind her ears. Who knew short hair could be so sexy on a woman? A hell of a lot sexier than a teased, sprayed tower with a fake flower growing out of the middle of it.

Although to be fair, Francesca isn't sporting the silk poinsettia tonight; nor is she wearing red.

Wait—what the heck is she wearing again?

Ralphie's eyes flick in the direction where she was standing, and finds the spot empty. He sees a flash of purple sequins—oh, right, purple—and realizes she's making a beeline for the ladies' room.

Uh-oh. That can't be good.

He should just take her home. Why is she here when she's obviously feeling like crud?

And why, when his fiancée is obviously feeling like crud, is Ralphie checking out another woman?

You're not, he assures himself, and looks away, wishing Lou would hurry up with his juice.

"Here you go, Rose," he hears Lou say.

Rose.

The name slams into Ralphie and he jerks his head around.

Oh. Lou's talking to the girl in the red dress. The one he was calling Rose Red.

Ralphie's mom was Rose, though. And whenever he hears the name, he thinks of her.

Wouldn't it be something if this woman's name turned out to be Rose, too?

Why would that be something? Ralphie demands uneasily of himself. It's not as though she has any connection to his late mother—much less to Ralphie.

She's just a stranger at the bar, and you'll never see her again, and hello, don't you have a fiancée to tend to?

"Thanks." Rose Red—who incidentally looks nothing like Ralphie's late mother—takes the two glasses Lou hands her.

"See you again." Lou two-finger salutes her.

"That depends . . . you don't have any candy back there, do you?"

"Sorry."

"Well, I'm thinking of heading home to my truffles pretty soon, so . . ."

"You're leaving before midnight? Pretty girl like you?" Lou, the old flirt, asks with a twinkle in his eye.

Ralphie finds himself bristling—and not just because Lou's a married guy. He can't help asking, "Hey, Lou, aren't you spoken for already?"

"What? Yeah, well, so are you, Chachi," Lou shoots back.

Chachi—he started calling Ralphie that back when he was just a kid, after the character Scott Baio played on

Happy Days. The show was long before Ralphie's time, but he caught it in reruns once in a while, and yeah, okay, he does look something like Chachi. But he wouldn't admit it to Lou and is glad the nickname never caught on with anyone else.

To Rose Red, Lou—who's big on nicknames even for complete strangers—says, "I figured you'd still be here on the dance floor when they play 'Auld Lang Syne,' kissing your sweetie."

"The only sweetie on my mind tonight is chocolate," she says with an easy laugh, and catches Ralphie's eye.

He finds himself smiling back at her.

Not that she was really smiling *at* him; she was just laughing and happened to look at him.

"If you hang around till midnight, Prince Charming might just show up and sweep you off your feet," Lou is telling her. "You never know."

She looks dubiously at the crowd and returns, "Sometimes you do."

"What," Ralphie pipes up, "you got a problem with married family guys and priests and senior citizens?"

She looks momentarily taken aback, then even more surprised when she realizes he's teasing.

"Of course not. This crowd? Every single gal's dream. It's just that I had my heart set on chocolate and pizza, and . . . well, you know how that goes."

"*C'est la vie,*" Ralphie says with a shrug.

"There's a lot of pizza here." Lou gestures toward the buffet table. "More pizza than you ever seen in your life."

"Yeah, but sometimes it tastes better out of a box," Ralphie can't help but say.

"Let me guess . . . a box from a little place just down the block called Big Pizza Pie, right?" Lou shakes his head and unscrews the cap on a bottle of Black Velvet to make a drink for someone.

"Exactly," Ralphie replies. "You can't beat Big Pizza Pie."

"You can't beat my wife Maria's pizza," Lou says, "and she made three of them tonight, so stick around, Rose Red, and I'll grab you a piece when I get a free minute."

"Yeah?" Rose Red looks at Lou, then, when he turns his back to fill a glass with ice, at Ralphie.

Ralphie has encountered his share of Maria Santarello's pizza, which as Pop used to say, counts cat hair among its usual toppings. He shakes his head at Rose Red, sticks out his tongue, and makes a slitting gesture across his throat with his forefinger.

She raises an eyebrow and mouths, "Thanks."

She throws a couple of dollars onto the bar, takes her drinks, and disappears.

"Never seen her here before," Lou comments, returning to Ralphie and shaking a fresh carton of orange juice.

"Nope."

"She's beautiful, huh?"

"Uh-huh."

"Wonder where she came from? I bet you dollars to donuts Manhattan."

"Maybe," says Ralphie, who was thinking the same thing.

He reminds himself that he has no business giving another moment's thought to the beautiful woman in red.

He has other things to worry about.

Like the MIA woman in purple.

"Here's that OJ, Chachi," Lou says handing him a glass. "Thanks for waiting."

"No problem," Ralphie murmurs, and wonders uneasily if Francesca's okay.

He looks around for her and is startled to spot an unexpected face in the crowd.

Madame Tamar again?

What is she doing here?

He watches her sipping from a full glass of white wine and notes that she doesn't seem to be enjoying herself much. She looks kind of . . . depressed.

Is she here alone, on New Year's Eve?

Why?

Trying to drum up new clients for her fortune-telling business, probably.

He remembers the business card she gave him the other night. She said they needed to talk.

He doesn't buy into any of that stuff, no matter what Dom and Mia say. Still . . .

It is a little unsettling.

Not unsettling enough to do anything about it, however.

Ralphie decides to forget about Madame Tamar. He has drinks to deliver and a fiancée who seems to be missing in action.

This isn't the first time Daria has walked into a ladies' room and found a presumably inebriated stranger sobbing her heart out.

It is, however, the first time she's seen a man in the ladies' room, which is just not right, even if said man happens to be dead as Marley's ghost.

She narrows her eyes at Sad Eyes, who gives her such a pointed look she blurts, "You're not supposed to be in here."

"I know!" wails the sobbing stranger at the sink, face buried in her hands.

Oops.

"Ralphie sent you in for me, right?" she asks Daria, who notices her nails are long and curved and polished the same purple shade as her dress, dusted in silver glitter to mimic the sequined fabric. Her generous cleavage—visible enough as it is—is also dusted in some kind of glittery powder.

Daria averts her eyes. "Actually, I just had to pee. I have no idea who Ralphie is."

"Oh." The woman peers miserably at Daria through soggy eyes rimmed by running mascara. "I'm sorry, I thought you were someone we know."

"I guess I have one of those faces."

"Yeah, you do," agrees the unhappy stranger, fumbling with the wet wad of tissue in her hand to blow her nose, loud and hard.

On that note . . .

Sad Eyes has vanished, Daria notes, and the bathroom is otherwise empty. She heads into a stall and has every intention of closing the door behind her.

But something makes her instead unspool a good length of toilet paper, step back out of the stall, and hand it to the stranger.

"Here," she says, "I don't see any Kleenex, but . . ."

"Thanks." She accepts it gratefully, blows her nose again, even louder. "I'm sorry."

"Nice to meet you, Sorry. I'm Daria."

The halfhearted quip—one of her sister Tammy's old standbys—is met with a blank stare, followed by an "Oh! I get it. That's funny."

It really isn't, and she's not laughing, but at least she's not crying anymore.

She's not drunk, either—at least, she doesn't seem it. Upset and disheveled, yes.

Daria wonders what happened, and decides she doesn't really want to know. She's got her own problems to resolve, not to mention her very own heartbreak kid on the other side of the bathroom door, drowning her sorrows in chardonnay and Ruffles.

"I'm Francesca Buccigrossi." The stranger transfers both the new used tissue and the sodden clump of more used tissue to her left hand and offers Daria her right. "It's nice to meet you, Daria."

Daria shakes her hand gingerly. "You, too."

Francesca sighs heavily.

"Are you . . . um, okay?"

"Yes," replies Francesca, who is obviously not the least bit okay. Black-tinted tears are rolling down her cheeks again.

"Are you sure?"

Francesca bobs her head so furiously that her hair, piled into a tall topknot, teeters and lists dangerously to one side.

"Okay, well . . ." Daria takes a step toward the stall again.

"Except . . ."

Here we go.

"I'm not really okay, I guess."

Surprise, surprise.

Daria glances longingly at the stall, then at the exit.

"Can I ask your advice on something?"

Reluctantly, Daria says, "Sure."

If only someone—say, Francesca's mother, or Dear Abby—would come in and rescue her.

"If you were engaged to the most perfect guy in the world, would you go through with the wedding?"

Talk about a no-brainer.

But it's obviously a trick question. And one that just happens to resonate with Daria.

"I'm not sure what you mean," she says cautiously.

Francesca emits another sigh, her sparkly cleavage just about heaving right out of her dress. "The thing is, I know he's totally perfect for me—everyone says so—and he thinks I'm perfect for him, too. Everyone says so. But things just don't feel right, you know?"

"You absolutely should break off the engagement if things don't feel right," Daria tells her firmly.

"I don't know. Maybe I just have cold feet—I've been feeling that way for a few months now and that happens to a lot of people, right?" At Daria's nod, she confides, "I was going to ask my fiancé for a little space a few months ago to, you know, get my head on straight. But then his father died suddenly, and how could I do it then?"

"You couldn't," Daria agrees, shaking her head. "That's rough."

"I mean, I might have cold feet, but I don't have a cold heart, you know? We did put off the wedding till next summer. I figured the extra time might take some pressure off me, and I would see that we really are perfect for each other like everyone says, but . . ."

"It didn't help?"

"No. I can't put my finger on what's wrong between us, either. It's like . . . Ralphie's been so serious lately. He never wants to have any fun since his father died."

No kidding.

Daria wants to remind her the poor guy—poor Ralphie—just suffered a loss and probably isn't exactly in the mood for fun, but before she can say anything, Francesca goes on, "I think he thinks I talk too much about silly things. Well, they're not silly to me. Like gossip columns and fashion."

Daria is starting to feel for poor Ralphie.

"And he laughs because I always wear my raincoat when we sit out in his back yard, even if the sun is shining, which is because there are all these pigeons around and one once pooped on me. I don't know . . . sometimes I feel like he just thinks I'm kind of . . . I don't know . . ."

Daria fights a smile and the urge to supply an adjective, certain Francesca won't find it flattering.

"Wacky," Francesca says.

Bingo! That's the adjective.

She does seem more than a little wacky. Not that there's anything wrong with that, but . . .

"Between you and me?" Francesca leans toward Daria as if they're the utmost confidantes. "Sometimes I think Ralphie's kind of . . . well, he's not *blah*, exactly . . ."

Blah? Daria thinks of her sister's beige Ikea couch. Functional, but definitely blah.

"He's just not as fun as I am," Francesca tells her. "I like to, you know, do things that are . . . I don't know . . ."

"Wacky?" Daria supplies helpfully this time.

"Exactly! Wacky—in a good way."

"Is there any other?" Daria asks, deadpan.

"And I'm trying to be understanding because I know he's going through a hard time, I really am, but it's really depressing to be around him and in that house with all his dad's stuff around. He's really set in his ways, but I mean, you've got to move on, you know?"

"He lived with his father?" she asks sympathetically.

Francesca nods.

Poor Ralphie.

"Yeah. He never got a place of his own. They have a really tight family. He actually wanted me to move into the house after the wedding. I can't do it. The place is still full of everyone else's stuff—his father's and his sisters' and brothers' and even his mother's, and she's been gone for years. I feel like it would never be *our* home. Like I would never really belong there, like I wouldn't even if I lived there for a long time. You know what I mean?"

Do I ever, Daria thinks.

She reminds herself that this isn't about her, but it's hard to ignore the memories of her own past.

"I just don't think I can break it off, though. I feel like he needs me."

"Listen, Francesca, you can't go ahead and marry this guy just because he says he needs you."

"Well, he doesn't *say* it, but it's obvious. And anyway, I do love him."

"That's not everything. Love doesn't matter in the end if things don't feel right."

"Maybe I really do just have cold feet, though. He's such a great guy . . ."

"You know what? I was once engaged to a great guy, too," Daria finds herself saying—thought it's not usually her favorite subject. "And even though my heart was trying to tell me I wasn't in love with him, I went through with the wedding because it seemed like the sensible thing to do."

"And . . . ?"

"And, long story short, it didn't work out." No need to go into the gory details.

"So you wish you'd never gotten married in the first place, then?"

"Let's just say I learned a lot from the experience. And I'm glad it's over." She glances at the stall again. She really does have to go.

"You know what, Daria?"

"What?"

"You're, like, the wisest person I've ever met. Thanks to you, I'm going to march out there and tell Ralphie it's over."

"Uh—right now?"

"*Right* now."

"But . . . I mean, it's New Year's Eve . . ." And some poor sap is about to get dumped in the midst of a big old party, thanks to Daria. "Maybe you should wait until tomorrow."

"I can't do that. Tomorrow's a holiday. There's this big pasta dinner at his place. It's a family tradition. I'm supposed to be bringing the braciole."

"The what?"

"Braciole. It's a New Year's tradition. You know—flank steak rolled around hard-boiled eggs and cheese and salami? Cooked in sauce?"

Daria, whose family wasn't big on tradition and who doesn't know flank steak rolled around hard-boiled eggs and cheese and salami cooked in sauce, nods anyway.

"Well, then, you should just wait till the holiday's over. Break up with him on the second. Or the third, even . . ."

"If I wait, I'll lose my nerve. Anyway, New Year's Eve is supposed to be out with the old, in with the new, right?"

"Er—right."

"And New Year's Day is all about fresh starts, right?"

"Right."

"So that's it. Thanks, Daria. Hope things work out for you." Francesca hugs her and sails out of the room to find her unfortunate soon-to-be-ex fiancé.

Oh, well.

As that cute guy named Chachi at the bar—the one the bartender mentioned was spoken for—said, in a charming Queens accent: *C'est la vie.*

Chapter
4

The bell jangles, as always, when Ralphie opens the door and steps into Big Pizza Pie. As always, the air is heavy with the scent of oregano and tomato sauce. And as always, an easy-listening radio station is playing in the background, one that features his father's favorite music from the twenties, thirties, and forties.

Tonight, the family restaurant—strung from ceiling to floor in red and green Christmas lights—is unusually quiet. The half dozen small tables, covered in red and white checkered oilcloth, are deserted, as are the stools at the counter.

The sign on the red-garland-draped door—scrawled on a piece of notebook paper in green Sharpie—reads WE WILL BE CLOSED NEW YEAR'S DAY.

Maybe next year, Ralphie thinks, *we should just be closed New Year's Eve, too. Even the regulars all have other plans tonight.*

Change. It's all about change these days.

Hanging beside an old framed poster of Cher and Nicolas Cage in *Moonstruck*, the green chalkboard bears a note—

"Try our new fruit antipasto!"—that makes Ralphie want to cringe.

His brother-in-law Joey Materi, wearing a long red apron, looks up from the *New York Post* spread before him on the counter.

"Ralphie! What are you doing here?"

Good question.

He isn't quite sure of the answer; just found his feet carrying him down the familiar block after he left Francesca at her parents' doorstep. She was crying. Funny, since she was the one who broke up with him.

"I came to relieve you," he hears himself tell his brother-in-law.

"What?" Joey shakes his graying head, the faint network of wrinkles around his eyes deepening in confusion.

"Yeah." Ralphie looks at his watch. "You've got about ten minutes to get over to the church hall if you're planning to kiss your wife at the stroke of midnight."

"Are you serious? You'll cover for me?"

"Sure." Ralphie reaches for an apron.

Joey's already untying his. "Don't you want to be there yourself?"

"Nah, I think Nina'd rather kiss you," he cracks.

"I meant—oh, that's right, Nina said something about Francesca being under the weather. She didn't make it tonight, huh?" Joey doesn't wait for a reply. "It stinks being alone at a New Year's Eve party."

"Yeah," Ralphie agrees, "it does. So go spare Nina. She'll be thrilled to see you."

"Thanks, you're the best."

"Ha, not everyone thinks so," Ralphie mutters under his breath.

Halfway to the door, Joey turns and stops short, looks Ralphie in the eye. "Hey . . ."

"Yeah?"

"Are you okay?"

Joey—who grew up next door and was like a big brother to Ralphie long before he married Nina and adopted Ralphie's baby—knows him too well.

"I'm fine."

"You don't look it."

Ralphie holds up his left wrist and gestures at the watch. "Nine minutes, Joey."

"It's a one-minute walk. I've got plenty of time. C'mon, what's going on?"

"Nothing, I'm good."

Joey hesitates.

If he were Nina—or Rosalee—he'd push and prod.

Thank God he isn't.

"Okay," he says with a shrug. "You know where to find me if you change your mind. I'll be back in an hour in case there's a rush when all the parties wind down."

"Don't bother, I can handle it. Go kiss your wife, have a toast, then go home to your kids."

Something Ralphie won't be doing so soon, after all.

"Thanks, kid. I owe you one."

The door jangles to a close behind Joey.

Ralphie plunks down on a stool, takes a deep breath . . .

And could swear he smells his father's favorite cologne mingling with the aroma of Italian cuisine.

It's so distinct that he looks around, half-expecting to see Pop standing there in his apron, ready to dish up a slice from the row of whole pies behind the glass case.

Wouldn't that be something? Pop would say he really didn't die, that it was all a bad dream.

Yeah. Right. That's definitely going to happen.

Okay, obviously, Ralphie's rattled. Is it any wonder?

His head is still spinning . . . and not from beer or champagne.

He was only a couple of sips into his second Bud when Francesca barreled over to him and told him they had to talk. Right that minute. Outside.

"I can't do it, Ralphie," she said, shivering in her skimpy purple dress, her breath puffing white in the December night air. "I can't marry you. I love you to death, but I can't marry you."

He has no clue what else she said after that, or what he said back.

Does it matter?

It's over.

It's over, and the diamond engagement ring he gave her is back in his pocket, and all he can feel is . . .

Relief.

You're off the hook.

Guilt stabs through him.

Off the hook? Is this what he wanted?

Maybe. Maybe he's glad she took the initiative to stop the wedding. Otherwise, he'd have had to do it.

But what if he hadn't figured that out in time? Then where would they be?

In about six months, married and living in a Bebe-connected condo on Steinway Street. That's where.

Thank God, Ralphie thinks. *Thank God she called it off.*

Granted, he did have tears in his eyes when he hugged

Francesca at her door, with her crying loud and hard. She kept apologizing.

"It's okay," he told her, hating that he felt like it really was.

He told himself he must be in shock. That as soon as it hit him, he'd be feeling like crap.

But now that a couple of hours have passed and the shock has worn off . . .

It's still okay.

Sure, he's sad—but it's a mixed kind of sadness, like when he was ten and his best friend Niko moved to the Bronx. In fact, he couldn't help but think of that occasion just now when he left Francesca at her door and walked away.

Before Niko moved, Ralphie used to feel as though his friend was cramping his style. All he ever wanted to do was ride bikes and talk about *Star Wars*, and he was no good at shooting hoops, which was Ralphie's passion. But their friendship was a habit.

Ralphie and Niko didn't hug goodbye the day the moving van arrived, and Niko wasn't sobbing hysterically, though he was crying, and yes, Ralphie had tears in his eyes as he walked away.

They dried by the time he got to Ditmars Boulevard.

Just as they did tonight.

He and Niko never saw each other again . . . and Ralphie didn't really miss him much, once he got used to it. That part of his life was over, they had outgrown each other, and it was time to move on.

This is different, though. Way different.

At least, it should be.

Shouldn't a broken engagement hit him harder than having a boyhood pal move to another borough?

Regardless of his ambivalence about the summer wedding, shouldn't he feel something stronger right now than this mellow sadness laced with relief?

Yeah. He should. He probably will.

Maybe it'll hit him hard tomorrow, when it sinks in.

Maybe—

The bell on the door jangles as it opens.

He looks up, half-expecting to see Nina or Rosalee. Word travels fast around here.

To Ralphie's shock, though, it isn't one of his sisters.

It isn't Pop, either, coming to say it was all a bad dream, even though the scent of his cologne really is stuck in Ralphie's head and seems stronger than ever right now.

No.

It's . . . *her.*

Blowing breathlessly in the door with cheeks that match her dress.

Rose Red.

"What are you doing here?"

Daria stares at him in surprise, then finds her voice.

"You just took the words out of my mouth," she tells him—Chachi, the guy the bartender said was already attached to someone. The guy who said *C'est la vie.*

C'est la vie, indeed.

"Aren't you at a party around the corner?" she asks, trying not to smile and not quite sure why she wants to.

"Aren't you?"

"Yes, but, see, I have this talent," she takes a few bold

steps into the pizzeria, "for being in two places at the same time. You?"

"Same exact talent, if you can believe that."

"I can't."

"Really. Right at this very moment, I'm also drinking a Bud and listening to the band play 'Shout.'"

"You're not dancing to it, though?"

"I'm not much of a dancer. How about you? I bet you love to dance."

"Especially to 'Shout.'" She hunches her shoulders and mimics it, whisper-singing, *"A little bit softer now, a little bit softer now* . . . Yeah, it's my favorite song of all time."

"Really?"

"Not really. I hate that song."

"Me, too. What do you like?"

"Everything the Rolling Stones ever recorded," she says promptly.

"That's it?"

"No, I mean, the Stones are my favorite, but I pretty much like anything and everything else."

"Except 'Shout.'"

"Except 'Shout,'" she agrees. "This is a good song. I love Frankie." She points at the speaker mounted up near the ceiling.

Frank Sinatra's voice spills from it: *"The best is yet to come, and babe, won't it be nice . . ."*

Daria tilts her head to the side, listening. "It's a good one for New Year's Eve, don't you think?"

"Sure," Chachi says amiably, but there's a flash of uncertainty in his brown eyes.

"So . . . what are you doing here?" Daria asks. "Seriously. And wearing an apron, no less."

"What does it look like I'm doing here?"

"Working."

He juts out an arm and points at her. "Bingo. You're a smart cookie."

"So I've been told."

She's flirting, dammit. With a guy who already has a girl.

It figures Chachi's taken. He's too cute, with an appealing down-to-earth, easygoing way about him, to be available. Especially in this neighborhood, where nice Italian boys are probably *de rigueur* for nice Italian girls.

"So you're a pizza guy, then?" she asks, charmed by the down-to-earth-ness of it all.

"Nah," he says, "I'm just filling in for my brother-in-law. It's a family business so I do that sometimes. Mondays through Fridays, nine-to-five, I'm an IT guy."

"What's that?"

"Information technology?" he asks, as if that'll mean something to her.

It doesn't. She shrugs. "I'm not very . . . technical. Or technological. Or whatever. Where do you work?"

"An accounting firm in midtown."

Huh. She kind of liked him better as a pizza guy. It made him seem more . . . her speed.

"What do you do?" Chachi wants to know in return.

"Right now?" Okay, that was a stupid answer. Of course right now.

The trouble is . . . she's pretty sure the real answer—"nothing"—isn't going to impress him, either.

Not that she's trying to impress him. Because, really, what does it matter what he thinks of her?

"My degree is in art." At least that's the truth. "And I've done various things with it. Right now, I'm an interior designer, with a new job lined up after the New Year." Also the truth.

"So how'd you happen to pop up here?"

"You mean—New York? Or the pizzeria?"

"Both, I guess."

She chooses the easier question. "I was walking to the subway, saw the sign, and remembered that I heard from *someone* that the pizza here is great."

"That, it is."

"Good. I'm counting on it, since I stopped in for a slice."

"My pleasure." He slides off his stool and starts rummaging around on the countertop. "There's a list of toppings somewhere . . ."

"Don't bother." She slips out of her coat—a vintage black velvet one she found at a thrift shop in the East Village. "I just like cheese and pepperoni."

Chachi stops rummaging. "No goat cheese or pineapple?"

"Maybe on a salad, but pizza? I just want regular pizza."

"And chocolate," he adds. "Right?"

Surprised he remembers, she agrees, "Right. But not on my pizza."

"I might be able to rustle up some of my Aunt Carm's homemade almond chocolate-dipped biscotti."

"You do, and you'll make my year."

"Talk about incentive." He goes behind the counter

and looks around. "Aunt Carm dropped off a boatload of biscotti over here yesterday. But I don't see it now. I bet Joey scarfed it all down or took it home with him."

"Joey?"

"My brother-in-law who runs the place."

"Except on New Year's Eve?"

"Pretty much. Sorry about the biscotti, but we do have pizza." He gestures at the glass-fronted case, where several pies sit waiting to be cut and reheated.

Chachi slips a big spatula beneath an enormous slice of pepperoni pizza, separates it from the rest of the pie, and slides it into the big brick wall oven.

Daria's mouth is already watering. She didn't eat at the party, other than a few handfuls of Ruffles as her sister and the late arrival Lenore held an impromptu and unofficial meeting of the lonely hearts club.

Daria wanted no part of it—regardless of her own lonely heart, which she prefers to keep to herself—and finally told them both she was heading home.

"You can't leave before midnight!" Tammy protested.

Wishing her sister would do the same—and be spared watching all those couples locking lips at the strike of twelve—Daria breezily said, "My pumpkin awaits," and left.

She fully expected to be sitting on the N train when midnight rolls around, but that was fine with her.

"Want anything to drink?" Chachi asks. "Sorry I'm fresh out of Irish Cream."

"Pop's okay."

He looks taken aback for a moment, then the light dawns. "Oh! I thought . . . I mean, we called my father Pop, so for a second there I thought . . ."

She switches to the local vernacular. "I meant soda. Not pop."

"You're not from New York."

"No. You're a smart cookie, too."

"Where are you from?"

"Well, I picked up 'pop' in Chicago, but that's not where I'm from."

"So where are you from?" he repeats.

"That," Daria says, taking the stool he vacated at the counter, "is an impossible question to answer."

"Because . . . ?"

"Because I'm a gypsy," she says simply, deciding she might as well tell him the whole truth.

What has she got to lose, anyway?

"Did you say you're a gypsy?"

"Yup. Literally and figuratively."

"Really." He balls a fist beneath his chin and looks intrigued.

She shrugs. "Sometimes I feel like there isn't a place on earth where I haven't lived at some point."

"So you're much, much older than you look, obviously."

"Twenty-seven."

"You're younger than I am, and I've only lived in one place."

"Here in Astoria?"

He nods. "In the same house. My whole life."

Her jaw drops. "I can't even imagine that. It must be so . . ."

"Blah?"

"Blah? No! I was thinking it was great."

Wow. Talk about always knowing where you belong.

"My fiancée calls it blah. Calls *me* blah, actually."

Daria is so bummed to hear Chachi mention his fiancée—God knows why, and anyway, it's not as if she didn't already know he was involved with someone—that it takes a moment for the rest of his sentence to register.

His fiancée calls him blah. And he's still living in his childhood home. Presumably right here in Queens.

Wait a minute.

Can it be . . . ?

No way.

That, Daria decides, would be too big a coincidence. *Anyway, his name isn't Ralphie. It's Chachi.*

"Did I say fiancée? I should say, my ex-fiancée, as of—" Chachi checks his watch "—about ninety minutes ago."

Daria gapes at him.

Yes way.

"Is your fiancée's name," she asks Chachi, "by any chance . . . Francesca?"

Okay, that's weird.

She knows Francesca's name.

Well, it's not weird, exactly. More like . . .

Interesting.

"Yeah," he says, "how'd you know?"

"Um . . ." She shifts around on her chair, looking a little freaked out. "I'm actually a psychic."

Obviously, she's kidding around. In a deadpan way.

"Yeah, right. So anyway, I'm Ralph," he says, and sticks out his hand, still wondering how she knows Francesca.

"Ralph." She shakes his hand slowly. "Not Ralphie?"

"Well . . . that's what my family calls me. And my

friends. And pretty much everyone else around here, which since I've lived here all my life is pretty much everyone I know, but I work in Manhattan and they call me Ralph there, thank God."

"Thank God? Why?"

"Because, Ralphie's a ridiculous name for a grown man." Not that he always feels like a grown man when he's around his family—especially his sisters.

"I don't think it's ridiculous. Not at all." She shifts her weight again on the stool, but she's not making eye contact, he notices.

Either she secretly does agree that Ralphie's a ridiculous name for a grown man, or she doesn't really believe he's a grown man, or something else is bothering her.

She hesitates, then says, "Your fiancée—"

"Ex-fiancée," he cuts in.

"Did she—"

"Hey," he cuts in again, "listen!"

". . . seven . . . six . . . five . . ."

On the radio, the midnight countdown is underway.

He looks at Rose Red, whose name he forgot to ask.

". . . four . . . three . . ."

Rose Red suddenly appears startled, and her eyes—piercing blue eyes—are not looking at Ralphie, they're looking past him.

Okay, she's apparently trying not to make eye contact with him. Maybe she thinks he's going to do something crazy at midnight, like . . .

". . . two . . . ONE! Ha-ppy New Year!"

Something crazy . . . like what?

Like kiss her!

Where the heck did that idea come from? It just popped

into his head, so detached from his own thought process that it's as if someone else said it.

Very convincingly, because for one wild, out-there moment, as the familiar opening strains of "Auld Lang Syne" fill the pizzeria, Ralphie is tempted to grab Rose Red and kiss her senseless.

But he doesn't.

Of course he doesn't, because she's a stranger and he's just been jilted and it wouldn't be the least bit appropriate, and anyway, the thought popped up out of nowhere and makes no sense whatsoever.

Kiss her?

Yeah. Sure.

And then what, Mr. Bright Idea? Get down on your knee and propose to her?

Then again . . . stranger things have happened.

To *Dominic*.

Ralphie would have said his perennial bachelor brother falling in love and getting married overnight was about as likely . . . as likely as . . .

As Pop coming back to the pizzeria tonight to ring in the New Year with his youngest son.

But it did happen—Dominic's whirlwind wedding, anyway.

Not Pop coming back here . . . though, come to think of it, Ralphie could swear his cologne really is wafting in the air.

Wishful thinking, he tells himself sternly.

And anyway, no matter what Dominic went and did in Vegas, Ralphie is not—repeat not!—going to kiss this woman just because the idea popped into his head.

"Hey, happy New Year," Ralphie says politely instead, pasting on a friendly smile.

"Same to you." She returns the smile, but only briefly before she looks past his shoulder again.

Ralphie swivels his head to see what she's looking at.

Nothing but the wall.

All righty then.

". . . *and days of Auld Lang Syne, my friend . . .*" In his head, Ralphie sings the lyrics along with the vintage orchestra on the radio.

Guy Lombardo. The music reminds Ralphie of Pop.

Pop used to talk about how back when he was first dating Mom, they spent one New Year's Eve dancing to Guy Lombardo live on the bandstand at the Roosevelt Hotel.

"And at midnight," Pop would say, with a faraway expression, "they played 'Auld Lang Syne,' of course, and I kissed your mother for the first time." A twinkle always sparked in his sad brown eyes when he added the ubiquitous, "I got her right on the lips, big smackaroo, and I thought she was going to slap me good and hard."

"Did she?" Ralphie would always ask, even though he knew the story's outcome.

"Nah, it was New Year's, and I was only doing what you're supposed to do at midnight on New Year's—kiss the beautiful girl you're with."

Fighting off a fresh wave of grief, he glances back at Rose Red. Now he knows why the errant thought of kissing her popped into his head. His father planted it there— years ago.

Meanwhile, Rose Red is still focused intently on the wall. Frowning at the wall, really. Kind of the way one would if one doesn't like walls and wishes this one would disappear.

Weird.

As "Auld Lang Syne" plays on, Ralphie tries to figure out if Rose Red is drunk—though she doesn't seem it, not the least bit—or just a harmless character, or . . .

Or what?

An escaped mental patient?

An undercover friend of Francesca's here to spy on him in the wake of the broken engagement?

Like *that* makes any sense whatsoever.

Like anything does.

He's standing here with the urge to kiss someone whose name he doesn't even know.

"Daria. Daria Marshall," she says when he asks, feeling a little awkward.

"Listen, Daria . . . did you say you were a psychic?"

"What?" she seems distracted.

By the wall.

Really weird.

"Did I say that?" she asks Ralphie. "I mean, I was just kidding. Of course I'm not psychic."

"Of course not. So . . . how did you know Francesca was my fiancée?"

"Oh, I overheard you mention her name. At the party."

Number one, he's pretty sure he didn't mention her name when they were standing at the bar together. Number two, Daria Marshall might be talking to him, but she's glaring at the wall as she does. Number three, he's supposed to be getting her pizza, treating her as he would any other customer.

Ralphie sighs inwardly and turns to the oven, wishing she could just be a normal, beautiful customer instead of a whacked out beautiful customer.

Maybe she's not really that whacked out, though. Maybe it's his imagination that she's—

"What is it?" she hisses behind him. "What do you want from me?"

Ralphie pivots, pizza paddle in hand. "What?"

She blinks, echoes, "What?"

"Did you say something?"

"No."

Liar.

Okay, so now she's *talking* to the wall.

"Did you say you wanted this to go?" he asks hopefully.

"The pizza? No, I was going to eat it here, but . . . maybe I should take it to go."

"No problem." He slides the slice onto a paper plate and turns back to her, thinking he'll just put it into a box and send her on her way. Bummer of a night, all around.

"Thanks," she says in a near whisper.

"You're welcome." He turns to see that she might not have been talking to him, after all.

But she's no longer focused on the wall, and her mood suddenly seems to have lightened considerably. Almost as if she's relieved.

On the radio, "Auld Lang Syne" has given way to Lena Horne singing a bluesy "What Are You Doing New Year's."

As Ralphie puts the pizza into a small box, he finds himself wishing Daria wouldn't leave. Or that he could see her again.

"How much do I owe you?" she asks, opening her little red evening bag. "I've got some cash in here somewhere. I borrowed this purse from my sister, and I can barely fit my phone in it, much less a wallet." She sets her cell phone, some keys, a small hairbrush, and a tube of lipstick on the counter and roots around in the bottom of the bag.

"Hey, listen, don't bother," Ralphie says. "It's on the house."

"What? You don't have to do that."

"I know. I want to. It's New Year's Eve."

She smiles. "Well . . . thank you. That's really sweet."

"Yeah. I'm a sweet guy. So where did you say you live?"

"I didn't. But . . . Manhattan. For now."

Right. She said she was a gypsy.

"I get the impression you're moving on soon," he says, and is glad to see those blue eyes looking solely at him now, not even casting a wayward glance at the blank wall.

"Probably. I've been staying with my sister." She starts putting things back into her purse. "But I can't hang out much longer."

"Where are you going?"

"Arizona, I think, or maybe . . . Australia." It almost sounds as if she's plucking random place names from an alphabetical atlas.

"You can't get much farther away than that," he comments. "Australia, I mean."

"Yeah." She drops the lipstick into her open bag.

"Although Arizona's far, too."

"Yeah." She picks up the hairbrush.

Enough with the geography lesson, there, Ralph.

One thing is clear: he's not going to be running into her again after tonight.

Unless . . .

He finds himself looking at her cell phone as she reaches for it.

Unless you ask her for her phone number.

Huh? What is with him tonight?

It's as if thoughts are being transmitted into his—

Whoa—loud crash in the kitchen.

"What was that?"

"I don't know," he tells Daria over his shoulder as he heads in that direction, hoping he doesn't have a prowler on his hands. It wouldn't be the first time someone's broken into the pizzeria, but it's not exactly a great way to open the new year.

Ralphie finds the kitchen empty, though. The back door is securely locked when he checks it.

A quick glance around reveals the source of the crashing sound.

Beneath a tall shelf, a large tin is lying on the floor.

A tin that just so happens to contain Aunt Carm's chocolate biscotti.

"Why'd you do that?"

Hearing Daria's voice, Ralphie turns and sees her standing in the doorway . . . looking, once again, right past him.

"I didn't do it. I was in the other room with you, remember?" Ralphie tells Daria incredulously.

"Oh, right—" She looks at Ralphie, who clearly thinks she's lost her mind. "I . . . uh, forgot you were in the other room with me."

She shoots another quick glare at Sad Eyes, who—standing beside the fallen cookie tin—doesn't even have the grace to look apologetic. He looks pleased, in fact.

He popped up in the pizzeria right before midnight, obviously following her around.

The odd thing is, he's changed since the party. Now she's seeing him in a pizza guy apron just like Ralphie's.

Anyway, she was relieved when he popped back out again just as Ralphie was asking her if she wanted the pizza to go.

She hoped he had called it a night.

But no, here he is wreaking havoc in the kitchen like a pouty, overgrown poltergeist.

Ralphie picks up the tin, the drugstore variety that has a nativity scene on the cover. Daria notes that there's a dent in the baby Jesus's manger. Nice. She glares at Sad Eyes.

Brow knit as he looks from the tin to the shelf, Ralphie mutters, "How the heck did this thing fall?"

"I have no idea," Daria says with a pointed glance at their unearthly visitor.

"Well, now at least I can offer you one . . . if they're not all crushed to bits." Ralphie opens the tin, peers inside, and shakes his head.

"Nope, they're hard as rocks. But biscotti's supposed to be," he adds hastily as he thrusts the open tin at her.

She helps herself. "Thanks."

Chocolate at last. Maybe that'll salvage what's left of the evening.

She can't help notice Sad Eyes's smug expression as she bites into the oblong cookie.

Obviously, this is what he wanted.

Why?

To butter her up for whatever favor he needs her to do for him here on the earth plane?

Whatever. All she knows is that this is the best biscotti she's ever tasted, and she tells Ralphie so.

"Everyone says that." He smiles. "Aunt Carm is a pretty good cook. She's my mother's sister and she likes to feed us. You should taste her almond paste cookies."

"Oooh, I love almond. You wouldn't happen to have any of those hiding around here, would you?"

"Nope, sorry. Fresh out." Ralphie leads the way back into the front of the restaurant.

Daria notices the ghost stays put, and gives him a warning glance over her shoulder.

Ralphie gestures at the pizza box he'd been about to hand her. "You know, that's going to be cold by the time you get it home."

"Maybe I should just eat it here, then."

"Maybe you should." He pauses. "Maybe I'll have a slice too."

"Yeah?"

"Yeah. Suddenly I'm starving. I guess being dumped by your fiancée works up an appetite."

She has to smile at the wry comment as she brushes the last biscotti crumbs from her hands, then licks a smidgen of chocolate from her fingertip.

"Wow, that was so good. Wish I had an Aunt Carm."

"No, you don't." Ralphie shoves another wedge of pepperoni pie into the oven.

"I don't?"

"Don't get me wrong . . . my aunt is a sweetheart. Like

I said, she looks out for us. But she's nosier than both my sisters put together."

"You have two sisters?"

He nods. "Nina and Rosalee."

"Both nosy?"

"They just feel entitled to poke around in my personal life, I guess since they pretty much raised me—especially Nina—after my mother died."

So his mom died when he was young. Nina's heart goes out to him, especially when she remembers that his father just died recently.

She feels another twinge of guilt, wondering if Ralphie's fiancée wouldn't have dumped him if she hadn't run into Daria in the bathroom.

But then, it was for the best, right?

Especially if Francesca's heart wasn't in it.

Daria can't help but wonder if Ralphie's heart was in it, either. He doesn't exactly seem distraught over the breakup.

Remembering the initial exhilaration she felt when Alan moved out, Daria decides Francesca couldn't have been the only unsatisfied party in the relationship.

So really, Daria did a good thing for both of them, urging her to break things off. A good thing for Francesca, a good thing for Ralphie.

Maybe even a good thing for you.

Okay, that's crazy. It's not as if she's going to pounce on this guy mere hours into his newfound bachelorhood.

A relationship with a freshly jilted fiancé—here in New York, no less—would be the mother of all fresh starts.

She doesn't need that.

All she needs is time alone to think . . .

She needs to get out of here, that's what she needs.

She picks up the box, then hurriedly scoops up her coat and evening bag, before she can change her mind.

Seeing her, Ralphie asks, "You're leaving?"

He seems dismayed.

Maybe she shouldn't leave, after all.

Yes, you should. And you shouldn't drag it out. You don't do goodbyes, remember?

"I have to go." She forces herself to put her coat on in a hurry, before she can change her mind. "It's late, and I'm beat, and . . . I've got some stuff to do at home."

Home?

Hardly.

But she will figure out where she belongs.

And she does know it isn't here.

And it sure as hell isn't with him.

"Well, it was nice to meet you," Ralphie says, and for the second time tonight, they politely shake hands.

"Nice to meet you, too."

"See you around."

"Yes."

No.

You won't be seeing him around at all, unless he's planning to move to Phoenix.

"Hey," he calls, "if you're ever in the neighborhood again . . . stop by for a slice. You know . . . if you're in New York for the holidays again next year or something, and you find your way over to Queens . . ."

"Thanks," she says. "I'll remember that. Same time, next year. If I'm in the neighborhood."

Daria allows herself one last look over her shoulder

before she steps out into the cold and closes the door behind her.

Ralphie smiles and waves at her. He seems lonely, standing there behind the counter in the empty pizzeria.

Well, that's not your problem.

Daria makes her way down the boulevard, past bars and restaurants spilling music into the chilly night air.

Talk about lonely . . . the elevated subway platform is totally deserted. Daria waits for the train, clutching her pizza box and wishing the train would come, wishing she weren't alone, wishing she had gloves.

You wouldn't need them in Arizona, she reminds herself. *That's where you belong.*

Why Arizona, though?

Because all your stuff is there, for one thing. Books, plants, photo albums, most of your clothes . . .

Then again, all her stuff has been with her pretty much everywhere she's ever lived, and that didn't make any of those places Home.

Still—you didn't even give Arizona a chance.

She had barely moved into her new place before she decided she missed Tammy, came east for a visit, and wound up staying three months.

Who, in the real world—the adult world—does that?

Aside from Daria's mother, anyway.

I love Mom, but I don't want to become her.

At last, the train pulls into the station.

It's filled with noisy revelers, fresh from the ball drop in Times Square. Daria steps aside as they throng the platform, traveling in clusters and pairs. No one, she notices, is solo tonight. No one but her.

And Ralphie.

Even Sad Eyes has left her alone . . . which is what she wanted, right?

This is the end of the line; the car is empty when she steps on board, aside from a sleeping man with a hand-written HOMELESS, PLEASE HELP sign on his lap. As she sits opposite him, she can't help but feel a kind of odd kinship with his transience.

As the conductor makes an unintelligible announcement, the train lurches into motion for the return trip to Manhattan.

Daria opens the pizza box, still pondering things.

Maybe she shouldn't have run away so quickly. From the party, from the pizzeria, from Ralphie, from Arizona . . .

Suddenly, it seems as though all she's ever done is run away.

In which case you need to stop.

You need to go back to Arizona and give it a chance.

But, a nagging voice protests, *wouldn't that just be running away from . . . New York?*

All right, and Ralphie too?

Would it?

Nope. Not at all, because she was in Arizona first and anyway, Ralphie has nothing to do with her decision one way or another. He's just a very sweet, very cute guy with whom she ushered in the new year.

Just like last year . . . remember? The beach, the Aussie.

Yeah, and it's not as if she ever saw the Outback hottie again, or even gave him much thought come January second.

That's how it is with New Year's.

Out with the old, in with the new.

Right . . . so wouldn't Ralphie be new? As in a new relationship?

No. Not if it stems from an old habit, she tells herself firmly.

Because really, New Year's is all about re-evaluating your life, making resolutions to change it.

And Daria is going to change hers. Break all those bad habits.

Okay, good. This is good.

Out with the old, in with the new.

So.

Arizona.

Not New York.

Not Ralphie.

That's the way it's going to be. The way it *has* to be.

Daria reaches for the pizza, then realizes her appetite is gone.

She closes the pizza box and hesitates only a moment before carrying it over to the slumbering vagrant. She gently sets it on the bench beside him.

There.

No longer does she possess a lingering trace of Ralphie. No tangible connection to him whatsoever. It's as if they never met.

Out with the old.

And now this poor man will have something to eat.

There are worse things, she reminds herself, than not quite knowing where one belongs.

She turns around and for an instant, sees a woman standing there. She's got gray hair and is dressed in clothes from an earlier era—late sixties, maybe, or early seventies. She smiles at Daria and gives an approving little nod, then turns a loving glance toward the homeless man.

That's his mother, Daria realizes as she vanishes again. She's watching over her son, worrying about his well-being. It's what parents do, even from the other side.

I really should call Mom. Wish her a happy New Year. See how she is.

Dad, too. Tell him I can't come visit him in Europe just yet, but I will when I can.

Daria decides she'll do all of that—tomorrow.

She'll call the airline, too. Check on flights back to Arizona.

And George—Daria really should check in with him. Find out how the construction is going, and whether he still expects to be open for business in a week or two. He'll be glad to hear she's coming back.

She feels better, having a plan to move forward.

In with the new.

The train is somewhere under the East River when she remembers her cell phone . . . still back on the counter at Big Pizza Pie.

Chapter
5

Ralphie's a crazy name for a grown man."

"No, it isn't," Daria protests. "Not at all."

They're alone together in the pizzeria, the entire rest of the world busy with other plans. She's wearing her red dress and he's in a suit, and everything would be perfect if she weren't feeling so guilty about causing Francesca to break up with him.

She has to bring it up, has to clear the air, so he can tell her to get lost . . . or thank her. She just isn't sure which.

She begins, "Your fiancée—"

"Ex-fiancée," he cuts in.

"Did she—"

"Hey," he cuts in again, "listen!"

". . . seven . . . six . . . five . . ."

On the radio, the midnight countdown is underway.

". . . four . . . three . . ."

A chill slips over her and she realizes they're not alone together, after all.

Over Ralphie's shoulder, by the wall, Sad Eyes is

*watching them. Not only is he watching them, but he's
speaking. To Ralphie. In a Queens accent.*

*"You know what you're supposed to do at midnight,
don't you? Kiss the beautiful girl you're with."*

Of course, Ralphie can't hear the ghostly voice.

"... two ... ONE! Ha-ppy New Year!"

*But as the familiar opening strains of "Auld Lang
Syne" fill the pizzeria, Daria is shocked to see that he
really does look as though he's about to kiss her.*

*She forgets all about Sad Eyes, and Francesca, and
the freshly broken engagement as she takes a bold step
closer to him, and he—*

She hears keys jangling in the corridor.

Tammy's home.

It's about time. She glances at the digital clock on the
television cable box and sees that it's almost four in the
morning.

She rolls over on the couch bed, her back to the door
as the lock turns.

She sincerely hopes her sister had a great night.

But not so great she'll want to wake Daria and tell her
about it.

Feigning sleep, she listens as Tammy fumbles her way
into the apartment, locks the door again, takes off her
shoes. She stumbles in the dark, curses softly, and disappears into the bathroom.

Good.

Daria is free to go back to yet another instant replay
of everything that happened between her and Ralphie
tonight . . .

And her fantasy ending involving everything that
didn't.

*   *   *

"Uncle Ralphie! Hey, Uncle Ralphie? You up there?"

Dripping from the shower, Ralphie wraps a towel around his waist and sticks his head out the bathroom door to answer his nephew. "Yeah, I'm here. What's up?"

"My mom sent me over to tell you she's coming over with spaghetti sauce and turn the oven on at 350 because Aunt Ro's bringing the lasagna. She's been trying to call you."

Yup, the phone's been ringing.

Nope, Ralphie hasn't been answering.

He's not in the mood to talk to anyone today.

He's not in the mood for a houseful of people, either, but it's almost noon and his family will be materializing momentarily.

With a sigh, he calls down to Nino, "All right, tell Nina I'll do it as soon as I'm dressed. And Nino? Will you tell her to give me a few extra minutes? I'm running late."

"Okay. See ya!"

The door bangs shut downstairs.

Ralphie shakes his head and grabs another towel. Rubbing his short dark hair furiously, he tells himself he'd better get into a holiday mood . . . and fast.

Any second now, Nina is going to descend on him with the pot of sauce, along with pounds and pounds of hand-cut noodles, followed shortly thereafter by Rosalee with her specialty: sausage lasagna. Both his sisters will want to know why Ralphie didn't pick up the phone when they called.

He probably should have. But he was afraid they'd mention Francesca and the braciole she's bringing, and then where would he be? Having to explain that there will be no braciole this New Year's Day . . . and no Francesca.

This, on top of no Nino Chickalini at the head of the table.

Oh, Pop. I wish to God you were here.

A tsunami of grief sweeps over him. They seem to hit out of nowhere sometimes, but today, there's a reason. Today marks another milestone without Pop.

Christmas was hard.

Last night was hard.

Today will be harder. A brand-new year stretches ahead, empty without his father's stolid presence. Uncharted territory. Despite the broken engagement, the loss of his father is what's bothering Ralphie today, more than anything else.

Will he ever get used to being nobody's son, an orphan? How can he ever fill the gaping void in his life? He's been robbed—that's what it feels like. Hell, that's what it *is*. He's been robbed of steadfast, unconditional love. Parental love.

Tears sting Ralphie's eyes, and he swipes at them with a corner of the damp towel.

Why is he having such a hard time getting past the grief and moving on? Harder, it seems, than his brothers and sisters. Is it because he's still single, without a spouse to lean on? Or because he's the baby of the family?

Is that it? Ralphie's never been through this before—not like his siblings have. He never knew their mother; missed her, yes, felt her absence all his life, envied his siblings their memories of her.

But you can't lose what you never had.

Ralphie *had* Pop. He was Ralphie's rock. And now he's gone forever.

He rubs his eyes again. He's got to pull himself together.

Maybe he should have taken Nina up on the offer she's made repeatedly over the past few weeks, to have the traditional New Year's gathering at her house next door.

It didn't seem right at the time. And it's too late to change things now.

Anyway, the operative word here is *traditional*. Chickalinis are big on tradition, and by tradition, the Chickalinis celebrate their holidays right here. They did Thanksgiving here, and Christmas, and they'll do New Year's, too.

Even if Ralphie is the only one left living under this roof.

This will most likely be the last holiday celebrated in the Chickalini home.

The new year has arrived, and they're planning to list the place as soon as possible.

The thought of strangers wandering through his home—let alone taking it over—makes Ralphie sick. But they've stalled long enough; it's not fair to his siblings to keep the place off the market and their inheritance out of their pockets.

Ralphie tosses the towel aside and glares at his reflection in the medicine cabinet mirror.

Is that all you care about? That you're going to have to move with or without Francesca nudging you?

You were going to marry her, for Pete's sake. Spend the rest of your life with her. Now it's over and all you're concerned about is the house?

The man in the mirror gazes back at him with sorrowful eyes that are strikingly similar to Nino Chickalini's.

Yeah, but Pop was always sad because he'd lost the woman he loved.

Not because he didn't love the woman he'd lost.

Ralphie turns abruptly away from the mirror and leaves the bathroom, padding barefoot down the short hall to his boyhood room.

It's the smallest in the house and faces the street. When Ralphie was a kid, you could still see out the window over the branches of the maple tree Pop had planted soon after he and Ralphie's mother moved in. But these days, unless it's the dead of winter—which it happens to be—the view is obscured by leafy boughs. Ralphie often considers cutting them back, but it seems wrong to tamper with Mother Nature—or maybe just wrong to tamper with Pop's handiwork. Especially now that his tree has outlived the man.

The bedroom is still crammed with twin beds and a lifetime worth of memorabilia: from boxes of baseball cards and yearbooks in the closet to basketball trophies still displayed on a long, high shelf.

You're a grown man, and you're still living like a kid.

In his own defense, he'd been originally hoping it would be temporary. He had a vague idea about redoing the room into a study or something if Francesca moved in, and they'd take over the master bedroom down the hall. His vague idea evaporated when Francesca informed him that she found it creepy to sleep in the room where Ralphie was, by all probability, conceived.

Back when she was still considering moving in, she thought they should knock down the wall between this room and the one next door, once shared by Nina and Rosalee. She wanted a master suite with a walk-in closet and steam shower or rain shower or some fancy shower she kept talking about.

For Ralphie, a regular old nozzle will do just fine. As will this regular old bedroom, indefinitely. Especially if it means putting off going through Pop's stuff—and his mother's, as well, still carefully preserved in the cedar chest and tucked away at the top of the master bedroom closet.

His sisters and Dominic have all said they're willing to help sort their parents' belongings. Pete even promised to fly back to New York and help when the time comes to put away a lifetime of memories.

Ralphie isn't ready to do that yet.

He isn't ready to move yet, either, with or without Francesca.

Well, with *is pretty much out of the question now*, he tells himself as he steps moodily into a pair of well-worn jeans.

And yeah, he's going to miss Francesca. Miss her companionship and her upbeat personality and her braciole.

Someday, Ralphie supposes, he'll find the right woman for him. Someone who's just as loving and family-oriented as Francesca was. Someone who's . . .

Five foot two, eyes of blue . . .

Ralphie's heard that old song on Pop's vintage radio station plenty of times through the years and never paid much attention. Now, though, the lyrics have been running through his head all morning, and God only knows why.

Okay, Ralphie knows why, too.

Daria Marshall happens to be five foot two—give or take an inch—with eyes of blue—the bluest eyes he's ever seen.

Yeah . . . so what?

The rest of the lyrics bear no relevance to Ralphie whatsoever.

Has anybody seen my gal?

Daria Marshall isn't Ralphie's gal.

She just happened to pop into his life at a vulnerable moment, that's all. And she popped right back out of it again, too.

He moves the clutter around on his bureau top, looking for his watch. In the process, he stumbles across a couple of things that give him pause: the engagement ring he took from his pocket in the wee hours of this morning, and the business card he casually tossed aside in the wee hours of Sunday morning.

Madame Tamar, Psychic and Spiritualist.

Remembering the thoughtful expression in her eyes when she said she wanted to have a word with him, he wonders now if she could possibly have foreseen . . . something. Francesca breaking up with him, for example.

Maybe she wanted to warn him about that.

And maybe you're as full of it as she is, he thinks in disgust.

He should just throw the card into the wastebasket.

He should . . . but for some reason, he doesn't. God only knows why, but he leaves it right where he found it.

The ring is a different story, though. He can't leave a diamond lying around the house. It's worth a couple of thousand hard-earned dollars. He should put it away until he can sell it or pawn it or do whatever it is one does with broken engagement rings.

For now, he opens his underwear drawer and reaches all the way in the back, where he keeps a wooden box with a carved top. He made it back in Cub Scouts, painstakingly etching a stemmed rose into the lid. The other boys carved fish and footballs and their initials into their boxes, and a few made fun of Ralphie's "girly" design, but he didn't care.

The rose symbolized his mother. Always has, always will.

Rose . . .

Rose Red.

She pops into his head for some reason, and he frowns. He really shouldn't be thinking about her right now. Not when he's got other things on his mind—not to mention, this diamond ring in his hand.

He opens the box.

Inside are a lifetime's worth of treasures: bottlecaps and seashells; a four-leaf clover he found and shellacked onto a rock; a crinkled final snapshot of his mother, hugely pregnant with him; the 1974 Dave Winfield Rookie Card his brother Pete traded to Dom and Dom traded to Ralphie; a lock of Nino's baby hair tied with blue ribbon.

Somewhere downstairs, a door slams.

So much for the memories.

It's time again to deal with the here and now.

He tucks the ring into the box and hastily returns it to the back of the drawer, slamming it shut.

"I did the stupidest thing after I left the party last night," Daria tells her sister.

"Yeah? What was that?" Tammy, who has finally staggered out of her bedroom at the crack of noon, pours herself a cup of black coffee at the kitchen counter. "Subway surfing? Russian roulette? One-night stand with a stranger?"

At the latter suggestion, Ralphie's face flits into Daria's mind. Again.

Okay, so it wasn't a one-night stand.

But she fantasized that it had been.

And when she finally drifted off to sleep after her sister's return, she dreamed it, too. It didn't fade with the early morning light, as dreams do.

No, the steamy images jarred her out of a sound sleep at dawn and lingered all morning, much to her dismay.

It's been a long time since she's had a sex dream.

A longer time since she had sex, for that matter.

That's probably why Ralphie got under her skin last night. A long drought will do that to a woman. What she probably needs is a good old-fashioned fling.

But it's not what I want, she realizes. No Strings Attached suddenly lacks a certain appeal.

"No," she tells her sister, "No subway surfing or one-night stands."

"What, then?"

Daria's gaze flicks to an apparition drifting past the doorway to the bedroom. It's been hanging around all morning, along with a phantom mouse she saw scurrying along the baseboards earlier. At least, she hopes it was phantom.

To her sister, she says, "I left my cell phone out in Queens. On a countertop in a pizzeria."

"You better go get it, then."

"The place is closed today." If Daria hadn't noticed the

sign on the door last night, she'd probably already be on the subway.

And not, she'll admit, just out of eagerness to rescue her phone.

She might run into Ralphie again, after all—somewhere other than in her an erotic dream, anyway—if she times it right. He's a nine-to-fiver in Manhattan, but maybe he hangs around the pizzeria at night or on weekends.

Yeah, Daria can live without her cell phone a little longer, if it means possibly seeing him one more time in the flesh.

Flesh.

That pesky sex dream pops into her head again.

"How's the coffee?" she asks Tammy brightly.

"Thick and bitter—kind of like me, in my middle age." Her sister pats her oversized waistline ruefully.

"That's because it's been sitting in the carafe on the burner for about five hours."

"Five hours? Why on earth did you get up that early?"

Why, indeed.

"I guess I was just worried about my phone."

"Well, you should call the place and leave a message so they can hang on to it for you until you get there tomorrow." Tammy adds darkly, "You don't want someone to find it and steal your identity, do you?"

"It's a cell phone. Not a wallet."

"Yeah, but what's programmed into it?"

"Good point. I'll leave a message." Daria heads for the phone to dial Directory Assistance.

"Ralphie! What the heck is going on?"

That's Rosalee's voice, bellowing from downstairs.

Ralphie knew the peace and quiet wouldn't last. Not with two sisters and a breaking news story.

He grabs a T-shirt from the stack of clean laundry in the hallway on his way to the stairs. "Happy New Year to you, too," he calls down to his sister, his voice muffled as he pulls the shirt over his head.

"Did you dump Francesca?"

Halfway down the stairs—and dragging his feet—Ralphie stops short. "Did I dump her? No! It was the other way around!"

"That's not what I heard."

He sighs and rolls his eyes to the ceiling—which, he notices, is lined with a new crack in the plaster, and an ominous water stain.

"What did you hear, Ro?"

"Bebe said—"

Oh, Lord. He should have known.

"I don't care what Bebe said," he cuts off Ro.

"Why are you always on Bebe's case?"

"Because Bebe's always on mine."

There's Ro at the bottom of the stairs, holding a huge tray of lasagna and wearing her zebra-print coat, shiny black high-heeled boots, a pair of oven mitts, and a frown.

"Look," he tells his sister, "it was the other way around. Francesca's the one who called it off. I'm the one who was left . . ."

He was going to say broken-hearted, but that's not entirely accurate. He's not broken-hearted.

He's the one who was left . . .

Just plain old *left*.

So he leaves it at that.

It's the truth.

"Really? Francesca broke up with you?" Rosalee's carefully made-up round face is troubled as she looks up at him.

"Really."

"I thought it was you. Just cold feet. I was going to remind you that Timmy had cold feet, too . . . and look at us now."

"It wasn't me."

Ralphie starts down the stairs, passing the framed family portraits his mother hung there decades ago: his parents on their wedding day, with Pop in a peg-legged sixties suit and Mom with her veil falling from a Jackie Kennedy pillbox hat; Nina in her white high school graduation cap and gown; Pete in his army uniform posed in front of a flag; a school photo of plump, adolescent Rosalee with braces; Dominic as a laughing toddler holding a red rubber ball.

The last photo, though, was placed there by Nina a few months after Rosemarie Chickalini died. It's just a snapshot, placed in a cheap metal frame from Duane Reade: infant Ralphie wearing only a diaper. He's lying on a changing table, an outstretched female hand holding him in place—Nina's hand, and the other must have held the camera.

Gotta love Nina, not even out of her teens yet when she stepped in to pick up where their mother left off.

In Ralphie's lifetime, as his siblings married and had children of their own, countless new photos have been displayed in the house. This wall, though, has remained untouched: a shrine to the original family unit that lived under this roof.

And now we'll have to take down the photos, pack them away, and sell the house.

Ralphie descends the stairs heavily, his hand stroking the silver tinsel garland wrapped around the railing.

Threadbare, having lost some of its luster, it's hung there every holiday season he can remember. He was teary eyed when he carried down the boxes of Christmas stuff from the attic, and almost broke down a few times when, with his niece and nephews helping, he decorated the house.

Six matching homemade red felt stockings hang on the wall beneath the stair treads, embroidered with both his parents' names, and his four older siblings'. A seventh stocking, not quite the same size or shade, slightly lopsided, and awkwardly hand-stitched with Ralphie's name, hangs at the end of the row.

Nina, again. She never wanted him to feel like an afterthought, or worse yet, like an orphan.

Ralphie swallows over a lump in his throat as he reaches his sister at the bottom of the stairs. Ro, too, took good care of him. She tried her best to mother him even when she was just a kid herself.

"Wait, Ralphie, let me put this down. It weighs a ton."

Ro goes to the kitchen, sets the lasagna on the counter, and is back in a flash. Her tone is considerably softer as she asks, "Are you okay, honey?"

"Hanging in there."

His sister gives him a hug, then runs her acrylic-tipped fingers through his hair, smoothing it like she used to when he was a kid.

"What?" she asks, at his frown. "It's sticking up all

over the place, and it's all wet. You're going to catch your death of cold."

"That's an old wives' thing."

"Yeah, well, I'm an old wife."

He smiles. Gotta love Ro.

"Listen," she says, "I'm sure Francesca's going to come around. It's probably just cold feet on her part."

"I don't think so."

"It happens all the time. Look at Nina! She fought Joey all the way to the altar. She thought she didn't want to get married, ever, and look at her now. Look at me. Timmy and I have been together since high school, but even he was nervous when it came down to making a commitment."

"It's not that," Ralphie protests. "I mean, with Francesca. The more I think about it—and believe me, I have been—the more I can see that we're just wrong for each other."

Rosalee dismisses that with a wave of fingernails that are just as long and polished as Francesca's always are. "Wrong for each other? Ralphie, she couldn't be more right for you. She's one of us. She fits right into the family. Has from day one. Pop loved her."

"Do you think I don't know that?" Ralphie rakes a hand through his damp hair, making it stand up again. "Maybe that's why I was trying so hard to make it work. Because Pop loved her. Because everyone did. Because she fit right in."

"But . . . you love her . . . don't you?"

"I care about her. A lot. I always will. Just . . ."

"Not like that," Ro says quietly, nodding. "Not like you should."

"No."

"I can't believe this. Did you tell Nina?"

"I didn't tell anyone."

Except Daria Marshall.

Funny how she keeps popping into his head long after popping into—and right back out of—his life. Twice. In one night.

Was it really just last night? Has it really only been fourteen hours or so since he first saw her—and a scant twelve since he last did? And if she had never crossed his path at all, would he be feeling more upset about Francesca?

That's a crazy thought—and one that's curtailed by a voice from the kitchen.

"You didn't tell anyone what?"

He turns to see Nina standing there, having just stepped in through the back door. Wearing oven mitts and holding a big pot of steaming spaghetti sauce, she glances toward the stove and groans before anyone can answer her question.

"Ralphie! You didn't turn on the oven to 350! Didn't Nino tell you to?"

"Yeah, but I didn't have a chance yet."

"And the lasagna's just sitting out on the counter. Where's Ro?" Nina disappears from view, in full hustle-bustle mode and still talking from the kitchen. "Oh, Mia's making a rum cake for dessert and—geez, Ralphie, you didn't boil the water for the pasta yet, either?"

Rosalee gives Ralphie a sympathetic glance.

"The homemade stuff only takes a minute to cook, Nina," he points out.

The only response from the kitchen: a clattering of

pots and pans, water running at the sink, the *click-click-click* and *whoosh* as a gas flame ignites.

Then Nina's back, pausing briefly to straighten a picture frame on her way. "Ralphie, you need to get the extra leaves into the table, and I'll find the tablecloths so that someone can get busy setting it. Ro, where are Timmy and the kids?"

"Still going around the block trying to find a parking spot. Where's your gang?"

"The kids will be right over with the noodles, and Joey's still down at the pizzeria."

"I thought it was closed today," Rosalee says.

"It is, but he had some paperwork to do and then he's boxing up some calzones and pizza to bring over. Last night was so dead there's a ton of stuff there. Which reminds me—" Nina turns her attention to Ralphie— "thanks for going over there and letting Joey come to the party for midnight."

"No problem."

"Really? I figured there must have been."

"Must have been what?" Ralphie asks reluctantly, seeing the gleam in Nina's eye.

"Must have been a problem. With Francesca. Otherwise, why would you have left so early?"

"I wanted to do a nice thing for you and Joey?" Ralphie offers, feeling like a little kid again, caught in Nina's maternal cross hairs. "You guys run yourselves ragged with the restaurant, so . . ."

"Oh, just tell her, Ralphie," Rosalee urges.

"Tell me what?"

"He and Francesca broke up."

"*What?*" Nina gapes at Ralphie. "Please say that's not true."

In the old days, Ralphie would have said *okay, that's not true* just to be a kid brother wise-ass.

Today, feeling old—and tired—he says simply, "Yeah, Neens, it's true. Sorry."

"Ralphie . . . honey . . ." She gives him a hug, then smoothes his hair. Ro learned from a pro. "A lot of men get cold feet, but—"

"It wasn't him," Ro puts in. "It was her."

"It was *her,* Ralphie? Not you?"

"Yeah, but it's okay," he says. "I'm okay."

Nina shakes her head sadly at him as if that can't possibly be true. "What on earth happened?"

"They think they're not right for each other," Rosalee puts in helpfully.

"What? You guys are perfect together. She fits right into the family."

Ralphie bristles. "She's not marrying the family, she's marrying me."

Only she's not.

"No, I know," Nina says hurriedly, "but . . . it's just, she's from the neighborhood and she's Italian and so family-oriented . . . she just seemed like the perfect girl for you."

Perfect. There's that word again.

Let Nina talk about *perfect* all she wants. Didn't she grow up to marry the boy next door? She and Joey were meant for each other—even if they were the last ones to figure it out.

And then there's Rosalee, with her burly husband whose devotion to the FDNY is second only to his devotion to her and the kids. Yeah, it took a few years longer than Ro would have liked for him to pop the question. But there's no doubt that they, too, were meant for each other. With their round faces and extra weight, Ro and Timmy look alike. They think alike, too, and act alike, and finish each other's sentences . . .

Like Nina and Joey, they belong together. So do Mia and Dom, and Pete and Debbi . . .

Ralphie's siblings have no idea what it's like to be with someone with whom you just don't click. Someone with whom there's no chemistry.

"Francesca's not perfect for me. She's all wrong. For me," Ralphie adds, feeling guilty again.

"Okay. So if Francesca's all wrong for you," Nina sounds incredulous, "what kind of girl *are* you looking for?"

Five foot two, eyes of blue . . .

Stop that, Ralphie commands his inner flapper.

To his sister—to both of them—he says with blunt force, "I'm not *looking* for any girl."

Or *gal,* for that matter.

There's a moment of silence.

In the kitchen, the pot of water makes a hissing noise as it heats up on the burner. Somewhere overhead, a jet makes a rapid descent toward the runway at La Guardia Airport.

"Ralphie," Rosalee says tentatively, "are you . . . you know?"

"Am I what?"

"Are you looking for a guy? Is that it?"

He raises an eyebrow. "What gave me away?"

His sisters exchange an eyebrow-raised glance of their own.

"Well," Nina pastes on a smile, "I have to say I'm a little surprised, but if that's what you—"

"Cripes, Nina, I'm not looking for a guy!" he cuts in, laughing. "I was kidding! I'm just not looking for anyone."

"Yeah, well, sometimes when you're not looking for anyone," Nina says with the air of one who knows all about these things, "is exactly when you find someone."

"Yeah, Neens, and if it weren't for a broken engagement, you wouldn't be where you are today," Ro points out.

"What? Joey and I weren't—oh. You mean Minnie. That's ancient history."

Ralphie's much too young to recall the day his brother-in-law was left at the altar—literally. The bride-to-be was Nina's friend Minnie Scaturro, who somehow got the calling and decided to join a convent, leaving Nina to pick up the pieces.

It was another fifteen years, though, before best pals Nina and Joey realized they were in love with each other.

"At least Francesca gave you plenty of notice, Ralphie," Ro tells him. "Think of what a nightmare it would be if she left you in the rectory at Most Precious Mother while Millicent played the wedding march over and over for a church full of people."

"Poor Joey." Nina shakes her head. "Even now, I cringe when I remember that day."

"It could've definitely been worse," Ro tells Ralphie. "Much, much worse."

"Yeah, I guess I'll count my blessings, then," he murmurs, and goes to find the extra leaves for the table.

"I hope they have voice mail," Daria comments to Tammy as the phone rings on the other end of the line, somewhere on Ditmars Boulevard.

"It's a business, right? Of course it has voice mail."

"Yeah, but this is more of a small, old-fashioned—"

"Big Pizza Pie," a male voice—as opposed to voice mail—answers briskly.

Daria's heart zings right out of her ribcage. "Ralphie?"

"No . . . this is Joe."

Ralphie's brother-in-law who runs the place, she recalls, and her heart bungees right back in again.

"You looking for Ralphie?" Joe asks.

"No! No!" she blurts, as if he's just accused her of something preposterous. "I'm looking for my wallet, actually. That's who I'm looking for. I mean, *whom*. I mean, that's *what* I'm looking for. That's all."

"Cell phone," Tammy says, at her elbow.

Daria scowls at her. "Shh!"

"Cell phone," Tammy repeats in a stage whisper. "You're looking for your cell phone."

"Hello, I know!" Daria stage-whispers back.

"You said wallet."

Oops.

Into the phone, Daria says, "Cell phone. I lost my cell phone there, last night, when I was talking to your brother-in-law. I mean, while I was waiting for my pizza."

Okay, she's making this a lot more complicated than it has to be. Why is she so rattled? She's met—and spoken to—hundreds, maybe thousands, of guys in her life. That this one is haunting her dreams makes no sense, other than the dry spell theory.

"Yeah, I found the phone on the counter when I got here," Joe tells her. "You're Daria, right? I called the first couple of numbers in the directory, but no one I talked to knew where to find you."

Story of her life.

"Yeah, well . . . I just moved," she tells Ralphie's brother-in-law. "Anyway . . . as long as you're open today, I guess I'll come out and pick up the phone."

Maybe Ralphie will be working again later, since it's a holiday.

"The thing is—we're actually not open. I just happened to stop in here to pick up a few things."

"Oh."

Joe must hear the disappointment in her voice—and assume it's because she really, really needs her phone—because he goes on, "Listen, though, I'll take the phone home with me—I live right around the corner from the pizzeria—and you can come there and get it if you're not busy today."

Daria's only plans were to hang around here with a bunch of dearly departed souls and a hungover sibling, but there's no need to—

"Oh, wait, I won't be home today," Joe amends, "I'll be at my brother-in-law's house—which happens to be right next door, though."

There goes her heart again. "Next door to the pizzeria?"

"Next door to my place. Everything's kind of claustrophobic in our family," he adds with a chuckle. "So do you want Ralphie's address?"

"Absolutely!" Daria snaps her fingers, gesturing wildly for Tammy to get her something to write with and on.

As her sister scrambles for pen and paper, Daria notices something—someone—out of the corner of her eye.

Turning her head, she sees that it's him again. Sad Eyes. Hanging around as though he's waiting his turn . . .

Or maybe just hanging around, because right now, he doesn't seem to need anything from her.

No, today his aura is more . . . settled. No beseeching glances, no spectral mischief. He's just . . . here.

And I'm outta here, Daria thinks as she hangs up the phone and tucks Ralphie's home address into her pocket.

Chapter
6

"The lasagna is awesome, Aunt Ro," Nino pipes up amid the clinking forks and china.

Ralphie, who has barely touched the food on his own plate, halfheartedly pokes his fork into a heap of sauce-covered noodles.

Rosalee smiles briefly and sips her wine. "Thanks. You eat your lasagna, too, Adam. And how about a meatball? You love Aunt Nina's meatballs."

"No, I don't."

Everyone chuckles at Adam's preschool bluntness. Even Nina.

Then it's back to clinking forks and china.

They're gathered, as always, around the dining room table, extended with two extra leaves and covered in a pair of slightly mismatched red tablecloths.

On the sideboard, Mia's homemade rum cake waits on the white pedestal plate perched above Ro's tray of M&M-studded Rice Krispy Treats. Beside the desserts: the old plaster creche. There's only one sheep these days, and poor Joseph's neck still sports the jagged crack where

Nina superglued his head back on after Dominic acciden-tally snapped it off years ago.

An array of pots, roaster pans, and platters line the table: lasagna, sausage and peppers, pizza and calzones, eggplant parm, and of course, the low, boat-sized bowl heaped with homemade noodles and sauce. The bread basket is lined in red and white checked cloth napkins and holds a golden heap of rolls Nina just took piping hot from the oven. Plastic two-liter soda bottles, a bottle of chianti, and a cluster of juice boxes are at one end of the table, a cut-glass bowl filled with iceberg salad is at the other.

"Is there any braciole?" Rose asks, and Ralphie looks up just in time to see her flinch. Someone obviously just kicked her under the table, and he suspects the guilty party must be one of his sisters.

"No braciole this year," Ralphie tells his niece. "Francesca was supposed to bring it, but since she's not here . . ."

"Maybe she'll make it next Sunday. I love her braciole. And you know those cut-out sugar cookies? Aunt Fran-cesca makes the best—"

"Have another meatball, Rose." Nina stabs one with a fork and passes it Rose's way.

"No, thanks. It's too bad Aunt Francesca's still sick. I wanted to tell her about—"

"Eat the meatball, Rose," her mother cuts in, looking as though she wants to stuff it right into her daughter's mouth.

"This is crazy," Ralphie speaks up, setting down his fork. "We should just tell them."

"Tell who what?" Nino asks, as the kids look cluelessly from one adult to the next.

Nina and Rosalee shake their heads at Ralphie, who ignores them. He never thought it was a good idea in the first place to pretend—just for today—that Francesca is still battling the flu.

Ralphie's sisters, who shooed their children into the living room with a game of Monopoly before mealtime, didn't want to "ruin the holiday" by making an announcement about the broken engagement.

Never mind that the holiday isn't exactly festive regardless of the state of Ralphie's love life. His father's place at the head of the table is symbolically empty. No one could bring themselves to sit there. Even Aunt Carm is absent this year, on a bus trip to Foxwoods with the Ladies' Guild from Most Precious Mother.

"Guys," Ralphie addresses his niece and nephews, "I know this isn't the greatest news, but Francesca—" He pauses to clear his throat.

"Did she die?" Adam asks with saucer eyes, and Ralphie realizes that's what they're all thinking, these poor kids, who just lost their beloved grandfather.

"No," he says gently, and wonders if maybe his sisters were right about waiting. But it's too late now. "She just decided—we decided—that it would be better not to get married, after all."

Yes, better not to put all the blame on Francesca, regardless of who broke up with whom. He doesn't want them to feel sorry for him. He doesn't even feel sorry for himself—unless he thinks about being the lone Chickalini left in this house that was once overflowing with family.

For a moment, the only sound is the college football bowl game blaring from the television in the empty living room, abandoned by the men when Nina announced dinner was ready.

"You mean we aren't going to see Aunt Francesca anymore, ever?" T. J. asks sadly.

"Probably not." Nina is somber. "But it's for the best, because Uncle Ralphie and Francesca both need to move on. I know you all really loved her, and so did Uncle Ralphie—"

"If he loved her," Nino cuts in, "then how come he's not getting married to her?"

"He doesn't love her that way, and she's just not his type," Rose says with all the wisdom of an adolescent girl who reads a lot of magazines. "What about movie night?"

"We'll still have movie night," Ralphie promises— though it was Francesca's idea to start the tradition with his niece and nephews.

One Saturday night a month for the past year or so, they've shown up with sleeping bags and DVDs to spend the night at the Chickalini house. Francesca always made popcorn and brownies, and could be counted upon to team up with Rose in favor of female-friendly movies like *High School Musical* and *Mary Poppins*.

"It won't be as much fun if it's just the five of us," Nino says wistfully, and adds quickly, "No offense, Uncle Ralphie."

Before Ralphie can comment on that, the doorbell rings.

"Maybe it's Aunt Francesca," T. J. says hopefully.

"They broke up, remember?" Rose sounds exasperated.

"Yeah, but she probably wanted to drop off the braciole."

En route to the door, Ralphie can only hope that it isn't Francesca—and that it isn't Bebe, either. She has a way of dropping by on holidays, or whenever she sniffs a family crisis in the offing. She'll want her salon to be the first in the neighborhood to have the inside dirt on the dissolution of the Buccigrossi–Chickalini nuptials.

But it isn't Bebe.

Nor is it Francesca.

For a moment, as he stands there with the door wide open, gaping at the newcomer, Ralphie is sure he must be imagining it.

But when she speaks, she sounds as real as she looks. "Yeah—hi—me again. Happy New Year. Again."

Standing opposite Ralphie on the concrete stoop of the Christmas-light-bedecked, vinyl-sided house on Thirty-Third Street, Daria is struck by the same feeling she had last night, when that crowd of festive people got off the subway in pairs and groups.

She's alone—quite literally out in the cold once again.

Meanwhile, beyond the open door, hung with a big boxwood wreath and red bow, is a genuine *home*.

Daria doesn't even have to lift a foot off the worn rubber welcome mat to figure that out.

From where she stands beneath a string of red and green outdoor bulbs, she can see the lamplit interior, cozy on this bleak January afternoon. There are framed photographs on tables and walls beyond the hall. Monopoly is in progress on the floor: four silver pieces are on the board, properties and cash for four players rim the edges.

Sports announcers jovially dispute a play from an unseen television set amid animated family chatter some-where nearby.

Daria, who skipped breakfast, finds herself salivating as she inhales the warm air spilling from the house, heavy with the savory, unmistakable aroma of marinara sauce and hot, yeasty bread dough.

Swept by a fierce longing, she momentarily decides Francesca Buccigrossi was out of her mind.

The place is still full of everyone else's stuff—I feel like it would never be our home. Like I would never really belong there, like I wouldn't even if I lived there for a long time.

So Francesca told Daria just last night.

A momentary glimpse into this household and Daria, on the other hand, can easily imagine belonging here.

Or maybe it's just that she *wants* to belong in a place like this, so fervently she can taste it as readily as the Italian cuisine wafting in the air.

A place like this?

This place. Right here. This unassuming house set right up close to its neighbors on either side, fronted by a statue of the Virgin Mary in a plastic grotto set in a rectangular patch of yard bordered by a low wrought-iron fence.

It feels like home.

Like I could really belong there. Like I'd give anything to just walk in the door and live here forever.

Belong here?

You don't, Daria reminds herself, taken aback by her intense reaction to the house.

He does.

And anyway . . . forever? Where did that come from?

You're always going around saying you don't believe in forever . . . remember?

She turns her attention to Ralphie, who's looking unabashedly bewildered in the doorway, asking, "What are you doing here?"

"Oh," she says, suddenly feeling awkward, "I take it your brother-in-law didn't—"

"Hey, Ralphie," a handsome man with graying dark hair has come up behind them, "this is Daria. She was in the pizzeria last night."

"I remember her." A faint smile touches Ralphie's lips.

"I forgot my phone there," Daria explains hurriedly to him.

"Huh?" Ralphie asks, clueless. Obviously he wasn't the one who found it.

"Yeah, and Joe"—the man who joined them has to be Joe, right?—"found it, and he told me to pick it up here."

"Only I not only forgot to mention it to you," Joe says, "but I forgot to bring the phone over. It's still next door, with the biscotti."

"Aunt Carm's famous biscotti?" Daria asks with a grin.

"Wow, she's good," Ralphie's brother-in-law says approvingly to Ralphie.

"Yeah, too bad Aunt Carm isn't here to eavesdrop. For once she might like what she overhears."

"Are you Uncle Ralphie's new girlfriend?" a child's voice asks.

Daria looks down to see an adorable little carrot-topped boy . . . and, coming up behind him, what is obviously the rest of Ralphie's family, all looking curiously at her.

Uncle Ralphie's new girlfriend?

Hardly.

"No," Ralphie says quickly, "this is Daria. . . ."

"Marshall," she fills in. "I'm just a—" A what? Not a friend, even. "I'm a customer."

"Who knows about Aunt Carm and her biscotti, no less." Joe turns to Ralphie. "How'd you find it? I had it hidden way up on a high shelf."

"I have my ways."

And you had a little help from Sad Eyes, Daria thinks to herself.

"Joey's a notorious biscotti hoarder," Ralphie tells her.

"Hey—the kids on the afternoon shift were plowing through it and I was trying to save some for the family today."

"Get outta here, you were trying to save it for yourself," a handsome guy says good-naturedly. "Admit it."

"You should talk, Dom." A striking brunette swats him in the arm. "You wanted me to cut the rum cake at home and leave half of it there so you could have it later for a snack."

"Not *half,* Mia. A *piece.*"

Dom . . . Mia?

They can't be the happy couple whose wedding Tammy not only attended just days ago, but claims wouldn't be married at all if not for her.

"His idea of a piece is half the cake," the brunette—Mia—explains laughingly to the others.

"You still think that's charming because you guys are newlyweds," a plump fortyish woman tells her.

Newlyweds. Dom and Mia.

It has to be.

The coincidence is so startling Daria knows that it isn't. A coincidence, that is.

There are no true coincidences—that's what her mother and Tammy always claim.

"Yeah, just wait a year or two," Joe is telling Mia.

"Or till you have kids," a big, jolly-looking red-haired man puts in wryly. "Then nothing he does will seem charming. Right, Ro?"

"Timmy! You make it seem like I'm not madly in love with you anymore." The fortyish woman laughs, then squeals as her husband's oversized, orange-freckled arms surround her in a bear hug.

She realizes Ralphie is watching her watch his family.

"Sorry," he says, "My family's a little nuts."

"Oh, it's okay, I'm sorry for interrupting your dinner." She means it to sound apologetic, but instead, it just sounds wistful.

"Hey, Nino, would you do me a favor?" Ralphie rests a hand on the shoulder of a boy who has to be Ralphie's nephew. He looks just like him.

"What is it?"

"Run next door and get Daria's phone. Where is it, Joey?"

"On the kitchen table, in a bag. It's got the phone in it, and the tin of biscotti."

"Bring that too, Nino."

"Can I go, Mom?" a bespectacled boy quietly asks the plump woman called Ro. "I want to see the electric guitar he got for Christmas."

"Okay, but if you're going, you're putting your coat on," she says firmly, and shivers. "It's freezing out there."

Ralphie says, "Yeah, you don't want to catch a cold, T. J."

Rosalee sticks out her tongue. "That's an old wives' tale, remember?"

"Yeah, and I also remember that you're an old wife."

Dom snorts and gives Ralphie a high five.

Ro rolls her eyes at them. "Timmy, beat up my brothers for me, will you?"

"Sorry, babe, you're on your own."

"Nina? Want to gang up on them?" Ro asks a quiet, amused-looking dark-haired woman who can only be Ralphie's other sister.

Nina and Rosalee—he told Daria they feel entitled to "poke around in his personal life" because they basically raised him after their mother died. Daria didn't miss the affectionate note mingling with his vexation when he spoke of them, and she doesn't miss Nina's tender glance at her brother before she turns to Daria.

"So listen, why don't you come on in. We were just about to have coffee and dessert. You should stick around . . . unless you have someplace else to be?"

"No . . . I have noplace else to be." Isn't that the truth.

"I want to go with T. J. and Nino, Mommy!" the youngest child—the one who asked if Daria is his uncle's girlfriend—says plaintively.

"No, you're too little. You stay here with us," Rosalee tells him.

"Please? I want to go!"

"Rose, would you take him for a walk next door with the boys?" Nina asks a dark-eyed beauty of about thirteen, who nods obediently and takes her little cousin by the hand.

A whirlwind minute later, the kids are out the door, Daria is in the door, and it's closed against the cold.

"Wow, it's quiet. So I'm Nina." She sticks her hand out to Daria. "I know you've already met my husband Joey. Our kids are Nino and Rose."

"Can I take your coat? By the way, I'm Mia Caloger—I mean, Chickalini, Ralphie's sister-in-law, and that's my husband Dom." She says her new name and the phrase *my husband* with a happily self-conscious little smile.

Chickalini.

So they are the same Dom and Mia.

And Ralphie is Ralphie Chickalini.

What a small world, Daria thinks, unsettled by the latest twist.

"I'm Rosalee, Ralphie's sister and T. J. and Adam's mom, and that's my husband Timmy over there thinking I don't see him sneaking another meatball with his fingers when he's supposed to be on a diet."

"Who said I'm on a diet? Not me," he replies affably around a mouthful.

His wife rolls her eyes, then adds, to Daria, "By the way, I love him madly even after all these years, even if he won't listen to a word I say."

They seem so comfortable together, she notes. The whole big clan of them—even Mia, the newcomer. This is the kind of family that embraces you, pulls you in. The kind of family anyone would be privileged to join.

Too bad Ralphie's ex-fiancée didn't see it that way.

Too bad? Her loss, Daria finds herself thinking.

She can't help feeling envious of Mia, who obviously got it right. Glancing at her again, Daria is seized by a premonition.

Hmm . . . so it won't be long before Mia's role as the newest Chickalini is usurped by the tiny addition she's carrying in her womb at this very moment.

Does she even know she's pregnant?

Well, I do.

It's early on, but Daria is certain of Mia's pregnancy, and it wouldn't be the first time she's known before the mother even does. Sometimes, her intuitive gifts part the curtains on people's private lives in ways she'd rather not experience. Not so with happy baby news like this . . . even if she may be the only one in the room aware of it.

"Are you hungry?" Nina asks. "Because we have a ton of food."

"Oh, no, thanks. It's, um, really nice to meet all of you and . . . see you again," Daria adds to Ralphie . . . and immediately wishes that hadn't slipped out.

Especially when she sees Ralphie's ears grow red, while his sisters immediately exchange a glance.

They're thinking I'm here because of him.

And they're thinking about Francesca—whom they all adored, she remembers.

She wants to blurt out that she does have to be someplace else, after all; that she'll just get her phone and be on her way and never darken the well-worn Chickalini welcome mat again.

But somehow, she just can't.

She wants to stay in this house, with him, with them. Just for a little while. She can't help it.

Just for a taste of what it would be like to belong here . . .

Before she goes back to the footloose life that's always seemed to suit her until now.

*   *   *

Daria Marshall might not be wearing a red dress or lipstick today, but she's still Rose Red, Ralphie decides, with her cheeks charmingly ruddy from the January cold. Or even "Sweet Gypsy Rose," to add another old song to the mix.

Still *five foot two, eyes of blue*, too.

But not his gal. Nope.

What he can see of her hair is wind-tousled beneath a blue knit cap that exactly matches the shade of her eyes, making them seem bluer, bigger, brighter. She has on a white ski jacket, jeans that are almost as worn as his, and Keds. Never in his life has Ralphie found down, denim, or canvas the least bit sexy, but on her, they are.

And when his mental warning mechanism automatically kicks into gear with an admonishment, his Inner Single Guy points out that he's no longer engaged. He's free to look.

Technically, he's free to do more than look, but this probably isn't the time or place to be thinking about that.

Joey drapes Daria's coat over the heap already on the hall tree and Nina leads the way toward the dining room, cautioning her to step around the Monopoly set on the floor.

Ralphie tries to see the place through her eyes and can't decide whether it's charming or an eyesore.

He sees her glance at the artificial tree in the corner of the living room, wrapped in colorful oval bulbs and hung with ornaments Ralphie's mother collected throughout her lifetime. He supposes this is the last time they'll be displayed as a collection; they'll have to be divvied up among the five of them, to hang on five different trees next year.

They reach the archway to the dining room, where their interrupted meal remains on the table. Daria seems to hesitate, and Ralphie sees her steal a glance in his direction.

"We were done eating," he tells her.

"Really?"

He nods, smiles, extends an *after you* hand.

He wishes he had been the one to invite her into the house for dessert. Maybe she thinks he doesn't want her here.

Do you?

Hell, yeah, he does.

More than he realized.

Maybe more than he should, just one day into his reclaimed bachelorhood.

Yeah, but the breakup was a long time coming. It's not like you have to go through an official mourning period, or something.

Inner Single Guy, I like the way you think.

Bottom line: he's really, really, *really* glad to see Daria again.

He's no psychic, but she seems glad to see him, too. She keeps darting glances in his direction—and so do his sisters. God help him, they don't miss a trick.

Neither does Mia, who comes to the rescue.

"Why don't we clear away the dishes," she suggests to Nina and Rosalee, "and start the coffee?"

"Good idea," Nina agrees. "I have no idea what we're going to do with all this leftover food. I hope there's room in the fridge."

"If not," Ralphie tells her, "get rid of that head of brown lettuce, and there's a gallon of milk that's got to be expired. There are some cartons of leftover Chinese food you can toss, too—I think they're maybe a week old, so . . ."

Rosalee sighs. "You're worse than Pop, Ralphie. You really need to learn how to take care of yourself better, especially now that—"

She breaks off.

Now that Francesca's gone.

That's what she was going to say.

Why didn't she? It's not like impulsive Ro to bite her tongue. Ralphie sees her glance at Daria.

Is it that she doesn't want to air Ralphie's dirty laundry with an outsider in their midst?

That sure hasn't stopped her before. Ro's notorious for spilling his personal business to whoever will listen . . . and of course, her pal Bebe is usually right there with an ear cocked for the juicy details.

There's an awkward silence.

Then Nina asks Daria, "Do you want something to drink? Wine? Soda?"

"No, thanks . . ."

"Juicy Juice juice box?" Ro adds teasingly, offering the one in her hand.

"Wow, tempting as that is, no, thanks," Daria replies with a little smile, "but I will have coffee if you're making it."

"Definitely." Nina heads for the kitchen with a black-and-white speckled roaster pan full of sausage. "We all need coffee after last night."

Ralphie sees Daria's brow knit as Ro and Mia, too, disappear into the kitchen carrying plates, leaving the men to lean back in their chairs around the table.

She's thinking we're a bunch of macho chauvinists, Ralphie realizes. It doesn't really matter what she thinks, but he finds himself wanting to explain.

Well, not really wanting to, but feeling like he has to.

He never had that feeling when Francesca first started coming around. She simply understood; it was the same way in her house.

"In case you didn't notice, my sisters are control freaks," he informs Daria.

She looks uncertain, unsure how to respond to that without insulting someone.

"If we offer to take over with the dishes," he goes on, "they think we'll do it all wrong."

"Yeah, so we gave up trying to help years ago." Dominic smirks. "And I must say, I really miss it."

"Yeah, right, you miss it like a big old wood splinter." Joey reaches for a two-liter plastic bottle of Pepsi and refills his glass.

"No, really . . . there's something therapeutic about having my hands in warm water," Dominic trills in a falsetto, wiggling his fingers at them. "And it does wonders for my skin. It's so supple, see?"

"Which one are you imitating?" Timmy wants to know. "Ro or Nina?"

"Both," Dominic says with a laugh. "*My* wife doesn't pretend to like doing dishes, though. Our pampered little heiress is still getting the hang of it."

"Mia's family won the lottery," Ralphie explains to Daria. "So in some ways, she was kind of spoiled."

"Till she married Dom. Now she's permanently slum-ming," Timmy says, and they all laugh.

All except Daria.

She's staring at the empty chair at the head of the table, Ralphie realizes.

Pop's chair.

He's here.

Sad Eyes.

Sitting right at the table, comfy as you please, as if this were a castle and he were the king.

Daria should have known he wouldn't stay put back at Tammy's place. Needy spirits rarely do. Next thing she knows, the phantom mouse will be scampering around under the table, too.

Such is life.

Her life, anyway. It's not easy to see dead people—especially persistent dead people with an obvious agenda.

Daria sighs inwardly and looks away, hoping Sad Eyes doesn't try any funny business to get her attention, like he did last night with the cookie tin. The last thing she needs is for him to start throwing the good china on the floor or, worse yet, pull the tablecloth out from underneath it.

She had a rogue wraith do that once, in the middle of a fancy Seattle restaurant where she and her ex-husband were having dinner. Alan, who as yet didn't know about his wife's so-called gift, blamed the waiter. That greatly amused Pocket Handkerchief, the real culprit and one of Daria's more bothersome spirits, a late con artist who still enjoyed stirring up trouble from the Other Side.

Sad Eyes, in contrast, doesn't strike her as particularly mischievous. Not at the moment, anyway. He's just sitting here as if he's enjoying the company of the Chickalini family, and their cozy, comfortable house. But Daria intends to keep an eye on him, as one never knows when the biscotti is going to start flying again.

"So did anyone make any New Year's resolutions?" Ralphie's brother-in-law Joe—whom they all call Joey—asks.

"Ro made mine for me, same as she does every year. She's afraid I'm going to keel over and leave her a widow. So I'm supposed to lay off the good stuff—fat, sugar, cholesterol, beer. She wants me to eat twelve different vegetables a day." Timmy's florid face wrinkles in distaste.

"I can't even think of twelve different vegetables," Dom says. "Do french fries and potato chips count?"

"What do you think?"

"I think you need to tell Ro to forget it."

"Listen to Ned Newlywed over there," Joe says with a laugh. "You'll learn, Dom. If Mia decides you need to start eating two dozen different vegetables a day, you'll be down at the green grocer in a flash."

"Nah," Dom says, "I'd rather take my chances on keeling over. And anyway, Mia's too busy getting ready to start that horticulture course to worry about what I'm eating these days. She's got orchids on the brain. What's your resolution, Joey?"

"To figure out if I can afford to hire some extra help at the pizzeria so that I can spend more time with Nina and the kids."

"We can all pitch in more," Timmy says.

Joe shakes his head. "You're all working full time as it is. Look at you, you're always doing overtime at the firehouse."

"Yeah. It's not easy."

"No. And life is too short. So my resolution is to figure out how to start living every day to the fullest," Joe says, "because . . . well, you just never know what tomorrow will bring. Look at Pop. One day he was here, the next . . ."

Their collective smiles fade on cue.

Daria sneaks a peek at Ralphie and realizes he's looking right at Sad Eyes.

For a split second she wonders if he, too, can see him.

Then she spots his faraway expression and realizes he's not looking at the ghost—just lost in memories.

"Enough with the New Year's resolutions," Dominic declares abruptly. "Especially seeing as I don't have one and don't want one. Too much pressure. So Ms. Daria, where in Manhattan do you live?"

She turns her attention to Ralphie's handsome older brother—who, while there's a family resemblance, seems nothing like his kid brother. Where Ralphie is low-key and unassuming, Dominic strikes her as outgoing and flirtatious, a life-of-the-party kind of guy.

She wonders what he—what any of them—would think if they realized Daria's sister takes full credit for the unexpected Dom–Mia elopement.

Not that she's going to mention it. Things are complicated enough without the Psychic Sister element thrown into the mix.

"I live in midtown," she tells Dom. "On Lex."

"That's a nice neighborhood."

She nods. "It is. It's not my apartment, it's my sister's. I've been staying with her for a few months, but I'm actually leaving soon."

"Yeah? Where are you going?" Timmy raises a burnished brow.

"Back out west. Arizona." She hopes she doesn't sound as halfhearted about it as she suddenly feels.

"Not Australia?" That comes from Ralphie, and she looks up to see him watching her with his head tilted to one side.

"That's not out west, that's down under," Timmy says. "Even I know that, and I was no social studies ace, believe me."

Something flutters in Daria's stomach at Ralphie's intent expression. "Well, I don't think I'll wind up in Australia," she says slowly. "But I guess you never know, right? I could end up there, or . . . anywhere, I guess."

"Must be that gypsy blood," Ralphie comments, eyes locked on hers.

"Must be."

Unsettled, she forces herself to focus anywhere but on him.

She glances from the sauce-stained tablecloth to the brass chandelier—which is draped in a few cobwebs—to the cluster of family photos on the opposite wall.

As she flicks her attention past the framed wedding portraits from different eras and a few vintage shots of ancestral faces, she realizes she's instinctively looking for one of Ralphie.

Ah, there—she spots a formal photo of the Chickalini kids.

There are five, she notes—another brother fits into the birth rank between Rosalee and Nina.

Why isn't he here? Did something happen to him? she wonders with a pang.

Okay, that's a little ridiculous, she chides herself. Maybe he simply has other plans today, or lives far away.

The latter is more likely. This isn't the kind of family that skips holidays together. If Daria were one of them, she finds herself thinking, she'd move hell and high water to get home for the holidays.

Another ridiculous thought.

She zeroes in on the picture again. It's easy to pick Ralphie out of the sibling lineup, even if she hadn't figured out he's the baby of the family. As a toddler, he had the same straight dark hair and big brown eyes, even those long, athletic-looking limbs.

Daria's gaze moves on to the next group picture, snapped a few years later, of the five Chickalini kids and a man who can only be their father.

Their father . . .

Oh. My. God.

It's all Daria can do not to gasp aloud as she recognizes the man in the picture, frozen on long-ago film with a familiar smile that doesn't quite reach his sad eyes.

Sad Eyes.

Sad Eyes and Ralphie's late father are one and the same.

No wonder he's hanging around the table as if he owns the place.

But why is he hanging around me? Daria wonders, and her mind races through the events of the last few days.

It's no accident, then, that she stumbled upon Francesca in the ladies' room last night; no accident that she then found her way to Big Pizza Pie; no accident, either, that she left her cell phone behind . . .

After, she realizes, the tin of biscotti mysteriously fell

in the kitchen before she could put the phone back into her purse.

In the cosmic scheme of things, there are no accidents, no coincidences.

Ralphie's father wanted her here.

Why?

Chapter
7

The biscotti, Rice Krispy Treats, and rum cake were swiftly devoured. The dessert dishes have been cleared—by Nina, Ro, Mia, and Daria, too. She insisted on helping in the kitchen.

Ralphie hopes his sisters didn't attack her with Twenty Questions under cover of running water. Not that it would be the first time that's ever happened. And not that their husbands—Dominic, too—didn't start firing inquiries at him as soon as Daria was safely out of the room.

Ralphie kept reminding them all that he barely knows her, that Joey's the one who invited her here, that he's just been dumped by his fiancée, for heaven's sake. But the guys seemed convinced he's interested in Daria.

Okay, so they're right.

They must be, because Ralphie's trying to figure out how to keep her here when the rest of them leave, without being too blatant about it.

He'd better work fast, because the New Year's celebration is rapidly drawing to a close. The bowl game is over and the kids have finished their Monopoly game, with

T. J. as the winner and little Adam melting down because he wasn't.

Now Ralphie's family is gathering their plates and platters and bundling into coats for the trip home—Nina and her family through the shrub border; Dom and Mia to the subway for a few stops; Ro, Timmy, and the kids to the Long Island Expressway.

Daria has her coat in hand, too.

Ralphie wants to grab it from her, tell her to stay. He isn't sure quite how to go about it, but if he doesn't, she's going to walk right out of his life for the second time in twenty-four hours.

Granted, she'll be doing that no matter what. She's moving away, after all. She's mentioned Arizona a few times.

Maybe a little halfheartedly, but . . .

Well, it's not as if she's going to suddenly opt out of her plan in favor of staying in Queens with a freshly jilted, soon-to-be homeless guy like him.

"Got your phone this time?" Joey asks her.

She pats the pocket of her jeans and grins. "Right here."

Don't go, Ralphie wants to say, but he doesn't dare.

Not with ten pairs of ears listening in.

"It was nice meeting you," Ro says as she zips little Adam into a hooded parka that obscures half his face.

"Nice meeting you, too."

Don't go!

"Your rum cake was absolutely delicious," Daria tells Mia.

"Was it? Good. I tried a new recipe Maggie gave me."

"Didn't you get a piece of your own cake?" Nina asks.

"No, I was too stuffed from dinner. I don't think I want to see another meatball or sausage for a week."

"I was going to tell you to grab some leftovers. The fridge is overflowing," Nina says.

"No, thanks. We have to eat again in an hour—my grandmother's making dinner for us."

Dominic groans. "I was going to say yes to leftover lasagna, but forget it. Her grandmother cooks for an army, too."

"What about you guys?" Nina asks Ro and Timmy. "Take some stuff."

"No way, we're on a diet." Rosalee answers firmly for both of them, and shoots a warning glance at Timmy, who's about to protest. "You take it, Nina."

"Can't. Joey filled our fridge with extra pizza and calzones and another entire antipasto. But you know what? You should take some food home, Daria," Nina suggests suddenly.

Ralphie wants to hug his sister, who has no idea she just made his night.

Or maybe she does, because he detects a certain gleam in Nina's eye when she turns to him. "Ralphie, take her into the kitchen and fix her one of those foil trays. I'd do it, but I'm done for today. Let's go, Joey. Come on, guys."

"Wait, when are we having movie night, Uncle Ralphie?" Rose asks. "You said we still could, even without Francesca, and I have the perfect movie for us to watch."

"What is it?"

"*Sleepless in Seattle*! It's this old movie I saw on TV the other night, and it's really good."

"It's also not all that old," her mother tells her with an eyeroll.

"Yeah, it is. It's about this guy and this girl who fall in love from far away, and on Valentine's Day, they meet up on the top of the Empire State Building just when Sam thinks Annie is gone forever, only she's—"

"That sounds like a girl movie," Nino cuts in. "Uncle Ralphie, do you think you can take me out to the Rockaways to fly my kite next weekend?"

"It's the dead of winter, Nino—don't bother Uncle Ralphie with that," his mother admonishes him.

"No, it's okay, he's not bothering me."

"You know what? I think winter is the best time of year to go to the beach," Daria puts in. "I used to live in Maine, and I think there's nothing better than going out to the water on a cold January day."

"You can come with us!" Nino exclaims. "Right, Uncle Ralphie?"

"Uh . . . sure. If she wants to." He doesn't dare look at Daria.

"She just said she does. So we can go next weekend, right? Can you come, Daria?"

"Um . . . well, I *think* I can . . ."

If Ralphie's not mistaken, his nephew just inadvertently set him up on a date. A date chaperoned by a kid with a kite, but a date just the same.

With a flurry of kisses and hugs, the family exodus is underway.

Daria stands slightly aside, as if she's trying to stay out of the way, but everyone stops to say goodbye to her, too. She's right near the open door, coat on, and Ralphie is almost afraid she's going to slip out with the crowd.

Then they're gone, and she's not, and Ralphie can't seem

to keep from smiling. For the first time today—first time this year, technically—he's feeling almost lighthearted.

He closes the door and locks it. As the deadbolt slams loudly into place, he realizes Daria seems a little taken aback.

"I'm not trying to keep my family out, specifically . . . it's just that this *is* New York, and you never know."

"I think you're more afraid of your sisters than you are of prowlers."

Feeling a little sheepish, he nods. "They're just a little overbearing, if you know what I mean."

"I have an older sister. I know what you mean. Especially now that I've been living with her."

"Is she single?"

"Widowed."

"That's too bad."

"Yeah. She never got over it."

"That's how my father was. For him, the moon rose and set on my mother, and when he lost her, so young . . . I don't think I ever saw him really, truly smile. I mean, he'd go through the motions, but you'd notice it didn't ever reach his eyes."

Daria nods, but she seems awfully interested in playing with the zipper of her coat.

Well, who can blame her? She doesn't want to hear his sob story, or his father's. She probably just wants to get her lasagna and get going.

"You do want a tray of food to take with you on the train, I hope."

She smiles, so genuinely that he decides she might not be in a hurry to leave, after all. "I never turn down a home-cooked meal."

"You did earlier," he reminds her.

"That's because I felt funny coming in and chowing down in front of your entire family when I was supposedly here to pick up my cell phone."

"You *were* here to pick up your cell phone. And anyway . . . my entire family's gone. Are you still hungry?"

"I shouldn't be, after a big piece of cake and a Rice Krispy Treat."

"But . . . ?"

"But I am kind of hungry. Okay, really hungry." She hesitates. "So I guess that means, yes, pack up some lasagna for me and I'll get out of your hair."

"You're not in my hair. My sisters were in my hair . . . literally," he adds with a wry grin, remembering the way Nina and Rosalee fussed with it earlier. "Not you. Stay and I'll heat up some stuff right now."

"But . . . I mean, do you really want to bother? We just cleaned up a big mess in the kitchen."

"*I* didn't clean it up. And yeah, I want to bother. Come on." He leads the way into the kitchen.

"You don't have to do this."

"I know. If it makes you feel better, I'm actually hungry myself."

"Already?"

"I actually didn't really eat much of anything today."

"With all this food around?"

"Freshly broken engagements can be a real appetite killer," he quips, then belatedly glances over his shoulder at her as they enter the kitchen.

She looks surprised at the candid remark. He wonders if he shouldn't have said that, and wonders why he did. Snappy comments are Dom's department; Timmy's, too.

Not Ralphie's. He's always been the more earnest one, the one who takes things to heart, as Nina would say.

Didn't it take him a long, long time to get over Camille after she had his baby—then broke his heart?

Come on, you know why you said it. You want Daria to know that you're hanging in there on the Day After.

Just in case she thinks he's devastated, or hoping Francesca will change her mind, that he's still in love with her . . .

I never was. And I wish I could come right out and tell Daria.

Maybe he can . . . in a roundabout way.

"You probably don't think I should be making light of a broken engagement," he says, opening the same old olive green fridge that's stood in the kitchen for decades. "I guess maybe I shouldn't be acting like it doesn't matter to me, because of course it does, but the thing is . . . it was over with me and Francesca, way before it was over. Know what I mean?"

"Definitely." Daria's expression makes him wonder if she knows from experience.

Intrigued, he wants to ask if there's a broken heart—or, who knows, maybe even a broken engagement—in her past. But that might scare her off.

"The thing is, with me and Francesca," he goes on, rummaging through the stacks of still-warm Tupperware containers and plastic food storage bags that cram the refrigerator shelves, "when we met, everyone expected us to hit it off, and we did, in a way . . . and I guess it just steamrolled from there."

"So it was never really right? From the start?" Daria

asks, as he hands her a container of pasta and a foil-wrapped calzone.

"Exactly."

Maybe if he keeps talking about his past relationship, she'll bring up her own. A woman as captivating and provocative as Daria Marshall doesn't come without a romantic past, and he's curious about hers.

Watching Daria set the pasta and calzone on the gold Formica countertop, he goes on, "Looking back now, I think Francesca and I were just going through the motions. It's a relief not to have to do that anymore. And maybe I'd feel a little more guilty if I were the one who had broken things off, but . . . it was her, so . . . I mean, thank God she somehow found the strength."

A strange expression crosses Daria's face. "Yeah," she murmurs, "that's good."

"In the end, you can't make yourself fall in love with someone, no matter how badly you want to. No matter how much easier your life would be if you loved them."

"No . . . I don't suppose you can."

There's a pause.

Ralphie realizes the subject needs to be changed in a hurry. He holds up a container. "Do you like sausage and peppers?"

"I like everything."

"Not everything."

"Everything."

"Nobody likes everything."

She shrugs. "Try me."

"Spinach."

"Oh, come on. Who doesn't like spinach?"

"I'm not crazy about it."

"I am."

"Liver."

"Fried with bacon and onions? Definitely."

"Without bacon and onions."

"I'll eat it."

"But will you like it?" he challenges, putting some smoked mozzarella and a deli container of olives on the counter beside a loaf of Italian bread.

"I told you, I like everything."

"Frogs' legs."

"Yum."

"Yum?"

"I used to live in New Orleans—they're a local delicacy down there."

"Sorry . . . I'm fresh out of frog legs—do you think this'll do?" he gestures at the food spread before them.

"This will definitely do. Who's going to eat all this?"

"We are."

We—Ralphie likes the sound of that.

He takes two plates from the cupboard. They're about the only thing in the kitchen that's not from another era. The everyday Corell plates their mother left behind were broken, one by one, years ago, so the Chickalinis have been through several sets since then. But the rest of it—the appliances, the dark cabinets, the white ruffled curtains with red rick-rack trim, the daisy-printed wallpaper—it's all intact, circa 1973.

Some unsentimental buyer is going to rip all this out the minute the house changes hands, Ralphie reminds himself with a pang.

"Here . . ." He hands Daria a plate. "Start filling it."

"Thanks."

She digs in and so does he, passing containers back and forth.

"Wow, this pasta is so light," she says, piling it on.

"It's homemade."

"The sauce?"

"Yeah, of course the sauce. The noodles, too."

"What do you mean, homemade?"

"My sister rolls them out from dough and cuts them. It's a New Year's Day tradition. My great-grandmother always did it, and my grandmother, my mother . . . and now my sister."

"Wow." She looks at him almost in awe. "That's really something. To go through all that work, every year, when you can just open a box from the store."

He isn't sure what to say to that. It's hard to tell whether she thinks they're all nuts.

"I mean . . . it's a real labor of love," she adds, softly. "And all these kids are going to grow up with that tradition, and maybe keep it going."

"Yeah, well . . . I hope so. Nina's teaching Rose how to do it. She always helps."

"Not her brother, though?"

Ralphie hesitates. How does he explain that in his family, it doesn't work that way? It's not that the men don't cook, because they do. But certain things are a woman's territory. That's just how it is.

Francesca got that. It was the same way in her family.

"I don't know, I wasn't there," he tells Daria, spooning extra sauce over his pasta. "Maybe Nino did help. He probably did."

She nods.

There's a pause.

"So where haven't you lived?" he asks. "New Orleans, Maine, Chicago, Arizona . . ."

"You're leaving out at least a few dozen places," she says with a smile.

"Like Australia?"

"No. I was just there last year for New Year's and I thought I might want to go back, but so far I haven't."

"Back for good? Or to visit?"

"To visit . . . to live . . . I've never gone anywhere 'for good.' Oops, did you want some?" She hands him a nearly empty jar of marinated artichokes.

He makes a face. "Nope, all yours."

"You don't like artichokes?"

"Uh-uh. Or spinach. Frogs' legs, either." He peers into another container, asking, "Don't you get tired of always moving around?"

She hesitates. "It's what we've always done, for generations. Kind of like you guys with the homemade noodles."

He wants to point out that she didn't answer his question, but something in her tone stops him.

Instead, he asks, "We—you mean, your family?"

She nods.

"So your parents . . . they were gypsies? Both of them?"

"Not the way you're thinking."

"What way am I thinking?"

"With tambourines and hoop earrings." She smiles.

Okay. So that was pretty much what he was thinking.

"You left out fortune-tellers with crystal balls and tea leaves," he adds, and a cryptic emotion flashes in Daria's eyes.

Oops—maybe he insulted her. After all, some members of his own family don't take lightly stereotypical comments about mistresses and the Mafia—even if his wayward uncle Cheech is notoriously rumored to dabble in both.

Before he can apologize, Daria tells him a little stiffly, "My ancestors came from Romania, and yes, they traveled around by wagon, but that was way before I was born. We used a regular old car, most of the time."

"So your parents moved a lot."

"My mother did."

"And your father . . . ?"

"In my family, men leave." Her tone is almost flippant, but the look in her blue eyes is not. "Oh, who am I kidding? In my family, men leave, women leave . . . everybody leaves. Myself included. And you can blame it on culture, heritage, gypsy blood all you want, but the truth is, it's just easier."

"To leave?"

"Yes."

Ralphie considers that. "Not always. Look at me. Look at . . . this." He waves the fork he's holding, gesturing at the room, the house.

She looks.

Then she nods slowly. "I guess you and I are opposites, Ralphie."

"I guess so."

Then again . . . maybe we have a lot more in common than we thought.

*   *   *

"Hey, it's snowing," Ralphie notices, glancing out the window.

Sitting next to him in the well-worn living room illuminated only by the glow of the Christmas tree lights and the television, Daria follows his gaze. Sure enough, flurries are swirling in the streetlight's glow.

It's hard to believe that it's only been a matter of hours since she first walked into the Chickalini house—or that at this time yesterday, she didn't know Ralphie even existed. Look at her now: sock feet propped on the well-worn coffee table beside two empty plates, a stack of magazines, and Ralphie's own sock feet.

Daria stretches and says reluctantly, "I guess I should hit the road."

"Don't go."

Ralphie's response catches her off guard, and for a moment, she wonders if she even heard him right.

Turning toward him, she decides that she must have.

And that it's a good thing there's an entire cushion-length between them right about now, because one glance into his dark eyes, and if she were sitting right next to him, she might be tempted to reach out and touch him.

How can she be so drawn to a man she barely knows? How can she feel so at home in a place she's never been before?

She forces a laugh. "I have to go sooner or later."

"Yeah, but not yet. You don't want to go out in that weather."

"I love snow. And it's not like it's a storm—just a few flakes."

"The game's not over yet."

"It's all but over," she points out, gesturing at the television set, where his favorite college football team is about to go down. "I'm not even a big football fan."

"I know, but you have to admit, you're having fun."

"I also have to admit that this is the laziest couple of hours I've ever spent in my life."

And perhaps the coziest and most comfortable, she admits to herself. But that doesn't mean she shouldn't venture back to the real world now.

"Sometimes a little laziness is a good thing," Ralphie points out.

"A *little* laziness?"

It's been a good couple of hours since they've budged from the couch. They ate their leftovers sitting right here in front of the Rose Bowl game, but not really watching it.

Mostly, they talked—easily, the way good old friends talk to each other. About what, Daria can't quite recall. Certainly nothing deep or meaningful or depressing, like his broken engagement or his father's death. She made sure to steer clear of anything too personal about herself, too. He still has no idea that she's divorced, or that she has a knack for seeing dead people—his late father included.

At least the family patriarch hasn't put in an appearance since she first saw him in the dining room and realized who he was.

Daria's been keeping an eye out, though, aware that he can—and probably will—pop up any second.

She just wishes she knew why—or what she's supposed to do about it.

"After the game's over," Ralphie says, "we can watch a movie or something."

"A 'girl' movie?" she asks slyly, and he grins.

"Yeah, like *Sleepless in Seattle*."

"I loved that movie," she says—and neglects to mention that there was a time when she lived—often sleeplessly— in Seattle. With her ex-husband.

"I liked it, too," he replies. "I even own the soundtrack. But don't tell my niece."

"I won't. And so do I . . . own the soundtrack, that is. I downloaded it onto my iPod for when I'm in the mood for something mellow."

"We can listen to it right now, if you want," Ralphie says. "I wouldn't mind something mellow."

"You have to be up early tomorrow for work, don't you?" she asks Ralphie, checking her watch.

"Yeah, but it's not like I'm going to bed at eight o'clock," he tells her.

"Do you like your job?"

"Pretty much. Do you like yours?"

"When I have one, you mean?" she asks wryly, and explains about George and his fledgling design firm back in Phoenix.

"You don't sound all that enthusiastic about it."

"No, I am—I mean, I love design. Maybe I'm just not very good at working for other people."

And maybe I don't want to think, right now, about living on the opposite end of the country from this cozy spot.

And from you.

"Open your own business, then," Ralphie suggests, as if it were that simple.

As if she hadn't already thought of it on her own, plenty of times.

It always comes back down to the same old issue, though.

"The thing is, to open a business, you have to be rooted in one place," she tells Ralphie, who ought to know. He mentioned that Big Pizza Pie has been in business all his life, and for quite some time before that.

Clearly, the Chickalinis are very big on tradition, on roots.

In their midst, a fancy-free woman like Daria would have a shorter shelf life than fresh mozzarella.

"There's something to be said for being rooted in one place," Ralphie tells her.

"I think I'd go stir crazy," she hears herself respond—and she doesn't miss the flicker of disappointment in his eyes.

But he sounds utterly casual as he asks, "So you're definitely leaving New York then, right?"

She nods firmly. "Right."

"Can I ask you a question?"

"Absolutely not," she says resolutely—then laughs at his expression. "I was kidding. Of course you can ask me a question."

"Why Arizona?"

"Because that's where my stuff is."

"You're kidding again, right?"

She wishes she were.

She opts to tack on the perhaps more conventional version of the truth: "I went out there to visit a friend of mine last August and decided I liked it."

"The desert. In the middle of summer."

She shrugs. "It's not so bad. And I hear the weather's

beautiful now, blue skies and warm—not blazing hot—sunshine, so . . ."

"So when are you leaving?"

She wishes she could feel as enthusiastically sure about it as she's managing to sound. "As soon as I can get a flight back out there."

"Are we talking tomorrow? Next month?"

"Something in between. I mean, I wouldn't want to disappoint your nephew."

She waits for the light to dawn in his eyes—along with an unexpected, welcome glint of pleasure—then adds, "You thought I'd forgotten about kite-flying on the winter beach, didn't you?"

"I wasn't sure you really meant it."

"I wouldn't make an empty promise to a little kid. Or to anyone, for that matter."

Is it her imagination, or is he suddenly sitting a little closer to her?

"I was thinking we'd leave here at around ten on Saturday morning," he says. "Head down to the beach, fly the kite, maybe stop for lunch on the way back at this great hot dog stand Nino and I love. Do you really want to go with us?"

He's sitting a lot closer; it's not her imagination.

"Sure," she says, in a voice that sounds a little more hoarse than her own. "If that's all right with you."

"That's more than all right with me."

Ralphie's feet are on the floor now, his body turned toward her. One arm stretches along the back of the couch, and she doesn't need supernatural abilities to sense that he's about to make a move.

Uh-oh.

She should probably stop him. . . . Shouldn't she?

Of course she should, regardless of how much she wants to slide closer to him, instead of away.

He's on an emotional rebound, vulnerable; she's about to make a permanent exit from his house, his city, his life . . .

What can possibly come of anything happening between them?

"You know what else would be all right with me?" Ralphie asks softly.

"Wait . . . let me guess." She forces herself to make light of it. "If Michigan scores a field goal for a comeback win?"

"That . . . and this."

As he leans in, Daria gives up. *You only live once,* she thinks, and closes her eyes.

She feels his warm hand cupping her face with unexpected tenderness; inhales the whisper-stir of his breath in the moment before his lips brush hers.

He kisses her thoroughly, as she hasn't been kissed in years—or perhaps ever before. Somewhere inside her, longing stirs to life with a fluttering of feather-soft wings. Physical longing, yes . . . but not just that.

Much more.

Her heart beats furiously, or is it the wings, consumed by the sudden urge to take flight?

She pulls back from Ralphie abruptly.

"I'm sorry," she says.

"You took the words right out of my mouth. I'm sorry." But he looks decidedly unabashed, she notices.

"I—I have to go." She swings her feet to the floor and hopes her legs won't give out on her when she stands.

"Are you sure?"

"Positive." She's up, and her legs are holding her. So far, so good.

She reaches down, starts to pick up the dirty plates.

"No," he says. "I'll get them."

"Unlike your sisters, I won't argue." She's already halfway to the door, stopping momentarily to grab her down jacket from the coat tree.

She shoves one arm into the sleeve but it won't go in readily. What's wrong with it? She's got to get out of here, before something happens.

She tries again. The sleeve is blocked.

Frustrated, she punches her arm in. Her blue ski hat shoots out the opposite end of the sleeve and lands on the floor.

Wordlessly, Ralphie picks it up and hands it to her.

"Thank you." She plants it on her head, zips her coat, fumbles blindly behind her for the doorknob. "I'm leaving."

"No kidding." He smiles faintly.

"Thanks for . . . everything."

"You're welcome."

She finds the knob, turns it, pulls it. Nothing happens.

Ralphie reaches past her and turns the dead bolt. "There. Now you can escape."

"That's not what I'm . . ."

Oh, isn't it?

Come on, Daria.

"Sorry," she says, stepping into the cold.

"For what?"

Leaving now . . . staying in the first place . . . she isn't quite sure.

Poised in the blustery glow of the overhead light fixture, she casts a last glance at the warm, cozy house, then at him.

"Listen," he says, "you look tired, and it's been a long day. I get it. Goodnight."

No. Not goodnight.

This has to be goodbye forever.

Even though she doesn't do goodbyes, and—as she told George what feels like a lifetime ago—doesn't believe in forever.

She can't make the same mistake twice in a lifetime. Ralphie represents all the things lacking in her own world . . . but that doesn't mean she belongs in his.

She has to flee, once and for all.

Unable to force the word *goodbye* past her lips, she gives a little wave, turns her back, and hurries down the slippery steps.

"See you Saturday," Ralphie calls, and she almost stops short.

Saturday.

That's right.

Nino, the beach, the kite.

She's not fleeing once and for all, after all.

"Just be here by ten o'clock," he tells her. "And dress warm. Goodnight," he calls again.

She hears the door close behind her.

"Goodnight," she answers softly.

Chapter
8

Which is closer, do you think?" Daria asks Tammy Friday night, hand poised on the computer mouse. "JFK, or La Guardia?"

"It's a toss-up," Tammy answers from her perch on the couch, not turning away from the repeat episode of *The Ghost Whisperer*.

"Really? La Guardia seems closer," Daria mutters.

Or maybe that's just because it's closer to Ralphie. The airport is right next door to Astoria.

Does she really want her last official glimpse of New York—as a semi-resident, anyway—to be his neighborhood?

"I'll check the fares from JFK," she decides, and begins scrolling through her flight options.

As the show goes to a toothpaste commercial, Tammy looks away from the television screen at last. "If I were you, I'd wait a few days. The airlines always have fare sales after the holidays are over."

"They're over."

"Barely."

"It's okay," Daria tells her sister. "I want to book this now. Tonight."

"Why?" Tammy asks. "So that you can show up at Ralphie Chickalini's house tomorrow morning knowing you already have an out?"

Daria offers her a grim smile. "If I didn't know better, I'd say you might be psychic."

"Ha. That was purely an educated guess, based on everything you've told me the last few days."

Wishing she hadn't opened her big mouth in the first place, Daria asks, "What was it, exactly, that you saw when you met Ralphie at the wedding?"

Tammy shakes her head. "I told you . . ."

"I know. Tell me again. Please. Aside from the black aura of grief."

Her sister sighs. "I just felt like he didn't like change . . ."

"I know, he doesn't. Not that part."

"And I saw this older guy standing behind him. That's it."

"An old guy with sad eyes, right? That's what you said."

"Right. An old guy with sad eyes," agrees Tammy. "Same as you saw. Ralphie's father, obviously."

"What do you think he wanted?"

"I have no idea, Daria. All I know is that it's pretty coincidental that I'm the reason his son Dominic found the love of his life and married her, and now you're going around kissing his other son. Maybe I should—"

"No, you shouldn't. I swear, Tammy, if you get involved like some cosmic matchmaker, I'll never talk to you again."

"Cosmic matchmaker?" Tammy looks insulted.

"I'm sorry. I didn't mean—"

"Yes you did, and you know what? That's fine. I promise you I won't get involved like some cosmic matchmaker, even if you beg."

"I doubt that's going to happen, and thank you for staying out of it," Daria says, and turns back to the computer to finish the reservation.

"You're the one who asked me about Ralphie. I was just answering your question."

"I know. And you did. Here's another one for you," Daria says quickly, hand poised over the keyboard, "What's Monday's date?"

"You're leaving on Monday?"

"Why hang around? I've got a job waiting for me." A job, a friend, a whole new life. When she got a hold of George the other night, he was thrilled to hear she's coming back. "Perfect timing," he said. "We should be up and running by Martin Luther King Day."

"I'll be there," Daria promised, determined to see this through. "Is your futon still open?"

When George hesitated, she immediately thought, *Uh-oh.* With good reason.

"Actually," he told her, "Barney's been sleeping on it."

"Big purple dinosaur?"

"Little French guy. Barney Saint Claire. He's new in town, from Paris, a friend of Evan's."

"And Evan would be . . . ?"

"Evan Dobbs. My new boyfriend, of course."

"Of course," Daria agreed, and tried not to sigh.

Now, Tammy nods reluctantly. "I guess you're right.

Why linger here if you've got a whole life waiting for you somewhere else?"

"Exactly."

Of course she didn't tell Tammy she's apparently going to land in the middle of an all-boy slumber party. Her sister will only try to convince her that her couch in New York is more comfortable than George's floor in Phoenix.

Maybe that's true, but Daria doesn't dare stick around. If she does, she might somehow convince herself that Ralphie Chickalini is the answer to her prayers—same as she did with Alan.

No way. This time, she's not going to allow herself to be blinded by a craving for conventionality. No way is she going to step into someone else's ready-made life just because her own lacks direction.

"Tam, do you ever look back and wish things had been different?"

"Every damned day of my life," her sister answers promptly, wearing the sorrowful expression she gets whenever Carlton crosses her mind.

"No, I mean . . ."

What she means—their childhood—seems so trite next to her sister's tragic adulthood.

"You mean Mom, and Dad—mine—and your dad?"

"That's exactly what I mean." She smiles at Tammy, relieved. "Don't you ever wish there had just been one dad?"

"That depends—mine or yours?"

When Daria hesitates, Tammy answers her own question. "I'll take yours. Mine is no prize. At least Dale stuck around."

"Not really. No one stuck around. Half the time Mom

was off visiting someone or other for weeks on end, and we had to stay with neighbors we barely knew, or whoever she could get to watch us, until you were old enough to do it yourself."

"I know, but I never minded."

Daria finds herself thinking of Ralphie's sister Nina, who raised him when their mother died.

Her own mother didn't die, but . . .

Maybe Daria and Ralphie have more in common than she realized.

Not that that counts for anything.

"You're saying you have no regrets, Tammy?" she asks. "You don't wish we'd had a nuclear family, a real hometown, homemade mashed potatoes? You don't think we missed out?"

"On homemade mashed potatoes?"

"On everything." Frustrated, she tries to figure out what, exactly, she's trying to say—and what she needs her sister to say in return.

"It's not like it's too late for all that, you know, Daria."

"Sure it is."

"No. Your childhood is over, but your life isn't. You can build all that for yourself. It sounds like this guy Ralphie is—"

"No," Daria cuts in sharply. "He's not."

"You don't even know what I was going to say."

"Yes, I do. You were going to tell me that he's exactly the kind of guy I need in my life, that he can give me all the things I've never had, that if I were with him, I'd feel like I really belonged somewhere."

Tammy stares at her for a long, hard minute.

Then she shakes her head slowly, the corners of her lips quirking a little. "No," she says, "I wasn't going to tell you any of that at all."

Daria feels her ears grow hot. "Oh."

"All I was going to say was that it sounds like he's interested in you."

"No, he's not." Daria shoots back, feeling ornery.

"No? So he kissed you because . . . ?"

Daria never should have told Tammy about the kiss—or any of it.

"You promised you'd stay out of it. And your show's back on," she mutters, gesturing at the television and turning back to the computer.

Jaw set resolutely, she types in Monday's date. Hits Enter.

Good.

New question . . . one way, or round trip?

She hesitates only a few seconds before clicking the obvious.

One way, of course.

She's out of here.

And Tammy's right. She can build a life for herself. She doesn't need some guy to do it for her.

She'll go back to Phoenix, she'll start her new job, she'll find a nice apartment, some new friends . . .

For the first time in her life, Daria is going to make sure she sees something through, completely on her own, from start to finish.

Mike's Diner is always jammed on Friday nights. Despite being on a first-name basis with the host, the four Chickalini siblings have to wait for a table.

Wedged into a crowded corner, Nina and Rosalee make small talk about the weather and the white sale at J.C. Penney and Dominic checks e-mail on his Blackberry.

Ralphie pretty much broods, but nobody calls him on it. They probably figure he's entitled, as a just-jilted fiancé.

The thing is . . . even now, after letting the breakup sink in for a few days, his heart has yet to hurt. Maybe he'd feel a twinge of regret if he actually saw Francesca, or spoke to her . . .

But he hasn't.

She's obviously determined to do this cold turkey, and frankly, he's glad. He figures she'll have to show up sooner or later to pick up some belongings she left behind at his house, and figure out what they're going to do about the attic full of shower gifts. When they parted ways the other night, she said she'd call him about it soon.

When he does see her again, he figures, they'll have more closure.

For now, Ralphie has all the closure he needs—not to mention further proof that the breakup was long overdue.

If he loved her, he'd be hurting by now. It's that simple.

The only thing that's hurting him these days is dealing with the loss of his father.

And the impending sale of the house, which—like it or not—he can't put off any longer. The day of reckoning has arrived.

Still, when at last he's settled into a turquoise uphol-stered booth with his brother and sisters, no one seems particularly eager to bring up the reason for the dinner.

Before and after they place their order, Dom fills them

all in on Mia's back-to-school venture into horticulture, Nina mentions that a boy named Theo has been calling Rose, and Rosalee frets over Timmy's upcoming shift change at the firehouse.

Ralphie arranges and rearranges the salt and pepper shakers and container of sugar and Sweet'N Low in the center of the table, not saying much of anything at all. He's not in the mood for small talk any more than he's in the mood for the conversational topic looming before them.

"Wow, all four Chickalinis out together on a Friday night?" Stavros, their favorite waiter, comments as he sets their plates before them. "What's the occasion?"

They look at each other.

"Well, actually, they're honoring me with the annual Brother of the Year Award," Dominic quips. "Again. You guys!"

Stavros congratulates him, tongue in cheek, and bustles on his way.

"Brother of the Year award?" Nina rolls her eyes.

"I'm sure the Brother of the Year isn't going to hoard all those french fries to himself, right Dommy?" Rosalee reaches across the table and grabs one.

"Hey! Why didn't you take the fries that come with your souvlaki?" Dom moves his plate out of his sister's reach.

"Because I'm trying to be good. I ordered double salad instead."

"Then eat it and leave my fries alone." Dom squirts ketchup all over them, then his cheeseburger, before wordlessly handing it to Ralphie.

He douses his own burger—sans cheese—then closes

the bun and, without asking, puts his pickle on Nina's plate, next to her Reuben wrap.

"Thanks," says Nina, who traditionally gets his pickles. He likes them well enough, but she loves them.

After all these years, the rhythm of eating together remains unchanged. At least something is, Ralphie thinks.

Nina bites into her wrap, then wipes her mouth with a napkin. "So . . ."

Here we go, Ralphie thinks, and fights the urge to halt his own burger en route to his mouth.

"Now that the holidays are over, we really need to get the house on the market."

And there it is.

Ralphie might have known it was coming, but the straightforward comment still manages to catch him off guard.

But they're here—the four of them, no spouses, no kids—to discuss the matter at hand, aren't they? Might as well get it over with. It's not as if there are any actual decisions to be made.

"Do we all agree on that?" Nina asks, and they nod.

But Ralphie can't help noticing that no one seems particularly eager to get on with the discussion.

Dominic scolds Rosalee for stealing another fry, and Rosalee asks Ralphie if she can have one of his onion rings. Then Stavros appears to ask if anyone needs anything, and it seems that they all do: more napkins, a beverage refill, mustard.

Finally, they've regrouped and Nina asks, "So . . . where were we?"

"Talking about getting the house on the market." Rosalee pokes through the olives and feta cheese clumps in her salad. "The first thing we should do is buy a little plastic statue of Saint Joseph and bury it in the yard."

"What?" The three of them gape at her.

"Bebe knows a Realtor who swears by it. A lot of people do. Saint Joseph is the patron saint of . . . I forget what . . ."

"Mortgages?" Dom asks with a snicker.

"Anyway," she goes on, shooting him a glare, "if you bury the statue upside down and facing away from the house, it helps you make a fast sale."

A fast sale? That's the last thing Ralphie wants.

Dom shakes his head. "That's insane, Ro."

"What, it works!"

"Just the same," Nina says patiently, "I think we'll go with a For Sale sign and a good Realtor."

"That reminds me, we should use the Realtor Bebe knows because—"

"No way," Ralphie, Dom, and Nina all say in unison.

Ro looks up in surprise. "What? You guys don't think we should use a Realtor?"

"Sure, we do. We just don't think we should use a Realtor who relies on deep-sixing Saint Joseph and has the slightest connection whatsoever to Bebe," Dom tells her.

"Why not? She's very plugged in."

"That's exactly why not," Nina says firmly. "Do we really need the whole neighborhood knowing our business?"

"They're going to know our business as soon as a For Sale sign pops up on the front lawn," Ro points out, and Ralphie cringes inwardly at that image.

"Mia knows a Realtor we can use," Dom offers. "John Fusilli. He's got an office off Astoria Boulevard."

"Any relation to Bon Bon Fusilli?" Ro asks.

"I think he's her brother."

"Ooh, I know her from CYO dances. She's a sweetheart. I haven't seen her in years. Okay, so he sounds good."

"Just because you know his sister Bon Bon?" Ralphie asks, feeling prickly. "What's with your friends, anyway, Ro? Bon Bon? Bebe? They sound like plushies on a kids' television show."

"Her real name is Bonnie, and Bebe has nothing to do with this, remember? Unless you'd rather use her friend, instead of Bon Bon's brother?"

"No, this is good," Nina says hastily. "Dom, can you see if Bon—I mean, John, can come by the house tomorrow afternoon?"

"Wait . . . tomorrow?" Ralphie protests, plunking his burger back onto his plate. "Why tomorrow?"

"The sooner the better. We just need him to take a look at the place and tell us roughly what we can ask."

"But . . . it's not in any shape to be shown."

"Ralphie, relax. We're not showing it to anyone but John."

"Yeah, but shouldn't he see it in prime condition?"

"Come on, do you know how long it's going to take us to get it into prime condition?" Dom asks.

"Prime? I'd settle for presentable," Nina says.

"Well, I hate to burst everyone's bubble, but tomorrow's no good for me."

"Why not?" Ro asks Ralphie.

"Because I have stuff to do. I play basketball on Saturday mornings . . ."

"At, like, dawn," Rosalie reminds him.

"Yeah, but I have stuff to do all day. I was going to take down the Christmas lights, and—"

"Pop never took the lights down until the Epiphany," Dom cuts in. "That's almost a week away."

"Yeah, well, Pop's not here this year." He hates himself for snapping; hates himself for resenting that Dom got to move out, move on, and leave everything at the house in Ralphie's hands.

"Take it easy, there, Ralphie." Nina pats his arm. "I know it's hard. And we all miss Pop."

Of course that's true. Ralphie knows in his heart that his sisters and brothers miss Pop as much as he does. But none of them seems to be struggling the way he is. They all have closer family to distract them, busy lives, homes of their own; Dominic is a newlywed, for heaven's sake. Of course the loss is hard on them, but not as hard as it is on Ralphie.

Or maybe, not as hard as you're making it on yourself, a little voice chides.

Ignoring it, Ralphie tempers his tone as he goes on, "And anyway, I'm taking all the kids kite-flying on the beach tomorrow . . . remember?"

"The beach? It's supposed to snow," Dom tells him.

"Not until late." Nina is trying to be the peacemaker as always. "So it's fine, Ralphie, go ahead and take the kids. I'll get Joey to take down the lights for you if you don't want to wait until the Epiphany, and I'll go over and take John through the house."

"No, Joey has enough to do. And anyway, I want to be there when the Realtor comes." He doesn't know why. Maybe because he's worried that if he's not there, the others will . . . what? Sell the house right out from under him?

Okay, that's not going to happen in a single afternoon, but still . . .

"Fine," Nina says, "then leave the lights on another day."

"It's going to snow on Sunday, too, and there are play-off games, and I want to—"

"So leave the damned lights on till spring, then!" Nina looks—and sounds—exasperated. Even she has her limits. "What time do you think you'll be back from the beach with the kids?"

"Not until late. By the time we take the subway all the way down to Far Rockaway, fly the kite, get something to eat—"

"Well, you'd better be back before four," Ro tells him decisively, "because Adam has to go to Ryan LaBianco's pool party."

"First the beach, now a pool party?" Dom shakes his head. "Am I the only one who didn't forget that it's January?"

"It's an indoor pool," Rosalee explains. "So, Dommy, just have this guy John come over to Pop's house after four. Okay?"

They all look at Ralphie, who shrugs. "Whatever. That's fine." He wants to add that it's not Pop's house anymore—not really.

But then, it's not his, either.

"I'll go call John now." Dom pulls his cell phone from his pocket and steps away from the table.

Nina and Rosalee exchange a glance at each other, then level their attention on Ralphie.

Story of his life.

"I know it's hard," Nina tells him, as he bites moodily into an onion ring.

"For all of us," Ro adds.

"But especially for you, Ralphie. You're the youngest, and . . . you hate change. More than any of us."

That Nina seems to get that doesn't help matters much, other than validating this oppressive feeling that's settled over him.

"If you're worried about dealing with everyone's crap that's left in the house, don't," Ro says. "Because we're all going to help. Timmy even said he can get a deal on a Dumpster."

"For what?" Ralphie asks.

"For all the stuff we're going to have to throw away when we clean out the house," Nina says gently. "You know a lot of it's going to have to go, don't you, Ralphie? I mean, this is New York City, none of us has extra room, and even if you wanted to, you can't take a houseful of old furniture and appliances to a little condo somewhere."

"You can keep whatever you have room for," Ro tells him. "We all will. But so much of it's just . . . junk. I hate to put it that way, but it is. Anyway, a couple of the guys from the firehouse said they'll help us move the furniture out when the time comes. And Pete's going to fly back if we need him, too."

"And if you're worried about having a place to go now that you and Francesca are—you know, you don't have to be in any rush," Nina says. "You're welcome to come stay with us for as long as you want."

"Nina, you don't have to—"

"Hey, it'll light a fire under Joey to finally get all those files from his old career out of the spare bedroom. I don't know why the heck he's kept them all these years in the first place. And the kids would just love to have Uncle Ralphie under our roof."

"Thanks, Neens, but . . . you guys have enough going on without taking in a boarder, so—"

"Ralphie, come on, a boarder? You know you're not—"

"No, I know, and I appreciate the offer. But when the time comes, I'll find a place."

The community message board at work is filled with notices for apartment shares and rentals. Ralphie checked it this morning, after he got the e-mail from Nina about this official sibling meeting tonight.

It really put a damper on his weekend plans. Not that he had anything else going tonight . . . but tomorrow is the beach with the kids, the kite . . . and Daria.

He's been trying for the past few days not to make too much of the outing, knowing it probably means nothing to her. She's going because of the kids, not him.

If she's going at all.

She left so quickly the other night that he didn't get her phone number . . . and unfortunately, this time she took her cell phone with her, so there was no reason for her to come back.

What if she never does?

Has anybody seen my gal?

The song has been running through his head for days, along with "Sweet Gypsy Rose," that Tony Orlando oldie that also reminds him of Daria.

Probably because that song's lyrics, coincidentally and fittingly enough, also ask if anybody's seen her.

Maybe somebody up there is trying to tell you something, Ralphie. Maybe you're never going to see her again. Maybe you're going to spend the rest of your life looking for her.

No. This isn't about the rest of his life.

This is about tomorrow.

All he knows is that Daria said she was coming—and that if she doesn't show up tomorrow morning, the kids are going to be bummed.

The kids?

Okay, *Ralphie* is going to be bummed.

But there's nothing he can do about that.

Either she shows up, or she doesn't.

Regardless of what happens tomorrow, she's getting ready to leave New York for good. So what does it really matter?

"All set," Dom announces, slipping back into the booth. "He'll see us there at four tomorrow afternoon."

"That was fast."

"Yeah. John is psyched. He knows the block. He said the location is a plus, because of all the trees, plus it's close to the subway and the stores." Dom could be reading from a real estate ad.

"Good. So we're all set, then."

Ralphie can't help but notice that Nina's voice sounds a little hollow.

Or that Ro's "That's great!" is definitely forced.

Or that Dominic picks halfheartedly at his fries.

They don't want to let go, either, Ralphie realizes.

Too bad there just isn't any other choice.

Chapter
9

The sky over Queens hangs low and threatening as Daria steps off the elevated subway platform on Saturday morning, the Rolling Stones blasting over her iPod earphones. She found that if she cranked the volume enough, she didn't have to listen to the annoying little voice in her head.

The one that keeps trying to warn her that she shouldn't be doing this. She should be back at Tammy's, packing a suitcase and daydreaming about . . . cactuses or something.

As she descends the steps from the elevated platform, Mick Jagger sings in her head about not getting any satisfaction.

Yeah, Mick, buddy, I know how you feel.

She's dressed warmly in suede sheepskin-lined surfer boots she bought in Australia, jeans, her down jacket over a fisherman's sweater, and a matching cream-colored knit hat. Still, the wind seems to go right through her, gusting and blowing a discarded supermarket flier around her feet as she emerges onto Thirty-First Street.

The desolate day reminds her of the lone winter she spent in New England.

After graduating from college in Boston, she moved up to Bar Harbor for a summer job at a children's camp, then fell for a local lobsterman and stayed till the following spring, when they broke up.

Just one in a long series of short-lived relationships—most of them, she has to admit even now, more fulfilling than her marriage.

Which begs the question . . .

Why am I bothering to do this today?

Ralphie Chickalini is another Alan.

That's why she thinks she's so drawn to him.

Why you think *you're so drawn to him?*

Hello? What about that kiss?

All right, so maybe it's not all purely in her head; maybe she really is drawn to Ralphie. It's human nature to want what you don't have, right?

And anyway, she once convinced herself she was crazy about Alan, too, right?

Yes . . . but not like this.

With Ralphie, it's a matter of chemistry, too.

That's still not enough to justify a relationship . . . not that she even has one with Ralphie. Or is going to have one with Ralphie, ever.

She's bought her plane ticket back to Arizona. One way, of course, departing from JFK first thing Monday morning.

So no matter what happens in the next few hours, there's no risk of Daria making the same mistake with Ralphie that she made with Alan. After she sees him today, he's history. Just like Alan, in a way—only without the lawyers and paperwork.

It doesn't mean she'll be alone forever—not that she believes in forever—or even for much longer.

When she gets to Phoenix, after she's found a new place to live and settled into her job, she'll start dating again. Who knows? Maybe she'll even fall in love. For real, this time, with someone who has everything in common with her.

Unlike Ralphie Chickalini.

Rounding the corner onto Ditmars Boulevard, she glances down the block toward the pizzeria. Looking over her shoulder in the opposite direction, she can see the steeple for Most Precious Mother. Again, she marvels that Ralphie and his family have lived and worked and socialized within a three-or-four-block radius for so many years.

That probably doesn't happen in Phoenix. Things are so spread out there; people more transient.

She thought New York was, too, but this tiny enclave in Queens is more like a small town, she decides, watching a couple of older women with shopping bags greet each other on the street.

In front of some homes and buildings, people balance on ladders, busily taking down lights and decorations. The curb is dotted here and there with stiff, discarded Christmas trees. Still, some holdout holiday lights, lit in broad daylight, provide a welcome glimmer of color on this gray Saturday morning.

Turning onto Ralphie's block, Daria is surprised—and pleased—to spot him sitting out on the stoop, waiting for her.

But as she draws closer, she realizes it isn't Ralphie at all.

It's his father.

Daria sighs inwardly as she approaches, wondering again why he's still hanging around. Lots of spirits are attached to their earthly residences, but she gets the distinct impression Nino Chickalini has a mission. One that involves her.

And I might as well just come right out and ask him what it is, she decides. *After all, you never know. I might actually get an answer.*

Some apparitions really can communicate verbally. Others just show up, drifting around. Still others convey messages to Daria through symbolism or telepathy.

Like Hank Biggs, who, as he later revealed to her, didn't show Daria *Hello, Dolly* as a sign for his wife to go ahead remarry. No, he was hoping to get his wife to go through with her planned move back to Yonkers, her hometown.

Hello, Dolly was set in Yonkers, of course.

But how was I supposed to know that? Daria wonders to this day.

Which is precisely why she hasn't attempted to deliver a ghostly message since.

And why she won't be mentioning to Ralphie Chickalini that his dead father is hanging around—much less that she can see him.

Not unless Nino reveals some earth-shattering information he has to get across to his family, via Daria.

She should find out, she decides wearily. Once and for all. She'll allow herself to focus on the energy and see what, if anything, comes through.

After jabbing the power button on her iPod and silencing her buddy Mick in mid-moan, she plucks first one, then the other, white earbud from beneath her cap.

Immediately, she hears a voice calling her name.

Not Ralphie's father's voice, though.

Turning in surprise, she sees that it's coming from his namesake, the other Nino, Ralphie's look-alike nephew. He's hanging around in the front yard next door, wearing a parka and boots, and munching on an apple.

"Uncle Ralphie said you might not show up," he calls to her.

"Did he, now." She wonders whether that could possibly have been wishful thinking on Ralphie's part.

It didn't seem, the other night, as though he didn't want to see her again. In fact, it was just the opposite. He acted pleased when she told him she was coming along on the kite-flying expedition.

Maybe "acted" is the key word there.

Or maybe he's since changed his mind.

Anything could have happened since then. For all she knows, he and Francesca are engaged again.

Though that shouldn't have anything to do with this, because it's not like this is a date, Daria reminds herself.

Just in case she momentarily forgot.

"I promised you and your cousins I'd come, remember?" Daria tells Nino. "I wouldn't blow you off."

"That's what I told Uncle Ralphie. I'll go in and get my kite ready. My cousins aren't here yet, but they will be soon. Do you want to come in?"

She looks back at Ralphie's house.

His father's spirit has vanished.

"No, thanks," she tells Nino. "I'll just meet you next door."

Ralphie answers her knock almost instantaneously. "Hey, there."

He certainly doesn't look disappointed to see her.

And she's definitely happy to see him . . . this one last time, she hastily reminds herself.

He's wearing a navy and black flannel shirt, untucked, over jeans and boots. There's an appealing growth of stubble on his cheeks, and he has a cup of coffee in his hand.

It's all so Saturday-morning-comfortable. So appealing. *Careful, there.*

"So you thought I wouldn't show?" she asks point-blank.

"Why do you think that? You said you would, so . . ."

"Nino said you weren't sure."

"Oh—well, I didn't want him to be disappointed in case . . ."

"I told you I never break my promises, remember?"

"Yeah, I remember." He opens the door wide. "I also remember you're moving to Arizona, so . . ."

"Not today, though."

He smiles. "Good. Come on in. Want some coffee?"

"Sure."

The house looks pretty much the same as it did the other day, with a few minor changes. There's no Monopoly game on the floor of the living room. The dining room is dark, quiet, and uncluttered, the table much smaller and only eight chairs, all matching, around it. The air doesn't smell of a home-cooked meal. The television is off; the radio is on, or maybe it's a CD—Van Morrison.

She loves Van Morrison.

She loves this house.

Loves being here again, loves seeing this man again, and to hell with the fact that he's all wrong for her. What does that matter, for one more day?

In the kitchen, she spots a white bakery bag sitting beside a crumb-covered wooden cutting board and an almost-full glass coffee carafe on the counter. The morning newspaper is spread out on the table.

"I've got bagels—they're fresh. I bought them on the way home from my basketball game," Ralphie tells her. "Did you eat breakfast?"

"I did, but . . ."

"You're still hungry?"

"I could eat. You play basketball?"

"Yeah, just with a bunch of guys from the neighborhood these days."

"You used to play more?"

"I played on the school team at Saint Bonaventure."

"You must've been pretty good."

"Decent. When I was a little kid, I had big plans to become a New York Knick. As you can see, it kind of fell through."

Yeah. Childhood plans have a way of doing that.

He peers into the white bag. "Do you want cinnamon, sesame, or poppy?"

"Sesame."

"Do you like cream cheese and lox?"

She *loves* cream cheese and lox.

Do they even *have* cream cheese and lox in Arizona?

"I like everything, remember?" she asks Ralphie, wishing they weren't off to such a smooth start.

Van Morrison, coffee, bagels just the way she likes them . . .

"I do remember," he tells her. "Too bad I'm fresh out of frogs' legs again. So have a seat."

Watching him at the counter, she decides—despite herself—that this feels an awful lot like a date. Even this early on a Saturday morning. Even with a gaggle of kids tagging along.

That's probably not a good thing.

Or is it?

Maybe you should just relax and stop worrying about every little thing, she scolds herself wearily.

What harm could there be in deciding to enjoy today for what it is? Regardless of what happens today, forty-eight hours from now, she'll be halfway across the country, and not looking back.

"How do you like your coffee?"

"Cream and two sugars."

"Hey, that's how I like mine," Ralphie tells her.

"I guess we have one thing in common, then."

"Is that all?" He brings two cups over to the table. "Just one thing?"

"Can you think of anything else?"

"Hmm . . . you like artichokes. I don't." He sits down in the chair adjacent to hers. "You're an interior designer. I'm not. You're a woman. I'm not. Nope, you're right. Not a thing in common besides the coffee."

She can't help but laugh.

And remember the kiss, when she sees the way he's looking at her.

As if he wants to do it again.

She wishes he would. Just grab her and kiss her and make her forget all the reasons this is wrong.

It's a small table. His knee brushes against hers beneath it.

"I got my plane ticket," she blurts, as if he just pressed a button. "To Arizona."

A shadow seems to cross his face, but not for long. He seems to be forcing a casual expression.

Okay, so either he could care less that she's leaving, or he doesn't want her to think he does care.

What does it matter either way?

It just seems important that he understand that their time together is waning. That this—today—is it.

"That's good. When is your flight?"

"Day after tomorrow."

"So soon? You must be in a hurry to get out there."

"Definitely. I mean, it's supposed to snow tonight," she adds, as if that has anything to do with anything.

"What?"

"Didn't you hear? We might get over a foot."

"I heard. So, um . . . you don't like snow? That's why you're leaving?"

"I love snow."

"But you just said—"

"No, I know, I just . . . I mean, it'll be good to see the sun." She's babbling, God help her. "The weather's supposed to be beautiful in Phoenix now, blue skies and sunshine."

"I know. Warm sunshine. Not blazing hot," he says, watching her closely. "You mentioned that the other night."

"Oh. Right." She takes a sip of her coffee, wishing

she hadn't brought up Arizona again. Because really, her plans have nothing to do with him, a man she's seen only three times in her life.

And besides, she sounds like she's trying to convince herself—and him—that she's glad to be going.

Which is exactly what she's trying to do.

So far, she's not convinced, and neither, judging by the look on his face, is he.

It doesn't matter, though, whether he believes her, and it doesn't matter whether she wants to go. She has to go. She's going.

Case closed.

"I was in Arizona once," he tells her. "In June."

"Yeah?"

"Yeah. It was blazing hot."

"I'll bet."

"I could never live there. I mean, I don't think I could live anywhere but New York, but if I did have to move, I couldn't live there."

Now he sounds as if he's trying to convince himself—and her—of something.

"You might surprise yourself, if you ever had the chance. To move, I mean. Not necessarily to Arizona."

"I don't think so. My whole family is here. My whole life is here."

"I don't blame you. I mean, you have no reason to pick up and go."

Neither does she, really . . . except that it's what she's always done.

And she, unlike Ralphie, doesn't have anything holding her here.

She can't bear to look at him another minute, so she

turns her head. Her gaze falls on the cool vintage appliance on the counter. She noticed it the other night, too. But then, she wasn't desperate to change the topic of conversation to a blender.

"Ooh, I love that," she says as if she's seeing it for the first time. "Where did you get it?"

He follows her gaze. "Get what?"

"The retro blender."

"Retro?" he laughs. "It's ancient. It was in my grandmother's apartment before we moved her to a retirement home. She probably bought it back in the forties."

"Does it still work?"

"I used it to make a strawberry milkshake the other day."

"Wow. There's actually a lot of great vintage stuff in here," she comments, looking around at the dome-topped chrome toaster, the rare Fiestaware serving pieces on a shelf, the cuckoo clock near the back door. "Some of this is rare, you know."

"No . . . really?"

"Sure. Collectors will pay big bucks."

An inscrutable expression crosses his face. "Maybe we won't need such a big Dumpster after all, then."

"Dumpster!"

"We're selling the house."

"Why?"

"I can't afford to buy out my sisters and brothers' shares. And anyway, my sisters basically said this stuff is all a bunch of junk." He waves a hand around the kitchen.

"What? You can't just throw away a Fiesta Red Disc juice pitcher."

"What are we supposed to do with it, then?"

"Are you kidding?"

"Believe me, this is the last thing I'd kid about."

"I'm sorry. I know. What I mean is, you can sell it."

"Where? At a garage sale?"

"No, a garage sale would be giving it away. The list price on something like that is over five hundred bucks."

Ralphie's jaw drops. "You're kidding."

"Believe me, this is the last thing I'd kid about," she says wryly, and is gratified when he offers a faint smile. "Look, I'm sure I can put you in touch with some dealers who—"

"You're leaving," he cuts in flatly, smile gone again. "Monday. Remember?"

For a moment there, she actually forgot.

"Well, I'm sure you can find someone."

He shrugs. "It really doesn't matter. I mean, it's just stuff, right?"

"That's not what I see when I look around."

"What do you see? A cash crop?"

"A whole lifetime of memories."

"Yeah," he says, a little hoarsely. "That's what I see, too."

"Oh, Ralphie . . ." She impulsively reaches out and clasps her hand over his.

He looks at her in surprise.

"I'm so sorry about your father," she says. *And your mother . . . and the house . . .*

He clears his throat, refusing to look at her. "Yeah, it was sudden so . . . I mean, he was getting up there, and he'd been having some health problems, and it wasn't his first heart attack, so I guess we should have all been prepared. But no matter what, it's hard. And it's only been a few months."

She murmurs something comforting.

"Maybe it would be different if I weren't living with him. But I saw him every day, you know? I mean, I took care of him, but in some ways—a lot of ways—he took care of me, too."

"Of course he did. He was your father."

She wishes she could tell Ralphie that Nino is right here with them.

He's standing behind Ralphie's chair, and his gaze is perhaps more sorrowful than ever before.

Ralphie's hand clenches into a fist beneath her fingers, trembling hard, as if he's struggling with all his might to contain the emotion.

"You need to let it out, Ralphie."

"What?"

"The grief. It's not good to hold it all in."

"What am I supposed to do? I'm not a little boy. I can't just go around crying my heart out."

"No, but you can't go around carrying all this sorrow with you, either. Your father wouldn't want you to suffer like this."

For a moment, seeing his father's ghostly hands settle on Ralphie's shoulders, she wants to just come out and say it.

Tell Ralphie that his father is here, in the house, in the room.

How would he react?

The same as everybody else. In sheer disbelief. He'd look at her as if he thinks she's crazy. They all do, but she especially doesn't want that reaction from him.

She watches Ralphie take a deep breath, hold it, and let it out with a shudder, as if expelling some of the grief with it.

No.

Regardless of the risk to her own image in Ralphie's eyes, she can't open the door to what might, in the end, only bring him more pain.

Whatever it is Nino Chickalini wants to accomplish in the mortal world, he'll just have to achieve on his own, without Daria as the mediator.

Chapter 10

Beyond the last stop on the A train, the crowded working-class neighborhoods, the deserted boardwalk, and the windswept dunes, the mist-shrouded beach at Far Rockaway is a study in gray on this January morning. The bleak horizon, the roiling ocean, the stretch of wet sand, even the icy air itself, meld into a monochromatic backdrop punctuated only by the colorful parkas worn by Ralphie's niece and nephews, and the red kite snapping overhead.

And Daria's eyes, Ralphie can't help but notice, as she glances in his direction, laughing at something Rose just said to her.

The shade of distant, tropical seas, Daria's striking eyes—like the hint of floral perfume that wafts from her whenever the bracing sea breeze blows in just the right direction—are a reminder that winter isn't all-encompassing.

"I want a turn, Uncle Ralphie!" Little Adam tugs the hem of his jacket. "Tell T. J. it's my turn!"

"It's my turn! I just got it from Rose," T. J. calls, turning the crank to let some line out as he walks backward, face tilted to the kite sailing the heavens.

"You're next, okay?" Ralphie promises Adam, as he watches Nino combing the beach for flat stones to skip across the water. Ralphie taught him how to do that here on this very spot years ago, when Nino was just Adam's age. It seems like only yesterday.

"I'm not next, I'm last," Adam grumbles. "I'm always last, 'cause I'm the youngest. It stinks," Adam hurtles a pebble across the sand.

Ralphie kneels down next to him, touched.

"It does stink, sometimes," he whispers in his nephew's ear. "I know. I'm the youngest, too, remember?"

Adam looks at him. "I forgot."

"Yeah. But you know what else? Sometimes it doesn't stink."

"When?"

"Uh, plenty of times," Ralphie says vaguely. He just can't think of any right now.

No, right now, being the youngest Chickalini sibling has few, if any, benefits.

Feeling Daria watching him, he looks up.

Rose is still talking her ear off, and she's nodding as if she's fully engaged.

But when her eyes collide with Ralphie's, he sees a warm tide of emotion that catches him by surprise, and he looks away.

This isn't good. She's moving across the country. He can't go and fall for someone who's moving across the country.

"So is it my turn now?" Adam is asking, with the typically short attention span of a kid.

"Let's let T. J. finish his turn first, and then it'll be your turn."

Again, Ralphie's gaze falls on Daria.

This time, she doesn't see him, though. Rose has momentarily stooped to pick up a flat stone to give to Nino, and Daria is looking out at the sea, as if she's lost in thought.

Is she thinking about the new life waiting for her out west?

If only she weren't leaving just yet, Ralphie can't help but think wistfully. If only this didn't have to end before it's even begun.

Then again . . . she's not leaving today. Or even tomorrow.

And it *has* begun . . . with a kiss still lingering in his memory.

So what if there's a predetermined ending to whatever it is he and Daria have started here? Like Joey said the other day, life is too short.

"Okay, Adam," T. J. calls. "It's your turn now. Come on."

"Yay!" Adam bounds over the sand and takes the spool from his brother.

Absently watching T. J. showing Adam how to turn the crank, Ralphie wonders if he should borrow his brother-in-law's New Year's resolution and start living for today.

He watches Daria good-naturedly receive a lesson in stone-skipping from Nino and Rose, who laugh every time she hurtles a stone at the water with all her might, only to have each one plunk to the bottom.

"Ralphie, help me!" she calls, shaking her head. "I can't get it right!"

He grins throws up his hands, and shrugs. "Practice

makes perfect." That's what he told little Nino, all those years ago.

But Nino had a whole summer of beach-going ahead of him.

There's no ocean where Daria's going.

She should stay, Ralphie thinks illogically, and again, the desolate feeling sweeps through him. Why does she have to leave? Why does everything have to change, and never, it seems, for the better?

Cut it out. You'll have plenty of time to miss her when she's gone.

Yes. Just like he'll have plenty of time to miss the house.

For now—for today—Ralphie is going to take a page from his brother-in-law's book. For once, he's just going to be in the moment.

Buoyed by that decision, Ralphie goes over to Daria and the others as Adam gleefully unfurls more kite line.

"They all sink," Daria tells him, another stone poised in her hand.

"Let's see."

She hurls it toward the water. *Plunk.*

"You have to flick your wrist, like this." Ralphie executes a perfect sidearm toss, and it skips several times before disappearing into a breaker.

"Oh. Like this?" She hurls another stone. *Plunk.* "Maybe this just isn't my thing."

"You think?" He laughs. She and the kids do, too.

"Come on, you can do it. I'll help you. Here." He hands her a suitably flat stone. "Try this one."

Plunk.

"You've got to angle your arm, like this." He demonstrates.

"Like this?"

Plunk.

He sighs and steps up behind her. Taking her wrist in his gloved hand, he arcs her arm back and forth a few times. "See?"

"I think so." She tilts her head to look back at him, and her hair flutters against his face. At that wisp of physical contact, his body tightens predictably. Feeling like a thirteen-year-old boy, he takes a slight step back, lest he embarrass himself.

"Go ahead," he says. "Try again."

Plunk.

"You really kind of stink at this, Daria," Nino tells her, and adds quickly, "No offense."

She laughs. "None taken."

"Uncle Ralphie, it's your turn," Adam calls, struggling to keep the kite spool in his hands as the wind whips it.

"What about Daria?" Rose protests. "She didn't get a turn."

"That's okay, I'm not pushing my luck today. I'm sure I'd turn out to be about as skilled at kite-flying as I am at stone-skipping."

Ralphie takes control of the kite from his nephew. "I'd say I'm just in time," he tells Adam. "You looked like you were about to be lifted right off your feet like Mary Poppins."

"I think Daria's kind of like Mary Poppins, don't you?" Adam asks in a confidential tone as Ralphie reels in some line.

"Daria?" Ralphie glances in her direction. The other

kids are still trying to teach her to skip stones, amid gales of giggles.

"In what way is she like Mary Poppins?" he asks Adam, going for a lighthearted reply. "I don't hear her singing about a spoonful of sugar."

Adam doesn't take the bait. "She's beautiful and she loves kids."

"How do you know that?"

"Because she's nice to us. And you're kind of like Bert."

"The chimney sweep?"

Adam nods vigorously.

"What, am I covered in soot again?" Ralphie attempts another quip. "I hate when that happens."

"No, but you're secretly in love with Daria."

Ralphie gulps and furiously turns the crank on the kite. "How do you know that?"

"Rose told me."

"Rose told you I'm secretly in love with Daria?"

"No! Rose told me Bert was secretly in love with Mary Poppins. She said—the kite!" Adam interrupts himself to shout, pointing overhead.

Ralphie looks up.

Oops.

His overzealous reeling snapped the line.

Untethered, the red kite soars into the sky.

Ralphie can only stand by helplessly, watching it go until it's swallowed by a bank of snow clouds.

"That was the best day ever," Nino declares as the six of them troop up Ditmars Boulevard from the subway station late that afternoon.

Daria is glad to see that he seems to have recovered from the lost kite episode, which threw all the kids—and their uncle—for a loop. Ralphie felt terrible about it. He promised to buy new kites for all four of them, and to take them out to the beach next weekend to fly them.

Of course, they wanted to know if Daria would be there, too.

It was Ralphie who spoke up before she did, telling them that Daria's leaving Monday morning for Arizona.

"When are you coming back?" little Adam wanted to know.

She couldn't bring herself to say never.

So she promised to let them know whenever she comes to town to visit Tammy. She made it sound almost as though she'll be here all the time. But she could feel Ralphie's knowing gaze on her.

Yeah, thanks to her, he knows that gypsies like to roam without looking back. He has no idea that she's longing for a different kind of life, and she can't possibly tell him. That would only put ideas into his head . . . and into hers.

Better to leave it all alone.

"Yeah, this was definitely the best day ever," Rose seconds her brother. "Uncle Ralphie, you're the greatest guy in the world."

Daria, bringing up the rear and holding little Adam's mittened hand, wholeheartedly agrees, but decides to keep her opinion to herself. It's okay for the kids to gush superlatives, but she doesn't dare join in.

There's enough tension sizzling in the air between her and Ralphie as it is. Every time their eyes connected on the beach or across the table at the hot dog place, something unmistakable was smoldering between them.

The last thing she wants is to ignite a fuse.

Oh, yeah?

Oh, hell, maybe that's exactly what she wants. Some satisfaction. A big old explosive reaction, something that will jolt some good sense into her—or maybe jolt the so-called good sense out of her.

Because seriously . . . is she really going to let herself turn her back and walk away from the most interesting guy she's met in—well, *ever?*

Why would she do that?

Because it seems like the sensible thing to do, considering the past. Right?

Right. You learn from your mistakes. You make sure you aren't drawn to someone just because he comes with all the trappings you ever wanted in a man, right down to the wholesome family scene lacking in your own life. Right?

Right. You realize that he's a flawed human being, not the answer to every problem you've ever had.

So you keep the guy at arm's length, and you plan to get the hell out of Dodge on the next available plane.

Yeah.

That makes a whole lot of sense. Really.

In theory, anyway.

If only she hadn't somehow left her iPod at Ralphie's place. Then she could have parted ways with him and the kids on the A train up from Far Rockaway, as she had originally planned before she realized—somewhere between the beach and the hot dog place—that her iPod wasn't in her pocket.

She knows she had it with her when she got to his place, so she must have left it on his kitchen table when they were having coffee . . .

Although she doesn't recall taking it out of her pocket.

But who knows? She was pretty distracted, having just glimpsed Nino hanging around out front.

Ralphie didn't seem all that disappointed when she realized she'd have to transfer with them to the N and go all the way back to Astoria. In fact, he looked so pleased that she wondered—but only momentarily—whether he could possibly have slipped it out of her pocket in the first place.

But of course, that's a ludicrous suspicion.

She just hopes he doesn't think she left it behind for an excuse to see more of him, especially after how the lost cell phone brought them together on New Year's Day.

He probably just thinks you're a complete idiot who can't keep track of her stuff, she tells herself. *And he's probably right.*

"What are we going to do when we get back home, Uncle Ralphie?" T. J. wants to know.

"*We're* not going to do anything, because *you're* going to a pool party somewhere," Ralphie says, then adds, "and anyway, I've got an appointment with someone."

He's trying to make it sound casual, like an after-thought. But it isn't.

Daria senses there's more to it than just that—and that he's reluctant to go into detail.

An appointment.

She wasn't planning on lingering—really, she wasn't—

but somehow, it didn't occur to her that Ralphie might have other plans even if she did want to hang around.

An appointment.

It's got to be a date, and he just doesn't want to say it in front of the kids . . .

Or in front of me.

Because the thing is . . . she'd have to be blind, deaf, and—not dumb—just plain old stupid not to notice that Ralphie is attracted to her.

And that, yeah, it's mutual.

So maybe she got her hopes up without even realizing it.

Then again . . .

It could just be her imagination that he's being cagey.

A fragile shard of hope remains intact, though in the shadow of teetering suspicion as she wonders where the heck Ralphie is going.

And with whom?

Francesca?

Daria finds herself almost wishing Ralphie would announce, right here and now, that he and Francesca are getting back together, if that's the case. Or that he's going out with someone new.

Then she'd have all the more reason not to look over her shoulder after she leaves New York on Monday.

"What kind of appointment is it, Uncle Ralphie?" Nino asks, as they round the corner onto Thirty-Third Street.

Ralphie looks a little uncomfortable, cementing Daria's suspicion. "Just a meeting with someone," he says vaguely, and crushing suspicion shatters her hope once and for all.

Yeah. A meeting-slash-appointment, a.k.a. *date*.

Well, he's entitled.

Remember, you can't—to quote the Stones—*always get what you want.*

"What I want to know," Ralphie expertly changes the subject, addressing T. J., "is how you're going to a pool party in the middle of winter. What are you, a polar bear?"

Adam, predictably, finds that hilarious.

"It's an indoor pool," T. J. protests.

"Even so . . ." Rose shivers and looks up at the sky beyond the bare tree branches that line the sidewalk. "I wouldn't want to jump into cold water today. It's going to start snowing like crazy any second now."

"My friend Ryan—he's the birthday kid—said the pool is heated," T. J. replies, but he's not looking particularly enthusiastic, heated or not.

"We're just teasing you, T. J." Ralphie pats him on the shoulder. "You'll have a great time. I wish I were going swimming in January."

"Daria's going to get to go swimming in January," Nino declares. "In Arizona. Right, Daria? You can swim outside all year round there."

"Right!" She tries to sound as if swimming outside the year round is the best thing that could possibly happen to a girl.

Yeah, right.

You can't . . . always get . . . what you want . . .

She really needs to get her damned iPod back, crank up Mick and the Stones, and be on her not-so-merry way.

"Hey, look," Rose cuts into her thoughts, stopping short and pointing down the block. "Something's going on down there."

"Is it our house?" Nino asks worriedly.

Her heart lurching, Daria realizes that the police car and fire truck, red dome lights flashing, do seem to be parked in front of their house.

Ralphie wordlessly breaks into a run.

Feeling little Adam's hand tighten in her own, Daria manages to find her voice. "I'm sure it's fine," she assures the shaken children.

"I'm scared." Rose clutches her arm. "What if something happened to my mom, or my dad?"

"No, I'm sure they're okay. Look . . . isn't that your mom right there?"

It is.

Thank God.

Daria watches as Nina meets Ralphie on the sidewalk, talking and gesturing a mile a minute.

She looks agitated, but definitely not distraught.

A few steps closer, and Daria can see exactly what's going on.

"It's okay," she tells the kids, heart beating in a wild burst of sheer relief, "Look, it's just a tree."

A tall maple in front of Ralphie's house bears a jagged pale yellow scar where an enormous leader branch was freshly ripped away. It apparently fell onto a power line leading from the street pole to the house and brought down the wire. Several firemen are milling around it, radios squawking. Nearby, Joe is talking to a police officer who's taking notes.

"Grandpa's tree," Rose says in dismay. "He planted it way back before my mom was even born."

Struck anew by the thread of continuity that runs through the Chickalini family's lives, Daria points out, "It's still standing, though. It was just one big branch."

"That's my climbing branch," Nino says in dismay.

"Well, look at the bright side. At least you weren't up there when it crashed down," T. J. tells his cousin.

When Daria and the kids reach Nina and Ralphie, he cautions them to steer clear of the debris, and states the obvious. "A tree limb took out a power line."

"It knocked out the electricity," Nina adds, "and broke a windowpane by the front door, see? It's a good thing you weren't around, Ralphie. You said you were going to take down the Christmas lights today. You could have been right there by the stoop on a ladder."

"Good thing you told me to leave the lights up till spring."

"Good thing you listened," Nina shoots back. "Listen, little brother, you'd better call and try to get Con Ed over here right away to get it up and running again. Or do you want me to do it for you?"

"I can do it."

"It must have been pretty windy for a giant branch to just rip away like that," Daria comments, gazing up dubiously at the gently swaying boughs overhead.

"That's the thing . . . it really didn't seem that bad out when it happened." Nina seems perplexed. "There I was in my kitchen, just putting a cake in the oven, when I heard this huge cracking sound. It was Pop's tree."

Nina sends all the kids into her house, away from the downed wire and broken glass, then tells Ralphie, "Oh, I called Dom and told him to cancel with John. We can't have him show up here in the middle of this mess."

John? That must be the appointment Ralphie mentioned earlier.

Daria is catapulted right back to the wistful, hopeful precipice.

So it's not a date. Not with someone named John, and the Chickalini siblings, all involved.

"I told Dom to reschedule for next week," Nina tells her brother. "I hate to put it off, but . . ."

"It's really not a huge rush," Ralphie says, so casually that Daria can't help but note that he sounds almost . . . relieved?

Whoever John is, Ralphie is obviously in no hurry to meet with him.

Maybe he's a lawyer, settling their father's estate. That would explain the reluctance on Ralphie's part.

"Oh, my gawd . . . what happened here?" There's Rosalee, calling from the open window of her car at the curb.

Nina goes over to fill her in as Ralphie and Daria survey the damage.

"I've got to get that jagged glass out of the window and cover it with cardboard for now." Ralphie pokes a shard with a cautious finger.

He's talking mostly to himself, but Daria offers, "I can help you if you want. I mean, I'm not in a big hurry to get back to Tammy's."

He seems about to protest, but then thinks better of it. "Yeah," he says with a nod. "Thanks. That's really nice of you."

Daria follows him around to the side of the house to make sure there's no more damage, feeling guilty that her offer wasn't entirely noble.

Okay, so maybe she wants to stick around a little longer for purely selfish reasons. Maybe she can't bring herself to leave just yet, especially under such frazzled circumstances. It's not that she wants a lingering goodbye scene . . . or any goodbye scene at all, for that matter. She doesn't do them.

Whatever. She's happy to have bought a little more time.

After ensuring that the downed wire is no longer live, the police and firemen are on their way.

"We should probably get a tree guy here to inspect the rest of it," Joe tells Ralphie as they all stand somberly looking up at the jagged break. "I'd hate to see it have to come down. I know that's Pop's tree."

"Pop's." Not *"your father's,"* not *"Nino's,"* but *"Pop's."* Daria can't help but notice that Joe, like his fellow in-law, Mia—and Rosalee's husband Timmy, too, for that matter—is an intrinsic part of the family.

Again, she feels a stab of envy, wondering what it would be like to belong in this world, for better and for worse. What it would be like to have known the sad-eyed man who obviously cared—still cares—so deeply about his loved ones? What it would have been like to have called him Pop?

You'll never know, she reminds herself with a pang.

"Come on, Joe. What does it matter if the tree comes down?" Ralphie asks darkly, and Daria looks at him in surprise.

"What do you mean?"

"I mean . . . think about it."

"Of course it matters. Pop planted that back when he bought the house, and it was just a little stick in the ground," Joe reminds Ralphie with the familiarity of someone who—if he wasn't there at the time—came along soon after. "The tree is part of his legacy."

"So is the house, but it's not like strangers won't be living here this time next year." Bitterness taints Ralphie's words. "For all we know, they would have thought the tree spoils the view and cut it down anyway."

Joe says nothing, just shakes his head and pats his brother-in-law on the back.

Daria stands by helplessly, wishing there were something she could do to make this better for Ralphie. For all of them. But there isn't. It's not as if she's sitting on a pile of money she can loan—or give—to Ralphie so that he can afford to hang on to the house. Unless one of the Chickalinis wins the lottery—as Mia's grandfather did, and lightning doesn't strike twice—they're going to have to put the house on the market. There's just no way around it.

It's not the end of the world . . . but Daria can see why Ralphie's feeling as though it's the end of his.

"I'd better go call Con Ed," he decides after a moment, and sighs heavily.

"Yeah, and I'd better get back to the pizzeria," Joe says. "I dropped everything and came running when Nina called earlier. I could hear sirens and I thought the worst. Good thing it was only a tree."

"Good thing," Daria agrees.

Ralphie is silent, looking at the jagged cut in the bark.

"See you later, Ralphie. You, too, Daria. Nice seeing you again."

"You, too."

"Mom! The stove buzzer's ringing!" Rose calls from

the stoop next door, and Nina, too, is on her way, bustling into her house with Rosalee at her heels.

Ralphie and Daria are left alone together with the splintered tree and shattered glass.

"I guess that's that." He looks at her. "Are you really going to help me with the window before you go?"

She hesitates.

You can't always get what you want.

Yeah, yeah. She knows. She's only going to help him fix the window, right?

Right.

"Sure, no problem," she tells Ralphie, and follows him into the house.

Chapter

11

There." Ralphie hands the roll of duct tape to Daria and steps back to admire his handiwork. "That'll hold overnight, right?"

"Definitely, unless there's a full-blown blizzard or something."

"Talk to my sisters, and they'll have you convinced there will be," Ralphie says wryly.

In the fifteen minutes since they stepped into the house, Nina and Ro have each called, Nina from next door, Ro from the car on her way to the birthday party.

They each wanted to tell him to come spend the night at their house if Con Ed can't get the power on before dark. And they both warned him that with snow in the forecast, Con Ed will probably be busier than usual.

His response to their offers: thanks, but no thanks.

He can hardly leave the house overnight with a windowpane missing. Cardboard and duct tape won't keep out potential prowlers . . . or so he told his sisters.

The truth is, he's not in the mood to see any more of his family today. Not that he doesn't love them, but they're a constant reminder of all he's lost . . . and all he's about to lose. He doesn't want Nina and Ro asking a million questions about Francesca or Daria, or looking at him as though they feel sorry for him.

He'd rather stay here in the empty house, even in the cold and dark.

Which is why he turned off his cell phone after the second call from his sisters. It's the only way they can get in touch, since all the phones in the house are cordless and thus, ineffective without an electrical outlet.

"Thanks for helping," he tells Daria.

"All I did was hold the tape."

"Don't sell yourself short. It's a key job," he says with mock gravity, and she grins.

Then the grin fades and she glances through the windowpanes that aren't covered in cardboard. The late afternoon shadows are quickly lengthening, and the house is dim. "I should probably get home. I've got a lot of packing to do, and—"

"Can't it wait? I was going to ask you if you wanted something to eat or drink." He wasn't, but hearing her say she's leaving made him realize he has to stop her, and the words came spilling out, courtesy of Inner Single Guy, whom he didn't even realize was lurking.

"I'm not hungry after those hot dogs," she says, "and I'm really not thirsty, either."

"Be a sport, Daria. It's not about your needs. Don't you realize there's a lot of stuff in the fridge that I'll need to use up pretty fast if the power stays out? Don't you know how wrong it is to let it all go to waste?"

She laughs.

"I'm so not kidding here," Ralphie says dryly.

"I don't know . . . It's going to get dark pretty soon, and . . . it's supposed to snow."

"Good point. People get snowbound here in Queens all the time. It's a big problem."

The smile is back, and Ralphie feels pleased with himself for making those amazing blue eyes twinkle.

Five foot two, eyes of blue . . .

"You're right. Okay, I guess I'll stay a little while."

"Thatta gal," Ralphie says.

My gal, Ralphie thinks.

"If worse comes to worst, I guess my sister can send a sled team for me."

"There's the spirit. How about a hot chocolate?" he asks, leading the way to the kitchen, feeling more light-hearted than he has in ages. "I know there's milk, and I need to use it up fast."

"Hmm . . ."

"Or a beer? I could use a beer, personally," he decides, peering into the darkened fridge. "But I know you're a chocoholic."

"That's all right, you don't have to bother. Anyway," she goes on, walking over to the table and looking amid the clutter there, "can you even make hot chocolate without electricity?"

"The stove is gas. So what do you say?"

"I don't know . . . the beer sounds good too."

"How about hot chocolate *and* a beer?"

"Mixed together? I'm not that crazy."

"You're not crazy at all."

"No? Then why," she asks, looking down at the table with a puzzled frown, "isn't my iPod here? I could have sworn this is the only place it could be."

He moves around some of the clutter. She's right. It's not there. "Maybe it's under the table," he suggests, bending to look.

Even in the low light, he can see that it isn't there.

"I guess I must have dropped it on the subway," Daria concludes glumly.

"I guess so," he agrees, straightening, though he's not sure how that could have happened.

It's not as if they're talking about something light and tiny, like a key in your pocket, that you could drop and not notice.

An iPod would make a thud, at the very least.

"This stinks. I had all my music on there."

"It does stink," he agrees.

First the kite, then the tree, now the iPod. In the grand scheme of things, Ralphie knows, it could be much worse, but still . . .

"Oh, well." Daria shakes her head. "No use crying over spilt milk. Speaking of milk . . . how about that beer?"

He laughs. "I thought you were going to say hot chocolate."

"That can wait. Right now, I just want to drown my sorrows."

Ralphie wordlessly opens two beers and hands one to Daria.

"Thanks." She swings her arm in a toast gesture. "Here's to you and what really was a very fun day."

"You stole the words right out of my mouth."

"You were going to toast to me and what really was a very fun day?"

"Something like that."

There's a moment of silence. Not awkward silence, but

the companionable sort, unmarred by the usual household white noise. There's no music in the background, no ticking clock, not even the refrigerator's steady hum.

"Here, sit down." Remembering his manners, Ralphie pulls out a chair for Daria at the table. His sisters taught him well. "Do you want a glass for the beer?"

She sits down. "Nah, I'm a bottle kind of girl."

He smiles, sits, and swallows some cold, fizzy beer, watching her do the same.

"Listen, I'm glad you came along with us to the beach," he tells her. "Thanks for going out of your way to be here."

"It was no big deal, really."

Maybe not to her.

"But . . ." She looks troubled. "I didn't get to say goodbye to the kids."

He shrugs. "Sometimes it's better that way. Goodbyes are hard on kids."

They're hard on everyone.

"I know, but . . . I hate to just leave."

"I thought that's what you do," he can't help saying.

"What?"

"You know . . . *Leave*. I thought you said it was easy."

"When did I say that?"

"The other day. When you were talking about Arizona."

She seems to be trying to recall the conversation. Either that, or she does recall it and she's trying to figure out what to say.

"Never mind, it doesn't matter," he says. "I just meant, it's better if you don't make a big deal out of going. For the kids."

She looks vaguely hurt. "I know . . . I mean, they barely know me, so . . ."

"That's not what I meant."

"What did you mean?"

What *did* he mean?

Why is he getting it all wrong with her, with everything?

Why can't he just come right out and tell her the truth?

"It's just that I guess I wish you weren't going."

Did that come out of him?

Whoa.

Apparently, *he* can't just come right out and tell her the truth, but Inner Single Guy can.

"I . . . I'm not sure what to say to that." She bites her lower lip.

"It's okay. I shouldn't even have said it. It's none of my business what you do or where you go. I just . . ." He trails off helplessly.

"You hate change. It's okay."

"Why did you say that?"

She blinks. "It's, um, obvious."

"Really? That's weird. Because this so-called fortune-teller said the same thing to me at my brother's wedding last weekend."

"She did?" She looks around hurriedly, needing to change the subject. "You know, getting back to all the stuff in the house . . . throwing it away or selling it to a dealer aren't the only two options."

"No? Why can't I think of any others, then?"

"You could keep it."

"Where are we going to put it? No one has room. Pete's not going to fly it overseas. Nina and Ro's houses are overflowing as it is, and Mia's place is picture perfect. She doesn't want to cram it with our old stuff. Even if she did, Dom is probably the least sentimental of all of us, so I doubt—"

"I don't mean the collective 'you,'" she cuts in. "I meant . . . *you*."

"Me? I don't even have a place."

"But you'll have to find one, right? And when you do, you can fill it with anything that means something to you."

"Everything here means something to me."

"Then move it all," she says with a shrug. "What makes you think you can't create a home somewhere other than under this roof?"

"It's not about the stuff. It wouldn't be the same."

"Nothing stays the same. Everything changes."

"Yeah, well, like you said—and like that fortune-teller said—I hate change. Okay?"

"Sometimes change is for the best."

"Most of the time, it's not," he says stubbornly, not knowing what's gotten into him.

"You can't say that."

"Why not?"

"Because it's not true. Look, it's all about fate. None of us would even exist if nothing ever changed."

"Yeah, and if I didn't exist, my mother would."

There.

He's spoken the words aloud at last, after a lifetime spent carrying around the guilt.

"What do you mean, Ralphie?"

"She died in childbirth," he says simply.

"I'm so sorry. I hope you haven't felt like you had to

carry around guilt for that for all these years," she adds, and he wonders, momentarily, if she actually read his mind.

No. That's impossible.

Daria Marshall is just a perceptive, caring person. Somehow, she's able to grasp what he's been through, far better than most people ever have . . . Francesca included.

His ex-fiancée once told him to stop beating himself up over his mother's death—that it had happened long ago, and he should be over it by now.

Those words stung.

An ache begins to build in the back of Ralphie's throat.

Maybe in the end, just as he couldn't forgive himself for not loving Francesca enough—or not loving her in the right way, if at all—he couldn't forgive her, either. For not understanding what it's been like for him to lose his mother, then his father; that you don't just get over it and move on.

"You've been through a hell of a lot." For the second time today, Daria rests a comforting hand over his. "I wish I could help."

"You *are* helping."

She just shakes her head and runs her thumb over the top of his hand, almost absently.

He notices, though.

Notices, and—after a moment—boldly turns his hand over, lacing his fingers through hers. He needs the comfort, needs the contact. Needs her.

She looks at him, surprised, but doesn't say anything.

"If you stay here," he says softly, "I'll cook for you."

"Stay forever . . . or just for dinner?"

Taken aback, he raises an eyebrow, and she looks embarrassed.

"I was kidding," she says, "obviously. You just seemed so serious, and . . . I don't know. I guess I wanted to make you smile. And anyway, I don't believe in forever, so . . ."

He forces a weak smile. "Well, since even *I'm* not staying here forever, I guess dinner is our only option."

"I really can't stay."

"But baby, it's cold outside."

She laughs instantly, realizing he's quoting the lyrics from an old Christmas song he knows by heart, courtesy of Pop's retro radio station.

"I don't know." She hedges. "My sister will be wondering where I am."

"Call her and tell her."

"Your phones aren't working."

"That's a really bad excuse. I have a cell phone . . . and so do you."

"True . . ." She looks at her watch, then out the window at the darkening landscape. "It really is getting late."

"Yeah, but you really can't move to Arizona without having tasted Chicken Ralphie," he tells her.

"What's Chicken Ralphie?"

"It's chicken—which I have in the fridge and need to use—combined with a lot of other ingredients."

"Such as . . . ?"

"Such as whatever else I have in the fridge and need to use before it all goes bad."

"Sounds appetizing."

"Oh, it will be. Well?"

She shrugs. "If I can't move to Arizona without trying it, then I'd better try it, because I'm leaving the day after tomorrow."

He tells himself that he shouldn't feel disappointed at that response.

At least she's staying.

Not forever, but for now.

And now is the important thing, remember? You're supposed to be living in the present, and the sooner you get the hang of that, the better.

Looking at Ralphie in the flickering light, Daria isn't sure whether to wish the lights had come back on, or be grateful they didn't.

The thing is . . . candles are romantic. No way around it.

Ralphie found a bunch of them, accumulated in cupboards and drawers through the years: scented jar candles, votives, tapers in elegant candlestick holders. He lit them everywhere—in the living room, bathroom, and especially here in the kitchen, where they illuminated the scene for cooking and now burn down, clustered in the center of the table alongside the remains of a delicious meal.

Chicken Ralphie consisted of chicken breasts sautéed on top of the stove in olive oil, onions, capers, tomatoes, black olives, and herbs, laced with pinot grigio. It seemed to Daria that he was just arbitrarily throwing whatever he found in the fridge into the skillet—and he probably was—but the result was impressive.

Now he's moved on to a carton of melting French vanilla ice cream as she finishes the last bite of her second helping of Chicken Ralphie.

"I honestly didn't think you could cook," Daria tells him, dabbing one last crust of Italian bread through the trail of sauce left on her plate.

"We all can."

"We all?" She looks around.

He laughs. "I mean my family. And no, they're not here, thank goodness."

You never know, she thinks, quickly glancing around for his father. Nope.

He holds out a spoonful of ice cream. "Want some?"

"No, thanks."

"I've got chocolate, too, in the freezer. By tomorrow it'll be soup, so if you want it . . ."

"No, really, I'm stuffed. So you all cook?"

"Sure. We have a restaurant, remember?"

"Yeah, but pizza's one thing. This dinner was a gourmet production."

"Thanks." Ralphie shrugs. "I guess Pop would be proud to hear you say that."

Don't be so sure he didn't, she thinks, looking around the kitchen again.

Aloud, she asks, "So your father was the one who taught you?"

Ralphie nods.

Yeah. She should have guessed as much. Nino did put in a brief appearance earlier, watching approvingly as his son diced and stirred.

She's starting to wonder if maybe he's just sticking around to keep an eye on things, though her gut still tells her it's more than that. Most spirits she's encountered have some kind of agenda. If Nino really is earthbound for a reason and needs her to help convey some kind of message, he'd better get a move on, unless he plans on following her to Phoenix.

It wouldn't be the first time she'd been tailed cross country by a wayward ghost.

Still . . .

You're not in the medium mode, remember?

Yes. She remembers . . .

But she also has a vested interest in the Chickalini family, like it or not. If there's anything she can possibly do to bring Nino—and the rest of them—some peace and closure, she should do it.

There's no sign of him now, though. It's just her and Ralphie, alone in the chilly, candlelit kitchen as the storm swirls outside.

"My brothers and I can all cook," Ralphie tells her. "Not that we do, much . . . but we can. My dad thought it was important that we learn. Why are you looking so surprised?"

"I don't know . . ." She tries to figure out how to phrase it without insulting him. "I guess I thought your family tended to take on more old-fashioned gender roles."

She's relieved when he breaks into a grin. "You mean because the women washed the dishes and the men just sat there?"

"How'd you guess?"

"I knew it! I knew you were thinking we were a bunch of chauvinists."

"I wasn't," she protests. Then adds truthfully, "well, maybe I was, a little."

"A little?"

"Okay, I was totally thinking you were a bunch of chauvinists. How are you not?" she can't help but challenge.

"Maybe we are. I never really gave it much thought until I saw the look on your face. What can I say? I know it's no excuse, but it's just the way things have always been done around here. My father thought we should all know how to cook, but he was old-fashioned about a lot of things. My brothers and I always took out the trash, mowed the lawn, stuff like that. The girls did the laundry and the dishes and—" Looking as though he'd better stop while he's ahead, he cuts himself off, concluding, "In your house, things were probably different."

"Well, in our house, nobody did the dishes, since we pretty much ate on paper plates—and never together. And not only did my father not cook, but my mother didn't, either. So yeah, things were different."

"That's good."

"You're kidding, right?"

"What?"

"I wouldn't call it 'good' that we ate on paper plates and no one ever cooked."

"At least you were used to it when you got out there on your own. Hell, at least you've *been* on your own your whole adult life. Unlike me."

Not entirely.

Is now the time to mention her short-lived marriage?

Before she can decide, Ralphie goes on, "Lately, whenever I come home from work to an empty house and make myself a sandwich and sit in front of the TV eating it . . . well, it's depressing."

"Well, that's understandable. You and Francesca were supposed to be getting married, so that's—"

"No, it's not about her. It's not that."

She rests her chin on her hand and levels a look at him. "Are you sure?"

"I'm one hundred percent positively sure. Yeah, I miss Francesca and I care about her and wish her well, but . . . her breaking things off is the best thing that could have happened to me. To either one of us."

"If it's not about her, then . . ."

"I don't know, I guess I feel like this isn't how it's supposed to be."

Is anything ever?

"How is it supposed to be, Ralphie?"

He pushes back the empty carton of ice cream and deposits the spoon on the nearest plate with a clatter. "Well, for one thing, my father should be here."

Daria has dealt with enough grieving loved ones in her life to know that he's still in the raw stages of loss.

Yes, he'll eventually learn to accept it, but who is she to counsel him about moving on?

She merely tells him, "You don't have to eat a sandwich in front of the TV every night, you know."

"I know. And it's not as if I'm incapable of taking care of myself. I'm a grown man."

Yes, and somewhere deep down inside, he's also the youngest child in a family of caregivers who tried desperately to make up for the one who was missing.

He has to learn to take care of himself, Daria realizes. Not just physically, but emotionally. Yes, he's capable . . . but he's still feeling his way in unfamiliar territory. He's got a lot to face in the months ahead, and he's going to have to do it head-on.

All the more reason for her to steer clear.

Ralphie rolls the edge of his blue placemat back and forth between his fingers, not looking at her. "I keep thinking, when I come home at night, what am I supposed to do, cook a meal for myself and eat it on china in the dining room?"

"You could."

"How would that help? I'd still be alone here."

She could tell him he'll get used to it.

That's not what he wants to hear.

It's not what he wants to do.

"Listen, Ralphie, you still have your family. I mean, even I can see that, as someone who's pretty much a total stranger. Your brothers and sisters and their kids . . . they're all around you, even if they don't live under the same roof. And they'll still be there for you, wherever you end up after you move out. Do you know how lucky you are?"

He looks up in surprise. "I guess maybe I forget sometimes."

"Don't," she says simply.

"What about you? You have your sister . . . you're close to her, right? It sounds like you are." He heard her end of the conversation on her cell phone earlier, when she called Tammy to say she'd be home late.

"I'm close to her where it counts." She taps her heart. "We stay in touch when we're living apart, but . . . it's just not the same."

"How about your parents?"

"You mean, am I close to them? Not particularly. My mother's kind of flaky." Understatement of the year. "She's in and out of touch, and unless I visit her wherever she happens to be living—which is Florida at the moment—we don't have much of a connection."

Ralphie feels sorry for her. She can see it in his eyes.

Maybe he's thinking it was better to have had an amazing mom you never really knew than to have a less-than-maternal presence on the fringes of your life.

Maybe she's thinking the same thing.

Even so, she finds herself saying defensively, "Still, she's my mother, and I love her."

"What about your dad?"

"Same thing. I mean, he wasn't around much, but I love him and he does love me."

"Of course he does. He's your father," he says in a mild, *I'm-not-arguing-with-you* tone. "Where does he live?"

"Italy. He's got a wife now and she's got kids . . ." She doesn't bother to mention that she's never even met her stepmother or stepsiblings. "I haven't seen him in a few years."

Whose fault is that? a little voice asks her. Not just her father's.

"That's too bad."

Judging by Ralphie's bittersweet expression, he's thinking that if his own father were anywhere on this planet, he'd find a way to get there.

Daria feels a twinge of guilt, remembering she never even called her parents to wish them a happy New Year. She really should. And she should visit them, too. First chance she gets.

Then again . . . it works both ways. They could call or visit her.

"It is what it is," she tells Ralphie with a shrug. "Is the offer still open for the chocolate ice cream?"

"All yours." He stands. She starts to rise as well, reaching for her empty dinner plate, but he holds out a hand. "I'll get the ice cream. And the dishes. You sit."

She protests, but he won't hear of it.

"Don't you think it's time I learned to amend my old-fashioned ways?" he asks, handing her a small round carton of gourmet chocolate ice cream and a spoon. "Anyway, it's my house and you're the guest."

"Yeah, but that doesn't mean I should sit here eating dessert while you clean up the kitchen."

"Sure it does," he says good-naturedly, and gets to work.

As he loads the dishwasher, scrubs the pans, and wipes down the stove, they talk. About ice cream flavors and Christmas and kites and kids.

"You have a great bunch of nieces and nephews," she tells him, dragging the spoon across the pooling fudgy surface of the ice cream as he settles across the table from her again. "And they obviously adore you. Especially Nino."

Some undecipherable emotion crosses his face. "Yeah."

"He looks a lot like you. They all do, but I mean, he's the spitting image of—"

"I'm his birth father, Daria."

She gapes at him, trying to process the words.

"My high school girlfriend got pregnant when we were sixteen and . . . long story short, Nina and Joey adopted him."

"I'm . . . speechless."

"Technically, you're not." He jerks a forefinger at her and says, with forced levity, "You have to speak in order to inform me that you're speechless. Which cancels it out."

"I . . . don't know what to say. That's what I meant." Her head is spinning, and it's her turn to set aside the ice cream.

"It was the right decision," he tells her. "Giving him to my sister and Joey, I mean. When Camille wouldn't marry me—thank God she had the sense to turn me down—and when she said she didn't want to keep the baby, I was hell-bent on raising him myself. It took me a while to realize that I'd be denying him exactly what I didn't have myself—the chance to be raised by a mom."

"Wow," she says softly, floored by the level of maturity it must have taken.

It wasn't as if he'd chosen the easy way out in handing over the baby for adoption. He actually offered to marry the girl, actually wanted to raise his kid when he was just a kid himself.

There she was, thinking Ralphie's this lost little boy, and it turns out he had to grow up pretty fast.

Remembering how Joe stood alongside Ralphie earlier amid the devastation in the yard, silently patting him on the back, she's touched anew. No wonder they're so close. It's about more than living next door to each other, or being in-laws.

Ralphie bestowed upon Joe and Nina life's greatest gift.

"I think it's pretty amazing . . . what you did." It's all she can do not to hug him.

"It wasn't easy. But it was the best decision I've ever made. And thank you."

"For what?"

"For getting it. Not everyone gets it. My buddies at the time . . . every one of them said I was nuts when I wanted to keep the baby. When I changed my mind, they all acted like I had been set free. To me, it felt the opposite. For a long time. I mean, I love kids, and someday—"

When he breaks off, she knows what he was going to say. Someday, he's going to have more children. Children who will have both a dad and a mom.

Some wonderful woman will come along to steal Ralphie's heart and slip into the family as seamlessly as Joe and Mia and the others.

And where will Daria be?

Maybe thousands of miles away. She probably won't even remember him, or this night.

A sudden gust of the wind rattles the pane above the sink, sifting grainy precipitation across it.

"It's getting pretty bad out there," Ralphie comments, eyeing the billowing white scene at the window.

"It is. I guess that means I should go."

He looks boldly into her eyes. "I was thinking that means you should stay."

"Why?"

"Because . . ." He leans across the table, so close she can feel the heat of his body. "I want you to."

"But—"

"Shh." He rests a fingertip against her mouth. "Don't."

"You don't know what I was going to say."

Frankly, she doesn't know, either. But the look in his eyes scares the hell out of her. If she let herself, she could fall hard for this guy.

Even after the conversation they just had, which

pretty much gave her every reason in the world why she shouldn't.

"I do know what you were going to say. You were going to tell me you have a lot of packing to do, or that you're leaving on Monday, something like that . . . right?" He leans closer, moving the fingertip from her lips, his own lips so near that if she moved a few inches forward, their mouths would be touching.

"Right." Her voice is barely more than a whisper.

"This isn't about what's going to happen later. It's about right now. One night, Daria. If that's all we'll ever have . . . then let's have it."

Oh, yeah. She definitely had it all wrong.

Ralphie Chickalini isn't a little boy in any way.

He's a man.

And she's in trouble.

"Okay," she says, "let's have it. One night."

Closing her eyes, she leans forward at last.

His mouth claims hers, hungrily, obliterating any ideas she might have had about taking things slowly.

He pulls her to her feet and she goes willingly into his arms, welcomes the length of his hard body crushed against hers.

She savors wine and vanilla sugar on his lips, and when his cool tongue dallies with hers, she drinks in the taste of him, drunk on the essence of him. They're spinning round and round, or the room is spinning, or maybe it's just her thoughts, whirling faster until she relinquishes the effort. She doesn't want to think, she wants to feel.

"Upstairs," he whispers, urgently. "Okay?"

Are they really going to do this?

"Yes."

The word escapes her without conscious effort, and it feels right.

He takes her hand and leads her through the candlelit rooms, then up the stairs and into the dark.

"This way," he tells her, feeling his way along the hall. "Careful. Do you want me to go get a flashlight? Some candles?"

"No . . . I don't want you to go. Don't go." She stops to pull him against her again and he kisses her deeply, pressing her back against a wall, his physical need blatantly evident.

He pulls her sweater over her head and casts it to the floor. The bra goes next. Waiting, aching to feel his fingers on a bare breast, she gasps when his mouth grazes her there instead. Grazes, then settles, warm and wet, and she threads her fingers through his hair, holding him against her until she can take it no longer.

When she moans, he lifts his head. "Here . . . come here."

He pulls her forward again, until her legs encounter the cushion of a mattress.

They really are going to do this, and if they don't do it soon, she's going to go out of her mind.

Oh, hell, she already is out of her mind, squirming against him as he lowers her onto the bed on her back, still kissing her. His rigid masculinity throbs against her feminine pliancy, suppressed by the layers of clothing, and then, with a swift tugging at buttons and zippers, the clothes fall away.

He stretches out alongside her and kisses her, long and

sweet, his tongue dipping into her mouth again and again in a rhythmic promise of things to come.

She strokes his back, his shoulders, his arms, revels in the bulk of muscles wrapped in warm silken skin.

Reality is a world away until the wind gusts, rattling the panes and somewhere, a salt truck rumbles along.

Jarred by conscious thought, Daria tears herself from his lips long enough to ask, "Do you have . . . anything?"

"Yes."

Cloaked in darkness, he rolls away—but not far; it's a twin bed.

She hears him open a drawer, fumble around. Then comes the unmistakable sound of a plastic wrapper tearing.

The bed springs creak again and, sheathed, he moves back over to her, then above her once more to kiss and caress her as a fire builds in the pit of her belly.

"Are you sure about this?" he asks raggedly, dragging his lips through her hair, over her neck, her collarbone.

It's all she can do to summon an affirmative answer that's mostly a moan, and guide him to her, inside her.

At the exquisite contact she bends her arms and throws them alongside her head. Propped over her on his elbows, he laces his fingers with hers, and there are no more words, just the ancient dance of bodies joined, intertwined.

His breaths come hard and fast against her cheek and she holds her own, caught up in the heated pulse building within.

In the moment before it comes to fruition, she feels his body begin to shudder. Ripples of pleasure explode at her core, and she clings to his shoulders as they ride out the storm together.

When it's over and he's lying, spent, in her arms, his head against her heart, he yawns contentedly and asks if she's sleepy.

"No," she lies, not wanting to close her eyes.

This is their night.

Just one.

The only one they'll ever have, and she doesn't want to miss a moment of it.

Chapter
12

Sunday morning dawns dark and stormy.

Daria awakens in an unfamiliar room to find herself alone in an unfamiliar bed beneath an unfamiliar window, shade pulled up to reveal an unfamiliar view.

Tree branches and swirling snowflakes . . . ? Where . . . ?

Oh!

An explicit memory of last night slams into her as if driven by a sixty-mile-an-hour wind.

Whoa!

She sits bolt upright and looks at the narrow, empty twin mattress beside her.

Where's Ralphie?

Last she knew, it was the wee hours and he was lying here, cradling her in his arms after their third . . . or was it fourth? . . . time.

He was sound asleep, his chest falling against her back with his even breathing.

She was wide awake, heart pounding, thoughts racing, courtesy of a post-passion adrenaline surge.

To keep herself from dwelling on the inevitability of

tomorrow, she replayed everything that had transpired between her and Ralphie from the start. Dissected everything he'd said—and hadn't said. Second guessed everything she'd said, and hadn't. Analyzed everything, start to finish . . .

This time, at least, there was no need to rewrite a fantasy finish.

For once, the fantasy had come to pass—and surpass. Last night was everything she could ever have imagined, and then some.

She didn't think she'd ever fall asleep, and didn't want to, but she obviously eventually drifted off.

Where, she wonders again, with a stab of misgiving, is Ralphie?

In the living room, Ralphie craves a cup of coffee and peers out the window at the transformed streetscape.

A billowing blanket of white has blurred geometric lines and obliterated the usual pervasive neutral shades of concrete and stone. Snow is still coming down, though not quite as hard as it was when he woke an hour ago to find Daria asleep beside him, a winter wonderland outside the house, and silent, chilly darkness within.

He climbed carefully out of bed so as not to wake her, though he did allow himself a few moments to watch her sleep, marveling that she really is here with him.

Downstairs, he used his cell phone to call Con Ed again, figuring he'd better do it now, with only one battery bar left. A blasé-sounding customer service rep said they'll get to him as soon as they possibly can. The weather has slowed service dramatically, as Nina and Rosalee predicted.

That's fine with Ralphie.

As long as the crippling storm is blowing through New York, the real world will be held at bay. He and Daria can stay right here in their own little cocoon . . . a cocoon that would admittedly be a lot more inviting with lamplight and heat and fresh-brewed coffee, the one thing he isn't equipped to make on his gas stove.

Outside, the neighborhood has stirred to life. Church bells are pealing over at Most Precious Mother, same as any other Sunday morning. Somewhere, a snowblower is humming, and Ralphie can hear the scrape of metal shovels against concrete from right next door.

A glance out the side window reveals Nino and Joey out there, bundled in parkas, hats, gloves, and boots, clearing the walks.

Ralphie is fairly certain they'll work their way over here next and hopes they won't pop in.

Who are you kidding? Of course they will.

One or some or all of the Materis invariably find their way next door on Sunday mornings before they all, Ralphie included, head over to ten o'clock mass together at Most Precious Mother.

Maybe Ralphie should just stick his head out now and suggest that they go to noon mass today instead, because of the weather.

You're going to mass today, after . . . last night?

The chiding voice in his head sure as heck doesn't belong to Inner Single Guy. No, it sounds suspiciously like Sister Mary Helen, his high school homeroom teacher.

You can take the boy out of Catholic school, as Dom used to say, but you'll never take the Catholic school out of the boy.

You're not a boy, you're a man. And you didn't do any-thing wrong.

Ah, there's Inner Single Guy. That's more like it.

Still . . .

Guilt tries to work its way into his consciousness as he listens to the church bells chime a Sunday morning hymn.

If Joe comes over, even if Daria stays asleep upstairs, Joe would spot her coat on the hook, put two and two to-gether, and get the wrong idea.

Well, the right idea, really.

Because it's not as though nothing happened between the two of them last night.

What *didn't* happen is more like it, Ralphie thinks, smiling to himself in the lingering afterglow, wishing his conscience wouldn't put a damper on things.

Anyway . . . a lot happened last night.

Not just physically, but emotionally.

Okay, so maybe he jumped into something without stopping to consider the consequences. Maybe it all went too far, too fast.

He's not prone to casual flings—doesn't believe in them.

But . . .

That's not what this was.

This was so much more, and he isn't taking it lightly.

For the first time in his life, everything fell into place. It felt right with Daria. The conversation, the connection, the attraction, chemistry, intimacy—whatever you want to call it. It was all . . .

Not perfect, he cautions himself. *Don't use that word. Even to yourself.*

Everyone thought Francesca was perfect for him—
even he did, in the beginning—and look how that turned
out.

Okay. So there's no such thing as perfect.

Perfect is dangerous.

This wasn't perfect; it was just . . . right. And good.
And promising.

I just hope she realizes that too, Ralphie thinks
uneasily.

But of course she must. For all her wanderlust, she
must know that you don't turn your back on a good thing,
a promising, once-in-a-lifetime thing.

You embrace it.

In this family, anyway, he thinks, considering his parents, his siblings and their spouses.

But what was it that Daria said, back on New Year's,
when he was first getting to know her?

*In my family, men leave, women leave . . . everybody
leaves. Myself included. And you can blame it on culture,
heritage, gypsy blood all you want, but the truth is, it's
just easier.*

But that's not how she was talking last night.

Last night, telling him about her childhood, and her
past . . .

She seemed wistful.

She doesn't want that kind of life anymore.

Ralphie heard it in her voice, saw it in her face. He
knows it, in his heart.

And so, he thinks resolutely, must she.

The bedroom is chilly—the electricity must not have
kicked back on again yet.

Reluctant to climb naked out from beneath the warm blankets, Daria looks around the room in the muted morning light.

There are two beds—the other neatly made, its headboard perpendicular to this. There are two dressers, too—one covered in clutter, the other almost bare, aside from a basket of folded laundry. She takes in the shelf lined with basketball trophies, another with books—mostly paperback thrillers—and wonders how much this room has changed, if at all, since Ralphie's boyhood.

He mentioned, as they lay talking about their childhoods in the middle of the night, that he and his brother Dominic shared the room as kids—and on and off as adults.

Daria detected a note of wistfulness in Ralphie's laugh when he speculated that those days are over for good.

So much in his life has changed drastically, and seemingly all at once.

All the more reason she doesn't dare entertain fantasies about staying here in New York, with him. Regardless of whether she's ready for a serious relationship—and that's debatable—there isn't a doubt in her mind that he's *not* ready.

Someday, maybe, he'll have worked through all of his issues and be ripe for love.

But when someday comes, Daria won't be here.

Unless . . .

No. You can't. You won't.

Wait around, longing for something that might never happen?

That isn't her style.

Neither are prolonged goodbyes.

She swings her legs around and her bare feet hit the floor, itching to carry her away before she makes another mistake.

In the kitchen rummaging around for a box of caffeinated tea—and jauntily whistling "Has Anybody Seen My Gal"—Ralphie hears a floorboard creak overhead.

He stops rummaging, and his heart jumps like that of a schoolboy about to see his first love.

That would be Daria, stirring at last.

Good. They have a lot to talk about.

Last night changed everything . . . and for perhaps the first time in his life, Ralphie welcomes change.

You were wrong, Madame Tamar, he thinks, a little smugly, whistling his way out of the kitchen. *I don't always hate change. Not when it's for the better. It's just that in my life, it rarely has been.*

When it comes time to get that Dumpster Rosalee keeps talking about, the first thing he'll toss into it is Madame Tamar's business card.

No, why wait?

He'll get rid of it today. Fitting, since today marks a new beginning.

With Daria.

Because of course she won't be moving away now. She'll need a place to live . . .

And so will you, he reminds himself. After all, not everything has changed. He'll still have to deal with selling the house.

He waits for the familiar sick feeling to sweep through him at the reminder, but somehow, the prospect doesn't seem nearly as horrible as it did. It's still sad, and it's still going to be difficult, but . . .

Maybe . . .

Okay, he's really reaching, really looking ahead, but . . .

Maybe when the time comes, he and Daria can find a place together here in Queens, or Manhattan, even.

Sister Mary Helen wouldn't approve, and his family probably won't approve, either, but what are they going to do about it? He's a grown man.

And for perhaps the first time ever, he actually feels like one.

All thanks to Daria, who walked into his life out of nowhere, and whom he fully expected to walk right back out of it again.

Thank goodness that's not going to happen now.

Her path crossed Ralphie's when it did for a reason. They were meant to be together. He was meant to find her now when he's in the midst of losing everything else.

After all, whenever God closes a door, He opens a window.

Ralphie has been hearing that phrase his whole life—from the nuns, from his sisters, from Aunt Carm—but never until now has it felt more fitting.

In the dining room window, he casts another glance out at the Materis's place next door, craning his neck to see if his brother-in-law and nephew are still safely shoveling their own walk. Nino must have gone inside to warm up, but Joey is still at it.

Ralphie turns away from the window and hurries toward the stairs, eager for the new beginning to be underway.

Hearing footsteps below and Ralphie calling her name, Daria falters in the doorway of the bathroom. Anxious to get moving, she just splashed water on her face and ran a toothpaste-covered finger through her mouth.

Anxious?

More like frantic.

If she doesn't force herself to go through with it and get out of here now, she might not get out at all. Not until it's too late.

You have to be strong. You have to remember it's the right thing to do. Look at what happened with Alan.

Do you really want to find yourself sitting in front of a judge with Ralphie Chickalini and a pair of opposing lawyers someday?

No. God, no.

That would be brutal.

This is going to be brutal, too, but . . .

In the long run, it will be less painful.

Not just for Daria, but for Ralphie, and that's what matters.

He's lost so much in his life. She can't bear to think of him hurting again, and all because of her. She cares about him, so much . . .

Too much.

But it isn't love, she reminds herself. *You don't even know what love is.*

Someday, though, she's going to find out.

Someday, she'll find herself in the right place, at the right time, with a man who's right for her.

This, she tells herself sorrowfully, is the wrong place, the wrong time . . .

And, more than anything, the wrong man.

"Daria?" Ralphie calls again, taking the stairs two at a time, before she can stray too far from the bedroom.

He reaches the top—and stops short at the sight of her.

Fully dressed, and walking so purposefully that for a moment he half-expects her to brush on past him, down the stairs, and out of his life.

But of course that's not going to happen.

That can't happen.

Not after last night.

She sees him, stops, smiles.

"Good morning," she says, and he should be reassured by the smile.

But he's not.

Because it's not a real smile. Her mouth is in the right position, but something—some hint of tension in her face, her voice, her beautiful blue eyes—sends a current of dread through him.

Still, he replies, "Good morning," and smiles back at her, as if everything is just fine.

Because it has to be.

He must be reading something into her tone, her expression, that isn't even there.

Because everything has changed for the better, for once in his life.

"How long have you been up?" she asks, running a

hand through her tousled, morning-after dark hair that somehow looks just right.

"For a while." He wants to move closer to her, take her in his arms, run his own fingers through that hair again . . .

But something is stopping him.

Something?

That same damned hint of tension, now working its way to her hand as it flutters back to her side, and her feet as she shifts her weight.

"Did you sleep okay?" he asks, casually, hating that it doesn't sound casual at all.

"I slept more than okay. I mean . . . it's past nine, right?"

"Yeah, but we were up past three."

Don't you remember why we were up past three?

Maybe she's embarrassed. Modest, in the glaring light of day.

Though the light of this day isn't all that glaring, and something tells him it isn't that.

It's more than that, and dread builds in his gut.

"I should go. I—"

"No, don't go."

Please don't go. You aren't going. You can't *go.*

She offers a tight smile. "I have to go sooner or later, Ralphie."

"Later. Later's good."

"No, my sister is probably worried, and—"

"She knows where you are," he points out.

Daria called home again late last night from her cell phone to say it was snowing too hard for her to make it back to Manhattan. It was a brief conversation, and her sister seemed to have no problem with it at the time.

"Why would your sister worry?"

"It's not just that. It's . . . I've got so much to do before I leave tomorrow."

Thud.

"What?" he asks, sounding—feeling—as though he's suffocating.

"What?" she echoes, looking confused . . . or maybe just uncomfortable.

"You're still . . ."

Leaving.

Tomorrow.

He can't even bring himself to utter the words.

Instead, he says, in a rush, "Come on, Daria . . . Phoenix? You don't want to live in Phoenix. You never did—that was obvious even the first time you brought it up, when I barely knew you. I know you now, and you know and I know that there's no real reason for you to get on a plane on Monday morning."

"No reason? I have a job there," she says softly, sadly. "And a very close friend, and a place to live, and—"

"And it's sunny all the time," he cuts in, trying to keep the anger from his voice. "Yeah, I know all about that."

He sees her glance at the window down the hall.

Encouraged when she doesn't snap back at him, he goes on, "You like snow, you said it yourself. And anyway, your sister is here . . ."

And that's not the point, dammit.

The point is that *he's* here.

But he doesn't dare even say it, sensing that it isn't enough. That *he* isn't enough.

He has to convince her.

He won't let her leave without telling her how he feels.

How do you feel? he asks himself, and the answer comes promptly.

Desperate.

He feels desperate.

That's wrong; this isn't how it should be.

He should be passionate, head over heels in love.

He plunges on, "Listen, you can find a job here, there are a million jobs in New York, and if you're tired of your sister's couch you can stay right here with me—not in that tiny bedroom; we can fix up one of the rooms down the hall, knock down a wall or something . . ."

He's babbling, Lord help him. Going on and on about knocking down walls while Daria looks more and more like she wants to crash through one, just to get away.

"Ralphie . . ." She reaches out, takes both his hands in hers. "You said it yourself . . . even you're not staying here."

Her fingers are ice.

Like her heart, he thinks grimly, refusing to meet her eyes.

"Please don't do this, Ralphie."

"Don't do what?"

"Don't make it hard for me."

Hard for *her*? That's rich.

"You know I have to go."

"So you're just going to walk away from me after last night."

"We said it would be our one night."

"I know, but . . ."

How could he have thought it had changed everything? It didn't change anything—not for her.

"Leaving has nothing to do with you. I think you're a great guy, but—"

"Oh, my God."

"What?"

"Please don't," he says flatly. "Don't give me the 'You're a great guy but' speech. I've heard it before—just the other night, as a matter of fact."

And somehow, it didn't hurt nearly as much coming from the woman to whom he'd been engaged for a few years.

Coming from a woman he's known less than a week, it's sucking the very life out of him.

"At least Francesca gave it a go," he hears himself saying. "She wasn't afraid of commitment. She wasn't afraid of getting married."

"What does that have to do with anything?"

"You don't believe in any of that, right?"

"I never said that, and you can't make assumptions on how I feel about commitment and marriage. You have no idea what I—"

She breaks off. Looks away for a minute, as if to gather her thoughts.

"Listen, you just can't compare me to Francesca," Daria tells him. "That isn't fair. Not to her, and not to me."

"I know. And I'm sorry." He shakes his head, trying to figure out how this all went so wrong, so fast. "I just wish you—"

"Ralphie, there's something you don't know about me,

okay? When it comes to marriage, I've been there, done that."

"What?" He wrenches his hands from hers, feeling as though he's been sucker punched. "Why didn't you tell me you were . . ."

"Divorced," she says flatly. "I'm telling you now. I've got an ex-husband in Seattle and a whole lot of bad memories, okay? So don't tell me I'm not willing to try. I tried. I failed. It's not something I can do."

And this isn't something he can do.

"I don't want to hurt you," she says, grabbing his hands again, squeezing hard. "Can't you see that? I don't want to stay, and try, and fail again. And this time you're the casualty. I don't want—"

"You know what? If you're going to go," he says wearily, pulling his hands from her grasp again, clenching them into inaccessible fists at his sides this time, "do me a favor and just go."

"Ralphie—"

"Please." His voice is hoarse. "Go."

She hesitates a moment, watching him.

He forces himself to hold her gaze, forces himself to memorize her face, telling himself he's never going to see it again and the day will come when he'll want to remember . . .

No, it won't. That day will never come.

You need to forget.

He closes his eyes.

Hears her walk away.

Down the stairs.

Out the door.

Only when it closes behind her does he allow himself to open his eyes, and look down at the empty hall.

His gaze falls on the cardboard-covered pane they repaired together yesterday.

Whenever God closes a door, He opens a window.

Yeah, well, not this time, Ralphie thinks, and swallows hard over a lump in his throat.

This time, the door closed and the window shattered.

Chapter
13

Don't forget these." Tammy comes out of her bedroom holding up Daria's favorite pair of earrings—big silver hoops she likes to borrow to create what she likes to call her gypsy look.

"Thanks." Daria tries to smile as she tucks them into a pocket in the lining of her full suitcase.

"You're welcome." In a terry cloth robe, fresh from the tub, Tammy rubs her damp hair with a towel, watching Daria lay a folded sweater on top of the pile.

"You're not going to need that in Arizona, you know."

"You're right." Daria takes it out. "Do you want it?"

"I would if I could fit into it, but . . ." She shakes her wet head ruefully and takes her hairbrush from the pocket of her robe. "Leave it here. You can wear it when you come back to visit."

Daria nods, not wanting to tell her sister it's going to be a long, long time before she dares to set foot in New York City again. She needs to put it behind her. Make a clean break.

Swallowing over a lump in her throat, she looks around

the apartment. The unplugged strings of Christmas lights hang like cobwebs from the moldings, the holiday greens are curling and dry, the poinsettias straggly and dropping shriveled yellowed leaves.

A novel she was reading is face down and open on the table; she picks it up, marks her place with the cover flap, and tucks it into her carry-on bag for tomorrow.

It'll be good to read a book. Take her mind off Ralphie.

As if.

Okay, so it's going to be a while before she stops thinking about him. Maybe she never will. Maybe he'll always be in the back of her mind, like an old scar that aches every once in a while.

"Am I forgetting anything else?" she asks Tammy, who is surveying the contents of the suitcase.

"I think you've got it all, but if you don't, I'll send it."

"Or just bring it when you come out to visit next month," Daria suggests.

"I didn't say I'm coming for sure."

"You didn't say you weren't. You need to start treating yourself once in a while . . . get out more, get away . . . maybe even date," she dares to add.

"Date! No way," comes the predictable response.

"Okay, so don't date. But it'll be good for you to take a vacation and see the sun for a change. And your favorite sister."

Tammy offers a sad smile that reflects the hollow feeling in Daria's soul.

"You have to come, Tammy. I'm going to miss you too much if you don't." When she speaks, she makes sure her voice is upbeat, just as she has since she blew in the door this morning, fresh from that heart-wrenching scene with Ralphie.

When Tammy pressed her, over hot coffee and bagels—with butter, no lox or cream cheese—for the details of her supposedly snowbound night, Daria made it sound utterly delightful, as if the whole family was there.

Not because she thought her sister would disapprove of her having spent the night alone with Ralphie—in Ralphie's bed—but because she knew that if she started talking about him at all, she'd cry.

It was all she could do to keep her composure on the subway home, and she couldn't even play the Rolling Stones as a distraction.

All day long, she's been half-expecting Ralphie to turn up at the door with her lost iPod . . . which isn't going to happen.

It's not even at his house, and even if it did turn up there—even if he did deign to see her again, if only to return it—he still wouldn't know where to find her.

She never told him where Tammy lives, or gave him her sister's phone number or even her name. She didn't call Tammy from his phone, either, so he wouldn't be able to trace it if he tried.

Why would he try?

He told her to go.

No.

That's not fair.

You said you were going, and he told you to go.

Which is for the best.

He's not in a good place in his life. She's known that all along. He's hurting, and lonely, and vulnerable. None of that is going to change anytime soon, so . . .

It's over.

He can't possibly find her, and she isn't going to go back to him.

"Ralphie? You here?"

Lying on the couch in the winter afternoon gloom, staring at the shadowy ceiling, he doesn't bother to answer his brother-in-law.

"Ralphie?" Joey stomps his boots in the hall, then sticks his head into the living room. "You are here. What are you doing?"

"What does it look like?"

His brother-in-law says nothing. Ralphie tries not to resent him, standing there placidly in the Christmas sweater his wife gave him. From where he sits, Joey doesn't have a care in the world.

Okay, that's not entirely true. But that's how it feels today.

"What are you doing here?" Ralphie looks back at the ceiling.

"Nina sent me over to tell you she made the sauce and dinner's at six, at our house."

"What?"

"It's Sunday, remember? Sunday . . . spaghetti dinner . . ."

"What about the storm? How are Ro and Timmy supposed to get here from Long Island?"

"They aren't. And Dom called and said Mia's not feeling good, so they're not coming, either. But all you have to do is walk next door, so Nina said to come."

"Yeah, well . . . I can't."

"What else have you got to do?"

"Wait for Con Ed."

"Alone, in the dark? And it's freezing in here. This is stupid. It's an outside repair job anyway."

"Not necessarily."

"So if they show up, you'll hear them and see them from our place. Come for dinner, and spend the night."

"No, thanks."

"Okay, then come to our place for dinner, and come back home afterward. Maybe you should just take a break from being Mr. Doom and Gloom."

"Maybe you should take a break from being Mr. Happily Ever After," Ralphie shoots back.

Joe nods thoughtfully, as if he's weighing his next words carefully.

"Listen, you should know . . . I saw her."

It takes a minute for that to sink in. When it does, Ralphie turns his head.

"I was outside shoveling when she walked out of here earlier," Joe tells him. "She was crying, so I didn't . . . she didn't see me."

"She was crying?" Ralphie repeats slowly, incredulously, looking at Joe again.

"Yeah."

"Really."

He would have sworn Daria just sailed out of here with her head held high, not giving him a backward glance.

Obviously, he was wrong.

But that doesn't change what she said, or did. It doesn't change the fact that she's leaving in a few hours to start a whole new life without him.

"So anyway," Joey says, "I know there's something going on between the two of you, and I—"

"Nope. Nothing's going on. Nothing at all. She's moving away tomorrow. Phoenix."

"Oh." Joey pauses. "Want to talk about it?"

"Nope," Ralphie says again, returning his gaze to the ceiling. "I'm good."

"You are definitely not good, pal."

Ralphie shrugs. He is definitely not. Big deal.

"If you feel like talking, you know where to find me. If you don't, I'm not going to push you."

"Thank God for small favors."

"Just . . . six o'clock. Dinner. Okay? If you don't come, your sister's going to think something's up, and you know she's going to come over here to see what it is."

Ralphie nods. Yeah, he knows.

Joey hesitates in the doorway, as if he wants to say something more.

Ralphie looks over at him. "What?"

"Just . . . Mr. Happily Ever After."

"Sorry." Ralphie shakes his head. "I didn't mean it in a bad way."

"No, I . . . it wasn't always a fairy tale, you know. For me. Me and Nina. You were around. You must remember . . ."

"What?"

"How hard it was for me to figure out that Nina and I belonged together. And how hard it was to make her see—once I figured it out—that I was her knight in shining armor, and Astoria was her kingdom, and that little house next door was her palace," he says with a faint grin.

Ralphie is bleakly silent, trying to remember.

That wasn't his finest era. He was just a kid back then,

with trouble at school, basketball on the brain, a pregnant girlfriend.

"Anyway, Nina didn't want anything to do with me or any of it. She was going to leave Astoria when you graduated high school, and she was never looking back. Never coming back. She figured her work here was done."

"Yeah," Ralphie nods, "I remember that. But then she had Rose, and she changed her mind."

"Exactly. About leaving. And about me."

"For what it's worth, Joey," Ralphie says, "I appreciate what you're trying to do here. But Daria's not pregnant, like Nina was. And she's not going to change her mind, like Nina did. There's nothing keeping her here."

"There's you."

Ralphie snorts and waves a hand in the air. "Look around. Look at me. Do I look like anyone's knight in shining armor? Does this look like anyone's palace?"

"Ralphie—"

"Hey, look at the bright side. I get to enjoy your fairy-tale ending by proxy. Tell Nina I'll be over at six. And *don't* tell her anything else. Okay?"

Joey shakes his head and sighs. "Okay."

"Hey, listen," Tammy breaks into Daria's morose thoughts.

"What?"

"Shh." Grabbing the remote control, Tammy raises the volume on the television, where the nightly news had been providing background noise until now.

". . . and while all three metropolitan area airports are expected to re-open later tonight," the local anchorwoman is saying, "there's no telling when the residual delays will ease up. If past storms are any indication, it could be several days before the airlines restore regular service. At JFK alone, thousands of stranded travelers clog the—"

"I hate to say it," Tammy tells Daria, "but your getting out of here tomorrow morning doesn't look so good."

"But I *have* to go!"

Oops. Daria's voice comes out a panicky register higher than usual.

"Relax . . . if you don't get out tomorrow, you'll go the next day."

"You heard what she said. It could be *days*."

"So?" Tammy looks more closely at her. "Why are you so frantic to get out of here?"

"I'm not frantic, I'm just . . . anxious. To start work. And see my friend George. And the sun."

"Oh, please." Tammy shakes her head. "I'm not that naïve."

"What do you mean?"

"Something happened last night, Daria. Admit it."

"What do you mean?" she repeats again. Too bad she's a lousy actress.

"I knew it! All the time you were going on and on about hanging out with the family over there, I knew you were full of it."

Daria raises an eyebrow. "What do you mean?"

Tammy nods. "I wasn't going to say anything, though. I said I'd stay out of it, and I always keep my promises. I figured whatever happened was your business, and that you'd tell me if you wanted to."

"Well, that's right."

"So tell me."

Daria lifts her chin. "I don't want to."

Tammy shrugs and starts to turn away. "If that's the way you want it . . ."

"I'm afraid," Daria blurts.

"To tell me?"

"No . . . I'm afraid that if I don't get out of here, I'm going to stay, and if I stay, I'm going to find my way back to him somehow, and I'm going to make the same mistake I did before, with Alan."

Tammy takes a moment to absorb the rush of words.

Then she says, "I thought it had to be something like that," and turns off the television, putting aside the remote.

"I'm an idiot. I knew this was going to happen, and I went ahead and let myself get involved anyway."

"Tell me all about it, honey." Her sister pats the couch beside her, and Daria fights back the tears.

She sits beside Tammy, wishing she could just curl up on the cushion beside her and let Tammy stroke her hair, the way they used to when they were kids and she'd had a bad day.

Tammy always had all the answers back then. Daria counted on her advice.

You still can, she reminds herself. *You never should have broken that habit.*

Tammy told her not to marry Alan, and she didn't listen. If she had, she would have saved herself a whole lot of heartache.

"Go ahead and talk, Daria. I'm listening," Tammy says gently.

So Daria pours out the whole story. All of it.

Tammy is silent, digesting the details.

And somehow, as Daria purges the anguish, she realizes she might have made room for something else.

Hope.

Again.

Tammy's going to tell me that I'm wrong about Ralphie, Daria realizes, watching her sister's face and second guessing her reaction. *She's going to tell me that I was crazy to walk away from him; that I should forget all about Arizona and march right back over there and give him—give us—a chance. She's going to say that's why Ralphie's father brought us together . . . not because he needed me to deliver a message to his family. Because he wanted me to get together with his son.*

Sure, a ghostly matchmaker would be hard for most people to swallow, but not Tammy, who after all credits herself—and her psychic powers—for a Chickalini marriage as it is. Who knows? She promised to stay out of it, but she might even take it upon herself to track down Ralphie.

If she does, Daria won't stop her.

Tammy will tell Ralphie to give Daria another chance.

If he does, Daria will take it.

She's exhausted herself, trying to find the strength to make her own decisions, then second guessing them every step of the way.

It would be a relief to let go; to put the matter out of her own hands and into Ralphie's, and her sister's, and, all right, the ghost of Nino Chickalini—

Okay, that's a little ridiculous.

It's a cop-out, is what it is.

She has to be accountable for her own decisions, her own actions.

If she finds her way back to Ralphie—with or without his, or anyone else's, help—then it was meant to be.

She's certain of one thing: she's not strong enough to walk away from him twice in a lifetime.

And who knows? Maybe she was wrong about Ralphie being in a bad place. Maybe it will all work out in the end. That's what Tammy is going to tell her. She just knows it.

She watches her sister brush her damp hair thoughtfully, working through the snarls as if she's untangling her thoughts as well.

Whatever she tells me, this time, I'm taking her advice. No matter what. She's older, and wiser, and she does this counseling stuff—albeit the psychic kind—for a living. Plus, she's my sister. She knows me better than anyone, and she's got my best interests at heart.

"Well?" Daria finally asks Tammy breathlessly, unable to stand the suspense and counting on her sister to save the day. "What do you think?"

"First of all, I think you should forget all about Arizona."

Daria exhales in relief.

So she was right.

Tammy is going to tell her that she and Ralphie belong together.

Her thoughts are already whirling, wondering what she's going to say to him when she gets there.

"Your heart was never in the Phoenix thing, Daria— that was obvious from the start. You should forget about it and stay here in New York. You can find a job here—"

"That's what Ralphie said," she breathes, feeling giddy.

"And you can stay with me."

Also what Ralphie said, but she doesn't tell her sister that.

Anyway, he still has to sell the house, so—

"But as far as Ralphie is concerned . . . you absolutely did the right thing."

Daria feels her entire body deflate.

"What?!"

"Like you said, he's been through hell these last few months, Daria. Even I could see it when I met him at the wedding. He's in a bad place. You don't need to be in a bad place with him."

"But . . . what if I can help him? What if that's why—"

"No, you can't," Tammy cuts in, before Daria can even suggest that Ralphie's father sent her into his life for a reason.

"Daria, it's going to take a helluva lot to pull him through what's coming with packing up the house, selling it, and having to move out on his own. Even if there were something you could do . . . Look, he's like a kid in so many ways. He's used to being taken care of, by everyone around him. They all tried to protect him, all these years—overcompensate for the fact that he didn't have a mother. Now he has to learn to take care of himself."

Hot tears sting her eyes. "I know. I said . . . I thought . . . all the same things. But then I let myself fall for him anyway."

"I can see why. I met him. He's handsome, and sweet, and all that stuff you like. And that family—I know how much you want a family like that, honey. But that's not a good reason to be with someone."

"I know." She wipes her eyes with the back of her hand. "They're so great . . . I guess maybe deep down inside, I wanted to be a part of all that big happy family stuff. It's like everything we missed out on, growing up."

Tammy pats her shoulder. "We had each other. Still do. I'm big, and I'm usually pretty happy, and I'm family, so . . . voilà! Big happy family."

"I know." Daria offers a weak, grateful smile. "I didn't mean you weren't—"

"I know you didn't. And I know it's not just about your wanting Ralphie's family. I know you want him, too."

"I don't know what I want anymore."

"Then listen to me. When I saw Ralphie that day at the wedding, his aura was so dark, and he was in such pain. There's more ahead for him. I saw it. For your sake, Daria, you have to stay away. You'll only get hurt. And if not for your own sake, stay away for his. He needs to focus on what he needs to do, and he needs to get his life together. This isn't going to be easy on him."

"I will," she says softly. "I'll stay away. For his sake."

Her sister looks closely at her. "Promise? Just like I promised to stay out of it and not be a cosmic matchmaker?"

"I promise." She sniffles, wipes her eyes. "I told myself I'd do whatever you told me to do."

"Good girl."

"But I can't stay in New York if I'm not going to be with him."

"Sure you can. You can look at it as staying in New York and being with me." It's her sister's turn to wipe at shiny eyes. "It's been too many years since we've had each other in our daily lives like this, Daria. It's felt good. Too good to let go again."

Daria nods slowly, looking at her sister. *She's all I've got. The one constant in my life. The only person who's always been there for me.*

"Look, I'm not saying you should stay here forever," Tammy tells her.

"Good. Because I don't believe in forever."

"Yeah, yeah, I know, I know. I just feel like this is the right place for you to be, for now. Okay?"

"Are you saying that as a psychic counselor?"

"I'm saying that as your sister who loves you."

Daria smiles through her tears and at last allows herself to curl up beside her sister, leaning her head against Tammy's ample, terry-cloth-covered body.

"So you'll stay for a while?"

"I'll stay," Daria agrees, "for a while."

"Promise me you'll give it a year."

"A year!" She sits up straight again. "You're kidding, right?"

"Nope. Not kidding. When was the last time you ever lived anyplace for a year?"

"I never have."

"Exactly." Tammy nods. "If you stay for a year, and it doesn't feel like home, then you can move on to Phoenix or Fiji or wherever the heck you feel like going."

"A year?" Daria protests. "That's a long time, Tammy."

"Right. It takes a while to put down roots and let them sink in, start to grow . . ."

Daria finds herself thinking of Nino Chickalini's tree.

If it was only going to end like this, she asks him silently, wherever he is now, *why did you want me there so badly? Why did you make sure my path crossed your son's? What was my purpose in his life, other than to complicate it?*

She doesn't know the answer.

And unless the spirit of Ralphie's father shows up again to fill her in, she probably never will.

"Did you get your flu shot, Ralphie?" Nina asks, her head in a cloud of steam as she breaks spaghetti into a pot of boiling water.

"Yeah, a few months ago. Why?"

"You don't look good."

Ordinarily, he'd respond with a sarcastic comeback, but he doesn't have the heart tonight.

"I feel fine," he lies.

"I don't think you do. Maybe you're coming down with something."

Let her think it. It's easier that way.

Ralphie focuses on the head of iceberg lettuce in his hands, tearing it into bite-sized pieces and tossing them into the big glass salad bowl.

He shouldn't have come.

He should have just stayed home and wallowed.

Nina stirs the pot. "So the kids had a great time with your friend yesterday."

There are any number of things he could say to that, beginning with, *she's not my friend.*

He says nothing at all.

The lack of a reply doesn't stop Nina. Has it ever?

"Rose said it's too bad she's moving away, because she thinks the two of you are falling in love."

Okay, that deserves a reply. And an eye roll.

He offers both. "That's insane."

"I don't know. Rose said you were hugging Daria on the beach—"

"What? I was showing her how to skip a stone!"

"And she said Daria was looking at you like she wanted to kiss you all day," she adds, sending a momentary little thrill through Ralphie until he remembers that she did kiss him. And kiss him goodbye.

Nina goes on. "Rose said—"

"Oh, for the love of God. Rose is a thirteen-year-old girl who's obsessed by people falling in love, Nina."

"Do you hear me arguing with that?"

No, but he's aware of his sister's eyes watching him shrewdly as he rips the lettuce to shreds. Self-conscious, he stops ripping and asks abruptly, "Where are the tomatoes? I'll cut them up."

"We're out. Do you have any left next door?"

"I have no idea."

"You have them, unless you've used them since I dropped them off the other day. Would you mind going to get them?"

"Not at all." He welcomes the chance to get out of this steamy kitchen for a few minutes, and away from Nina.

"Here . . ." She rummages through a utility drawer. "Take a flashlight. It's dark over there."

"I don't need a flashlight. I know where the tomatoes are. I know every inch of that house in the dark."

"Take it," Nina insists, thrusting the flashlight at him.

He takes it. It's easier than arguing.

"Take your coat, too. It's freezing outside and you're getting sick."

That, he ignores.

He isn't getting sick.

He *is* sick. Heartsick, sick of his life, sick of thinking about Daria.

What more is there to analyze? It's not all that complicated. She was here, and now she's gone, and that's that.

He steps out into the still night. The sky is starless and there's no moon, but the banks of snow are luminescent. Night sounds seem muted by the crystalline blanket; the city has yet to stir back to its usual cacophony . . . but it will, all too soon.

This is the rarest of nights in New York, and Ralphie could have shared it with Daria, had she stayed.

But she's not going to miraculously reappear, like Meg Ryan on the top of the Empire State Building at the end of *Sleepless in Seattle*. This isn't a chick flick. Things like that don't happen in real life.

In real life, you love and you lose.

Except that you didn't actually love *her,* Ralphie reminds himself as he wades across the snowy yard and up the drifted back steps. *"Love" is way too strong a word. That was just infatuation. Just a fling.*

He should have known better.

He *did* know better.

They said it would just be one night.

He stubbornly neglects to turn on the flashlight as he moves through the dark, chilly kitchen . . . until he slams his hip into the edge of the table.

"Ouch! Dammit."

What is that doing there? He could swear the table should be a few inches over to the right.

Only he didn't move it, and it didn't move itself, so . . .

So maybe you don't know every inch of this house in the dark, after all, he tells himself, irritated. *What does that prove, anyway? That you love it? That you shouldn't have to move?*

He turns on the light and aims it at the table.

There, illuminated in the beam, is something that shouldn't—*couldn't*—be there at all.

Daria's iPod.

"What the . . . ?" Ralphie picks it up, turning it over and over in his hands.

It wasn't there yesterday. He and Daria searched everywhere for it. They set this table, ate at it. He cleared the table himself.

No way was there an iPod on the table at any point.

How could it just miraculously reappear?

It couldn't.

Except that it did.

Maybe someone found it, and sneaked into the house, and left it on the table . . .

Yeah, because passengers who find expensive lost items on New York City subways always trace the owners and creep anonymously into their homes at night to return their possessions.

And anyway, this isn't Daria's home, and no one could possibly trace her iPod here, and the house is locked . . . *and why are you wasting time even thinking about a possibility that just couldn't happen?*

Deciding to momentarily forget about the how, Ralphie turns his attention to the *what now?*

What is he supposed to do with this thing?

What *can* he do?

Return it? He has no clue where to even find her. He doesn't know her sister's last name, or where her apartment is—other than that she lives in midtown, on the east side . . . along with tens of thousands of other people.

All right, then.

Later—much later, when he can bring himself to set foot into his bedroom again, where the sheets are presumably still rumpled and smelling of Daria's perfume—he'll bring the iPod upstairs.

He can stash it in the wooden box in his dresser, fittingly, along with the broken engagement ring and other relics of his past.

Looking at it in his hand, Ralphie absently turns on the iPod. After a moment, the rectangle lights up with a Now Playing screen.

The Rolling Stones' "You Can't Always Get What You Want."

Isn't that the truth, Ralphie thinks, standing alone in the dark kitchen, Nina and the tomatoes forgotten.

Chapter
14

Say hello to Uncle Ralphie, June. Hi, Uncle Ralphie!"
Mia waves the baby's pink-mittened hand at her brother-in-law as she steps over the threshold on a blustery Saturday morning.

"Hey, sweetie girl." He takes the pink-snowsuited bundle from her arms. "Is that a tooth I see in there?"

"Yup," Mia says proudly, closing the door behind her and shivering a little. "It's cold in here."

"The heat was on the fritz in the night, but I got it working again. So tell me about the tooth!"

"Her first one. It came through last night."

"No wonder she was so fussy on Christmas." He plants a kiss on June's cherubic pink cheek. "You poor little thing. That hurt, didn't it?"

"My grandmother kept wanting to rub whiskey over her gums—that's what they always used to do for teething babies back in Sicily, she said—but Dom and I wouldn't let her."

"How is Nana Mona doing, anyway?"

Mia's grandmother is a recent widow; her husband passed away just before Father's Day—two weeks before the birth of his first great-grandchild.

The baby wasn't due until late July, but Mia went into labor a few weeks early, maybe due to the stress of losing her cherished grandfather, who had raised her. His real name was Carmine, and that was what Mia and Dom were going to name the baby if it was a boy.

When it turned out to be a girl, they went with June, after the unexpected birth month—and her great-grandfather's nickname. Carmine Calogera Junior was always called Grandpa Junie for short.

"Nana Mona's hanging in there," Mia tells Ralphie as he turns the baby toward her so that she can unzip the snowsuit. "You know how it is. It's not easy."

"No, I know. It's not."

Losing someone you love is cruel and difficult.

But you do get through it, and past it, eventually.

"I know it's a cliché, but time really does heal all wounds," Ralphie tells Mia. He adds, with a wry grin, "Time, and extensive therapy."

"Are you still going to see Dr. Garland?"

"Every Tuesday night. She's helped me figure out a lot of stuff."

"I'm glad you got over that stubborn Italian male thing and gave it a try," Mia says as she gently pulls her daughter's arms from the quilted down sleeves. "It's not the worst thing in the world to admit you need help, or to talk about what's bothering you to a capable outsider."

"It's not the easiest thing, either," Ralphie points out.

But anything is better than what he went through last winter and early spring. It took him several bleak, depressing months to accept his sister-in-law's advice that he go see a grief counselor.

And it took him countless sessions with Dr. Garland before he began to peel away the protective armor and work through the loss not just of his father, but his mother—and his child, as well.

Though he's always thought he had handled the whole Nino thing like a champ and put it behind him, he realizes now that that wasn't the case. He never quite grasped the emotional impact of putting up his son for adoption. Instead of dealing with it at the time, he suppressed the pain, telling himself that he'd made the best decision for everyone involved—for Nino, for his sister and Joey, and for Ralphie himself, who headed off to college and tried to put it behind him.

As Dr. Garland pointed out, yes, he made the best decision—that isn't an issue. But that doesn't mean it didn't hurt.

For nine months now, Ralphie has been working through his emotions: from being raised a motherless child to giving up a child of his own to the raw pain of Pop's death and getting ready to sell the only home he's ever known . . .

And, ultimately, to the heartache of losing Daria.

That didn't come up for a while in his psychotherapy sessions. And when it did, he told the doctor he was sure it was a minor episode in the grand scheme of things, because he had only known her about a week.

Dr. Garland didn't see it that way.

"Some people share more in a week than others do in a lifetime," was how she put it.

All right. So what he felt for her was valid.

All he could do was mourn that loss, like the others, and move past it.

Ralphie's finally learned that you can't go through life thinking about what might have been.

You have to accept what is, and go on.

He's done his best, for months now. Not that he doesn't suffer a pang of regret when bittersweet memories pop up to throw him for a loop.

Getting the house ready for the market was a nightmare, forestalled by complications right up to and including June's unexpected early birth.

The Realtor, John, advised the siblings to "stage it" for the buyer. That meant weeding out the household clutter, including going through their late parents' belongings and dividing mementos with his siblings. Ralphie's share of what they're keeping is tucked away in the attic.

Next, the whole place had to be painted inside and out—which, in the hot and humid New York summer, sans air conditioning, was a challenge.

Finally, in late July, a For Sale sign was planted in the yard, beneath the leafy boughs of Pop's surviving tree.

None of that was easy, but Ralphie got through it, and he's in a much better place now.

Most importantly, he got here entirely on his own, without counting on anyone else to carry him through.

Mia has been a godsend, though. He's found an unexpected friend in his sister-in-law, who can be a caring confidante without the bossy and proprietary edge his sisters bring.

"So to what do I owe the pleasure of this drop-in visit?" Ralphie asks Mia, as he tickles his niece's soft baby neck.

"Hmm? Oh. Dom said the pipes were leaking again."

"So he sent you over to do some plumbing maintenance?" Ralphie asks, half-amused, half-puzzled.

"No, I came over on my own."

"Really. So you've got a wrench in the diaper bag, or what?"

She smiles faintly. "No wrench."

"I don't get it."

"I didn't think you would. Let's go into the kitchen and make some coffee, Ralphie. I need to feed the baby, and we have to talk in private, without your brother and your sisters around."

"What's so private about the plumbing?"

"It's not just the plumbing. It's the heat, too, apparently, along with everything else that's been going on around here the last few months."

He doesn't have to ask her what she means by that.

He's dealt with one household mishap after another lately. Electrical shorts, cracked plaster, broken appliances, clogged drains.

"You took down the Christmas tree already," Mia observes, looking into the living room as they pass.

"Not exactly. John Fusilli was here yesterday with a prospective buyer and it tipped over."

"What do you mean it tipped over?"

Ralphie shrugs. "It just fell, John said, while they were standing here in the living room. Some of the lights broke so I had to throw away the whole strings because they're so old you can't find replacement bulbs anymore. And a few of the old ornaments broke, too."

"Oh, no."

"Oh, yes. Anyway, I took the whole tree apart last night and boxed it up with the decorations."

Also not an easy job . . . but easier than last year, when he had to do it in the wake of Daria's departure. Back then, he was thinking the old Christmas tree and ornaments had just seen their last holiday in this house.

Who ever thought it would take this long to sell?

There was a time when he only wanted to stall the process. But now that it's underway, it seems that every day that passes makes it a little easier to get used to the idea of letting go. The house feels less and less like the haven it once was . . . especially when it feels at times as if it's falling apart around him.

"That's so bizarre . . . that it just fell like that." Mia frowns thoughtfully, staring at the spot where the tree had been.

"Freak accident," he replies with a shrug, leading the way to the kitchen.

"One too many."

"The other stuff has nothing to do with that. This is an old house. Things are going to need repair."

"Constantly?"

"What do you want me to say to that? It's like a run of bad luck."

"No, it isn't," Mia says. "The place is haunted, Ralphie. And we have to do something about it, because it's never going to sell if we don't."

*   *   *

"I don't know . . . I still like the red better," Tammy concludes, as Daria casts a critical eye at the full-length mirror.

"You don't think the black is more sophisticated?"

"Maybe, but the red is more you."

Daria tilts her head, looking again at the black sheath. "He's kind of a sophisticated guy, Tammy."

"Be yourself, Daria."

She smiles. "You sound like my mother. Well . . . not *my* mother . . . as in *our* mother. I meant, you sound like someone's mother."

"Yeah, well, I probably would have been a good one," Tammy says with a sad smile.

You were to me, Daria thinks fondly.

Aloud, she says, "It's not too late, you know. If you met someone and opened your heart to—"

"No," Tammy says firmly. "How many times do I have to tell you I'm not going down that path? I'll settle for being a great sister . . . and a great aunt, someday."

"Maybe just a great sister." Daria shakes her head and looks at the dress from a different angle.

"What, Mr. Sophisticated isn't up for fatherhood?"

"For one thing, that is way premature. I've only been going out with him for a few weeks, and his name isn't Mr. Sophisticated, it's Dan."

"I think Mr. Sophisticated suits him better."

Daria thinks so too, and can't help but smile at that. "For another thing, he's not the type. But I really don't think I am, either."

"You're not his type?"

"No, I meant I'm not the motherhood type."

"Sure, you are. You just haven't met Mr. Right yet."

Mr. Right.

Even after all this time—a year, almost—an image of Ralphie Chickalini flits into Daria's brain.

She has no idea why. It's not as though he was Mr. Right.

No, and it's a good thing she saw the light and moved on. Despite the tumultuous beginning, the past year has been the most settled and gratifying of her life.

Though the trial twelve-month period is almost up, she still has no desire to move on.

Partly because New York's frenetic energy agrees with her. The city seems to reinvent itself daily, with a restless rhythm that matches her own. It's not easy for a person to feel stagnant here.

And then there's Daria's job at a Soho design firm. The place specializes in eclectic style—which is what drew her to their help wanted ad last February. The offbeat clients are right up her alley and she's been feeling creative and productive, more professionally gratified than ever before.

But it's Tammy's steadfast presence in her life that has made the biggest difference of all. They might not be a big happy family, but they're a tiny happy family . . . living in a tiny, tiny space.

Daria's finally going to be looking for a place of her own come January. The thought of her name on a long-term lease no longer makes her cringe.

Too bad Mr. Sophisticated sometimes does.

She's been dating him for a few weeks now. She keeps hoping something will click between them, but so far, it hasn't. Not on her end, anyway. He's handsome and well-off and prone to adventures—like jetting off to the islands on a whim to go deep sea diving—and he's crazy about her.

That's the part that makes her cringe.

She can't help but feel guilty that she doesn't feel the same way. If she could make herself fall in love with him, she would, but it doesn't work that way.

She should probably just tell him she can't see him again, and she intends to . . . but not until after the New Year's Eve gala they're attending at a fancy midtown ballroom.

No way does Daria want to sit home alone on that particular night, remembering what happened exactly a year ago.

And no way is she going to wear a red dress to the gala . . . even if it's not the same red dress she had on last New Year's Eve.

"I'll go with this," she tells Tammy, turning from side to side in the mirror to give the black sheath a last look. "You can't go wrong with basic black."

"You're right." Tammy goes back to the open magazine on her lap.

Daria returns to her sister's bedroom, where she strips out of the black dress and puts it back on its padded hanger. Returning it to the closet—jammed with both her clothes and Tammy's—she hangs it alongside the red dress she wore last year.

It hasn't been touched, shrouded in protective plastic.

If only she could do the same with the memories that pop up every now and then.

The time she spent with Ralphie was fleeting, just a few days out of her life. So why can't she shake the whole episode from her consciousness? Never before has anyone—or anywhere—lingered in her mind the way Ralphie and the Chickalini world have done.

She hasn't ventured into Queens since that fateful stormy day, and it's not like there are physical reminders here in Manhattan. She doesn't even work in his neighborhood, so they certainly aren't going to bump into each other on a deli line some lunch hour.

It's not that she wants that to happen . . .

But at least she'd know, then, how he is.

She wants him to be well. That's all.

But he's vanished from her life as if he were never there at all.

For that matter, so has his father's spirit.

It's just as well.

Tammy's business is booming, but Daria still has no desire to entertain wayward spirits and relay messages from the Other Side, for business or . . .

Well, it never was a pleasure. That's for sure.

"Hey, are you hungry? You know what I feel like eating for dinner?" Tammy calls from the next room. "Pizza."

Pizza.

Big Pizza Pie.

"What do you think?" her sister wants to know.

"Sure, why not." Daria steps back into her jeans.

Tammy sticks her head into the bedroom, phone in hand. "I'm going to call Ray's and order. Pepperoni and mushroom okay this time?"

"How'd you guess?" Daria looks around for the sweatshirt she earlier discarded somewhere on the floor. "Pepperoni and mushroom is exactly what I'm in the mood for."

"I'm a psychic, remem—" Tammy breaks off as the phone rings.

She looks down at the Caller ID window.

"What?" Daria asks, seeing her sister's bemused expression. "Wait, don't tell me. Ray's a psychic, too, and he's calling you to tell you the pizza's on the way."

"No, it's . . . just a client," Tammy says, heading toward the living room as the phone rings again. "One I haven't heard from in a while. I'll take it in the other room."

"Fine, just don't forget to order the pizza when you're done. I really am hungry."

"Right." Tammy answers the phone. "Madame Tamar speaking."

Daria locates her sweatshirt and pulls it over her head.

In the next room, Tammy is saying, "Yes . . . no, it's good to hear from you again, how is everything?" Long pause, and then, "I can do that, if you're sure you . . . yes . . . no, tomorrow is fine. Just tell me the address and I'll be there. Okay, thanks. See you then."

Daria sticks her head into the living room to see Tammy just sitting, holding the phone in her lap, a faraway expression on her face.

"So now you're making house calls?" Daria asks, frowning. "Do you think that's safe?"

"It's a favor," Tammy replies, "for an old client."

"Then why do you look so stressed about it?"

Tammy blinks. "Do I? I'm not stressed."

Yes, she is. Daria watches her thoughtfully.

"Okay, what did you want on that pizza? Sausage and peppers?"

"Pepperoni and mushroom. Are you sure you're okay?"

"I'm great."

But Tammy doesn't meet her gaze as she dials the phone to place their order.

Hmm.

Tammy isn't the only one who's psychic around here.

Something's up. And Daria would be willing to bet it involves a guy.

Maybe her sister has finally come to her senses and realized that nobody should be alone forever.

One thing is certain—whoever was on the other end of the line just now was no ordinary client.

"I can't believe we're actually going to go through with this," Ralphie tells Mia early the next afternoon. "And on your wedding anniversary, no less. Shouldn't you be home with your husband?"

"Our real wedding anniversary is in October—we celebrated it then. And anyway, it's good for your brother to figure out how to take care of June on his own." Mia peers out the front window at the street. "Plus, we're celebrating our reception anniversary on New Year's Eve, while Uncle Ralphie babysits . . . remember?"

How could he forget?

Spending the night with his baby niece is the perfect way to usher in the new year.

The only reason Mia and Dom agreed to the plan was that he pointed out that he has no desire to join the rest of the family at the annual party at Most Precious Mother. Even Joey is going, having decided to close the pizzeria for a change.

But Ralphie won't be ringing in the New Year with everyone this time.

"Too many bad memories of last year," Ralphie told his family, and they exchanged knowing glances.

They figured he was talking about Francesca jilting him—and that's how he wanted it.

Little does anyone know that a year later, Ralphie has nothing but fond memories of his former fiancée, who, local rumor has it, just got engaged at Christmas to a nice guy from Bensonhurst. He wishes her all the best.

It's the memories of Daria that he wants to avoid.

But of course, his family has no idea she ever meant a thing to him. To them, she was just another wayward stranger passing through the Chickalini fold, welcomed as warmly as they would anyone who showed up at their table.

Even the kids stopped bringing her up after a few weeks into January.

Of everyone, only Joey realized she meant something to Ralphie. Whenever he asked about her, Ralphie assured his brother-in-law that he was doing just fine, and long over his little fling.

Whether or not Joey believed him is unclear, but at least he's long since dropped the subject. He seems even more preoccupied than usual lately with his family, and work.

"Listen," Mia says, "if you change your mind at the last minute, Ralphie, don't worry about us. We don't have to go out on New Year's."

"No, but you want to, and I don't. So—"

"There she is!" Mia says excitedly, leaning in to the window.

Ralphie looks over her shoulder. That's her, all right. Madame Tamar's bulky form is wrapped in a long black wool coat that whips around her ankles in the wind. She's wearing a black scarf draped over her head and sunglasses that are hardly necessary in the midday December gloom. Maybe she's trying to be mysterious.

"Here goes nothing," Ralphie says, and rolls his eyes.

"Don't say that. You promised you'd cooperate."

"It was a weak moment. I never should have let you talk me into it."

"You sound just like your brother."

"If Dom knew what we were up to—never mind Dom, if Nina and Ro had any idea that you're bringing in an exorcist—"

"Oh, please! She's not an exorcist, Ralphie."

"All right, a ghostbuster."

"She's not a ghostbuster, either. She's a psychic medium who's coming to rid the house of negative energy."

Ralphie shakes his head. "You really think it's haunted?"

"Got any other reasonable explanation for what's been going on?"

"It's an old house. Things break down."

"Break down? Things are going haywire around here!"

"Ghosts are not a reasonable explanation," he reminds Mia.

"Even you admitted it was possible."

"Only because you made it seem so logical at the time."

"That's because it is."

"No, it isn't."

"Well, it's too late now. She's almost here. And we're about to find out for sure."

"I think this is ridiculous. We would have been better off buying one of those little plastic Saint Joseph statues Rosalee keeps talking about, and burying it in the lawn upside down and facing the house."

"Facing away from the house, and how is that any less ridiculous than this?"

"It isn't. That's the point. And you said yourself that this is ridiculous, so—"

"You know that's not what I said, and listen, if Madame Tamar doesn't think there are any ghosts here, we'll try your statue thing. Okay?"

"All right, all right," Ralphie grouses and follows an eager Mia toward the door to usher in Madame Tamar.

He only hopes that this time, she'll focus on the matter at hand, instead of on Ralphie and how much he hates change.

Which he doesn't, anyway. Not anymore.

He knows now that change is an unavoidable part of life, and he can deal with it from here on in, thank you very much—without any help from Madame Tamar.

"I'm torn between the trout with wild mushrooms in a port wine reduction and the sautéed breast of duckling in a tarragon lime sauce," Mr. Sophisticated informs Daria from across the white linen tablecloth. "You?"

I'm torn between telling you right here and now that I can't go out with you on New Year's Eve, and waiting until after New Year's Eve to tell you I can't go out with you ever again.

"I don't know . . . I can't decide," Daria murmurs, pretending to study the menu as Dan sits there in his cashmere sweater and Gucci loafers, waiting.

The elegant old townhouse is fairly crowded for lunch on a winter afternoon, and ordinarily, Daria would appreciate the candlelit ambiance. But today, for some reason, she can think only of a far less elegant old house across the East River, and another candlelit meal.

"Well, what do you feel like eating?"

"The Chicken Ralphie sounds good."

"Chicken Ralphie?" Mr. Sophisticated echoes, looking blank.

"I mean, ragout. I'm sorry. Chicken ragout!"

Mr. Sophisticated scans his menu. "Hmmm . . . that does sound good."

Daria bites her lip, absently watching a female spirit in a shirtwaist and Gibson girl hairdo—undoubtedly an erstwhile occupant of the house—as she drifts through the room.

"What if I get the trout and you get the chicken and we share both?"

"I can't do this," Daria blurts.

He blinks but, with impeccable breeding, says smoothly, "I'm sorry, you don't have to share. That was rude of me to suggest."

"No, it wasn't. But it's rude of me to keep going out with you like this, when I know it's not going to go anywhere."

Mr. Sophisticated blinks again. "Pardon?"

"I'm sorry, Dan . . . I can't keep going out with you. You're a great guy, but—"

She breaks off, remembering.

Don't give me the 'You're a great guy but' speech, Ralphie lashed out at her.

Dan merely says mildly, "Go on?"

"I can't go to the New Year's Gala with you. It's just not . . . right. Between us. It's not you, that's not the problem, you're not—"

You're not Ralphie.

That *is* the problem.

This isn't going to solve it, but it will make her feel better not to keep stringing along a nice guy like Mr. Sophisticated.

"I'm sorry," she says, and shakes her head sadly at him. "It's just . . ."

"There's someone else," he says kindly. "Right?"

"Right," she lies, because it's easier that way.

Leading Madame Tamar from room to room is not unlike leading the Realtor from room to room, Ralphie decides as they reach the second floor.

He feels just as dubious and resentful as he did when John first came through the house, just as wary of the stranger's critical eyes—now that the sunglasses have been removed—sweeping through the place.

Mia abandoned them a few minutes ago in the kitchen, when a frazzled Dom called to ask her something about the baby. She's still downstairs on the phone, coaxing him step by step through whatever it is he's trying to accomplish with little June. It seems that for the second time in his life, Ralphie's brother has met a female he can't charm with a smooth line alone.

"This is—this *was*—my parents' room," Ralphie says, holding open the door to the master bedroom.

Madame Tamar steps into a room that is, by today's standards, small and modestly furnished when it comes to master bedrooms.

To Ralphie, it looks impersonal as a hotel room, with the bureau tops bare and the closet door ajar to reveal an empty pole and shelves. The familiar quilted bedspread has been replaced by a patchwork quilt John thought was "cozier," and the heavy drapes gave way to sheers that let in more light.

"There was a lot of sadness in this room," Madame Tamar comments. "It's a lonely room. A lot of tears flow here."

Ralphie nods. He doesn't remember it himself, but Nina told him that back when Pop was a new widower, he often audibly cried himself to sleep.

"The rest of the house, it's happier," she tells Ralphie. "There's a good feeling there."

"Does that mean it's not haunted?"

"No. That means it's happier."

"So it is haunted?"

"I wouldn't say *that*."

"It's *not* haunted?"

"I wouldn't say that, either."

Exasperated, Ralphie asks, "What *would* you say?"

"I would say . . ." She is clearly weighing her words. "I would say that there is a presence in this house that doesn't want to let it go so easily. That's why you've been having this trouble."

For the first time, Ralphie allows himself to put aside his skepticism and voice the thought that's been in the back of his mind since it all started.

"It's my father, isn't it? The presence."

Madame Tamar hesitates.

Ralphie sees her looking off into the empty corner of

the room beyond his shoulder . . . as if it isn't empty at all.

He stares hard at the spot too, willing himself to see something. Feel something.

But he doesn't.

It's just an empty corner of an empty room in a house that isn't yet quite empty, technically speaking, but might as well be.

Mia breezes back in. "Sorry about that, I—" She stops short and looks from Madame Tamar to Ralphie. "What's going on?"

"Pop is here, apparently . . . and he doesn't want us to sell the house."

"I knew it!" Mia says triumphantly. "That's exactly what I thought!"

That's exactly what he thought, too . . . only he didn't even realize it until now.

"I didn't want to say anything to you, Ralphie," Mia says, "because I thought it would bother you."

"You did say something. You said the house was haunted."

"I didn't say by your father."

"You thought it, though?" When Mia nods, he asks, "Why? Did you see him, or hear him, or something?"

"No. I just thought it made sense that he wouldn't want the house to be sold."

Ralphie nods . . . though he doesn't know why that theory doesn't quite ring true. His father always had to have known that his children would have to sell the house after he was gone. Why would he—or rather, his spirit—now be tormenting them to scare away prospective buyers? It doesn't change things, only prolongs the inevitable.

Sooner or later, the house will sell.

Wouldn't his father have more important things to do in the afterlife than worry about a material earthly possession changing hands?

"Why didn't you tell me you thought it was Pop's spirit making trouble?" Ralphie asks Mia, discarding the *why* for now.

"For one thing, I didn't think you believed in ghosts. You always seem so skeptical whenever I talk about how Madame Tamar brought me and Dom together."

Ralphie casts an eye toward Madame Tamar, who doesn't look surprised to hear that.

"No offense," he tells her.

"None taken."

"I was skeptical, I'll admit it. And I didn't believe in . . . you know, any of that supernatural stuff. But things change. People change."

"So you believe now?" Mia asks, as Madame Tamar regards him thoughtfully, while keeping one eye on the corner of the room.

"Maybe," he admits. "I mean, I can't see God, and I believe in Him. I guess it's easier to think that Pop is still out there somewhere, looking out for us, than that he just ceased to exist."

"The love doesn't leave us when people pass," Madame Tamar says softly—and so emotionally, he's caught off guard. "They're still with us, all around us. They don't want us to hurt. They want us to heal."

Ralphie swallows hard. There was a time when he wouldn't give credence to a word this woman said. But nothing has ever made more sense to him.

"I was afraid it might upset you if I said I thought your

father was the one who was haunting the place," Mia tells him.

"Better him than some random ghost," Ralphie says with an offhandedness he doesn't really feel. If he let himself, he could cry, right here and now, in this room where his father shed so many private tears.

"It's kind of nice to think that Pop's hanging around here, isn't it?" Mia wraps her hands around Ralphie's upper arm, leaning against him.

"Not if he doesn't want us to sell the house. Is he . . . here now?" Ralphie tentatively asks Madame Tamar, who is still transfixed on the corner.

She simply nods.

"Tell him . . . tell him we don't have a choice about the house. We just can't keep it." Ralphie swallows hard, forces himself to continue. "Doesn't he know that?"

"He knows. But he knew you needed time, Ralphie."

"That's what he was doing?" he asks, stunned. "Giving me time?"

They don't want us to hurt. They want us to heal.

"Without our stuff—and without our family here, together—this is just four walls and a roof. I get that now," he says raggedly. "I'll carry the important things with me wherever I go."

"It's hard, Ralphie," Mia says gently. "It's the only home you've ever had. Everyone understands that. Your father probably understood it most of all."

He nods, takes a deep breath. "I'll be okay . . . wherever I end up living. I'll carry Pop right here with me, just like he always did—like we all did—with my mom." He taps his heart. "Right here with all the memories and all the love."

Mia sniffles and wipes her eyes.

"If my father's really here ... can you tell that to him?" he asks Madame Tamar, who smiles at last with suspiciously shiny eyes.

"He is here, and you just did."

Then she looks back at the empty corner with a nod and a smile.

"He just didn't think you were ready to let go yet," she tells Ralphie. "He thought you needed to hang on a little longer."

Ralphie clears his throat and pushes his voice past a wall of emotion. "I did need to. But now ... I can let go. I have to."

"No, Ralphie, you don't," Mia says. "Dom and I were talking, and ... look, we can afford to buy out everyone's share, and you can live here."

"Mia, you can't do that."

"Sure, I can. My inheritance is—"

"No, I mean, I can't let you do that. I don't want you to do that. It's an incredibly generous offer, and a year ago—hell, maybe a few days ago—I probably would have taken you up on it."

"Ralphie, I want to—"

"No, listen, hear me out. I've been letting other people take care of me my whole life, because it's easier that way. And I can't go on doing that."

"We all want to do it because we love you."

"If you love me, then force me to stand on my own two feet," he returns, and hugs her. "Really, Mia, I meant what I said. It's just a house, and ... it's time to move on."

"Are you sure?"

He nods. "If I stayed here, it'll always feel like it belongs to someone else. I told you—people change. I'm not the same person I was. I don't need that anymore. I don't need to be taken care of. I need . . . I don't know what, but it isn't the house."

"Your father is relieved to hear you say that," Madame Tamar announces. "He's smiling now, and whistling."

"Dom told me that he used to whistle sometimes," Mia says. "He said that it always made him feel good when he heard it, because it meant your father was happy for a change, instead of sad and lonely."

"Yeah," Ralphie smiles, remembering. "That's exactly how it was. I'd hear him sometimes from my room in the morning. He'd whistle old songs when he was shaving and getting ready to go to the pizzeria."

"Which old songs?" Madame Tamar asks thoughtfully, her head cocked, as though she's listening to something Ralphie and Mia can't hear.

"Oh, I don't know . . . stuff they used to play on his favorite radio station. Frank Sinatra, Dean Martin."

"He's whistling an old song right now," Madame Tamar tells him, "but it's older than that. From the Roaring Twenties, I think."

Ralphie's heart skips a beat at that. "Really. What song is it?"

Somehow he knows, before Madame Tamar replies.

"I don't know the exact title, but I know some of the words . . . *Five foot two, eyes of blue . . . buh-buh-buh-buh-buh-da-buh . . .*"

"I know that song—Grandpa Junie used to sing it to me when I was little!" Mia exclaims, and sings the title, "Has Anybody Seen My Gal."

"That's the song." Madame Tamar casts a meaningful

gaze at Ralphie. "That's the song your father's whistling. Know it?"

"I . . . think so," Ralphie manages to say.

If there was a lingering doubt in his mind about Madame Tamar's gift, and whether his father's spirit is really here, it's gone now.

Pop is here. Ralphie can't see him, but he doesn't have to. He knows his father is here . . . and he knows what he's saying.

All this time, he's been thinking it was too late for him and Daria.

That it would be impossible for them to find each other again, and make a go of it.

But—as he catches an unmistakable whiff of his father's cologne in the air—he now realizes that nothing's impossible.

Daria is on her couch-bed poring over the real estate classifieds when Tammy returns from her so-called client house call late Sunday afternoon.

"How'd it go?" she asks, looking up from the ad she's in the process of circling—a studio apartment in a doorman building on the west side.

"It went great!"

Tammy's reply is so enthusiastic that Daria is certain she was right about her sister being up to something . . . perhaps involving a man.

"You seem awfully happy for someone who just came from a business appointment," she observes, wishing Tammy would just confide in her.

Not that she blames her, really. Maybe Daria shouldn't have nagged her so much about dating again. Maybe now

Tammy is reluctant to say anything because she doesn't want Daria to get her hopes up.

Tammy balances on one foot, taking a tall black boot off the other. "Well, you know . . . my business is other people's pleasure. It makes you feel good when you help someone get their life back on track."

"Hmm. So Miss Lonelyheart is all healed?"

"What makes you think it was a *Miss* Lonelyheart?"

Bingo! "Ms. Lonelyheart, then? Mrs.?" Daria baits her.

Tammy smiles mysteriously and shakes her head.

"What, it was a *Mr.* Lonelyheart this time?"

"Right."

"So what did you tell him? That no one should be alone, and that eventually, a person can get past anything—even a broken heart—and that it's time to move on to someone new?"

"Oh, I didn't come right out and say that, actually," Tammy says, tossing her coat over the back of a chair. "It wouldn't be right for me to meddle."

"Meddle? I thought he hired you to counsel him," Daria says, wishing Tammy would just come clean.

Tammy shrugs. "I just helped him see the light about a few things. He'll figure out the rest of it on his own."

"How can you be so sure about that?"

"I just have this feeling." Tammy flashes that enigmatic smile again, then goes into the bathroom and shuts the door.

Daria just hopes her sister doesn't get hurt. It's been years since she lost Carlton, and she's always said he was her one true love.

How can anyone ever measure up to that?

With a sigh, Daria flips a page in the paper to see if she missed any good listings.

Nope . . . these aren't rentals, these are sales.

She's about to turn back again when an ad catches her eye.

ASTORIA: DITMARS AND 33rd. Two-story well-loved home in leafy family neighborhood, close to train and shops. 3 BR, 1 B.

Sure there could be other homes for sale in that neighborhood that match the description, but . . .

Well-loved. Leafy family neighborhood.

This is the Chickalini home.

There isn't a doubt in her mind.

So.

Ralphie really did it.

He put the house on the market.

He's moving on at last.

So are you, Daria reminds herself.

She's freed herself from Mr. Sophisticated, and she's going to find a place of her own to live, and . . .

And put down roots. Here in Manhattan.

A stone's throw away from Queens.

She sighs and closes the paper, then looks up to see that she's not alone in the room.

A man is standing there, watching her.

It takes her a moment to recognize him. It's the eyes, she realizes, when she comprehends who it is. His eyes are so different. They're no longer sad.

Now they glimmer with light and warmth, as if all is right, at last, in the Other World.

Daria can't help but smile at him, and he smiles back.

Then he nods knowingly, as if the two of them share a little secret.

Then he reaches out his hand . . . but not toward Daria.

A woman has appeared beside him. A beautiful woman with dark hair and a gentle smile and Ralphie's kind eyes. She slips her hand into her husband's, and Nino casts one last look at Daria before he and his wife fade away, together at last.

And in that moment, the message is clear, and she knows what she has to do.

Chapter
15

New Year's Eve
Astoria, Queens

Good night, honey." Ralphie gently sets the pink bundle into the portable crib Dominic set up earlier, in Ro and Nina's old bedroom.

"You're my favorite uncle, Uncle Ralphie," he mimics the answer in a high-pitched voice. "And the smartest and the nicest and the most handsome uncle in all the land! Good night! Sweet dreams."

Ha.

Sweet dreams are all he's been having lately—and they're all about Daria Marshall.

He checks his watch as he tiptoes back into the hall. It's past eleven.

This time last year . . .

"Cut it out," he scolds himself aloud.

He promised himself earlier that he wouldn't spend the entire night dwelling on what might have been.

But he can't help it, really.

He was so certain he was going to find her somehow. For the last couple of days, he's been on the Internet and on the phone, searching everywhere he could possibly think of, going only on the meager clues Daria provided about her past.

He spent the better part of today calling every single interior design firm in metropolitan Phoenix, asking— hopefully—to speak to Daria. There was never a Daria on hand, so he would then ask for George.

A couple of times, a George actually came to the phone, but it was never the right George.

Ralphie would begin with, "I'm calling about Daria Marshall . . ."

And the clueless George on the other end of the line would say, "Who?"

And Ralphie would hang up, discouraged.

He'd been so sure that if he just tried hard enough, he'd be able to find her. That it was meant to be.

Maybe he was wrong.

He gives the slumbering baby a last look, then leaves the door to the bedroom open a crack and heads down the hall. As he starts to descend the stairs, he realizes it suddenly seems chilly in the house. That's strange—he turned it up higher than usual tonight because the baby was coming.

Uh-oh.

Maybe the furnace is acting up again. There hasn't been a household incident since Madame Tamar was here, but that doesn't mean it was resolved for good. Nino Chickalini was nothing if not stubborn.

"Pop?" Ralphie asks, standing alone in the darkened hall. "Is that you? Are you here?"

No reply.

But it is definitely drafty, and for no apparent reason.

Ralphie backtracks to his bedroom to find a sweatshirt.

The twin beds, bureaus, and shelves are intact but the books, photos, and trophies are gone—packed away in boxes in the attic. This room, too, has been staged for prospective buyers . . . staged to look generic and welcoming, as though anyone could move right in and claim it for their own.

That bothered Ralphie at first . . . maybe it still does, in a way.

But that doesn't mean he wants to stay here.

He shivers as he opens his dresser drawer to look for a sweatshirt, thinking he should probably turn up the thermostat even higher for the baby's sake. The last thing he wants is for her to catch a chill and get sick.

Hey, that's an old wives' tale. He smiles to himself. *And I'm not an old wife.*

No, but someday, if he's lucky, he might have one.

It won't be Daria.

He'd been hoping for a miracle, but she's vanished, and there's no way to find her. The only hope now is that she might somehow find her way back to him . . . but how can that happen?

Even if she had a change of heart, he won't be living in this house much longer. She could always track him down through Nina and Joey next door, or the restaurant . . .

But something tells Ralphie that the true end of an era is upon the Chickalini family. This morning, when he was having coffee in Nina's kitchen, she said something about needing more space. Maybe a house in the suburbs, somewhere near Ro.

"Now that you won't be living right next door, I don't feel so attached to this house, either," Nina said, looking around the small kitchen.

"But it's so far from the pizzeria, and Joey works so late . . . wouldn't the suburbs be inconvenient for him?" Ralphie asked with a pang.

"I don't know . . . we'll see," Nina said vaguely.

Ralphie's been thinking about the exchange all day, and has come to realize that Joey might not want to run the restaurant forever.

He used to be a finance wiz. Maybe he misses his old life—and all the money that went with it. It's not as though he hasn't voiced, with increasing frequency, the stress of having two kids and college just around the corner.

The bottom line, Ralphie realizes now, is that his family is in flux, and even if Daria came back to Astoria to look him up someday, she might not find him.

He pulls out a well-worn hooded Knicks sweatshirt. When he went through his dresser getting rid of stuff, he couldn't bear to part with it.

Nor could he part with the wooden box he carved back in boy scouts. That's still here in the drawer, untouched in almost a year now.

He finds it and opens it.

Lying right on top is Daria's iPod.

He takes it out, running his fingers over it, remembering.

Of course, the battery will have run down.

He presses the power button anyway . . .

And is startled when the screen blinks to life.

Okay, so these things hold their charge a lot longer than you'd think.

NOW PLAYING: MAKE SOMEONE HAPPY, JIMMY DURANTE, SLEEPLESS IN SEATTLE SOUNDTRACK.

Huh?

That's odd.

That wasn't the last thing playing when Ralphie put the iPod away a year ago.

No, it was a Rolling Stones song. "You Can't Always Get What You Want."

He remembers it well, because the lyrics seemed so fitting at the time.

Puzzled, he presses Play, raises the headphones to his ears, and listens.

"Where's the real stuff in life to cling to? Love is the answer . . ."

Whoa.

Ralphie lowers the earphones abruptly.

Talk about fitting.

So fitting that he looks around the room, half expecting to see his father's ghost standing there.

Madame Tamar told him and Mia that just because they couldn't see Pop, it didn't mean he wasn't there.

"If you talk to him," she said in parting, "he'll hear you. You don't need me around for that."

"Pop . . ." Ralphie's voice seems to echo in the empty room. "Are you here? Are you doing this?"

No reply.

Of course not.

Heart pounding, Ralphie raises the earphones again.

Jimmy Durante is still singing: *"Someone to love is*

*the answer . . . Once you've found her build your world
around her . . ."*

Ralphie lowers the earphones, a slow smile spreading
over his face.

"Okay, Pop . . . I hear you loud and clear. I just wish I
knew what you wanted me to do about it. I mean, this isn't
Sleepless in Seattle. It isn't Valentine's Day, and I can't
just go up to the Empire State Building and—"

Suddenly, an idea pops into his head.

Probably the most farfetched idea he's ever had.

But it might be worth a shot . . . if he hurries.

This close to midnight on New Year's Eve, Ditmars Boulevard is fairly quiet. The city's revelers are all celebrating
indoors or across the East River in Times Square.

Daria's heels make a hollow sound on the stairs as she
descends from the elevated platform. The N train rumbles
off into the distance, heading back down the track toward
the city.

She glances at Manhattan's glittering skyline in the
distance, where the Empire State Building glows a festive
red and green.

This is crazy.

What is she doing here in Queens?

She should be over there, across the river, eating popcorn and watching the *Twilight Zone* marathon with
Lenore and Tammy, who—if she does have a secret boyfriend—seems awfully content to spend New Year's Eve
apart from him.

Daria told her sister and Lenore that she was going
down to Times Square to watch the ball drop.

She was afraid they'd ask to come along, but she should have known better. They're seasoned New Yorkers.

"Are you sure you want to deal with that madhouse?" Lenore asked dubiously.

"Just be careful, and watch your wallet," Tammy advised, and if she suspected Daria's Times Square story was a cover, she didn't let on.

Maybe Daria should just turn around and go back now, before she makes a fool of herself in front of Ralphie or his family . . .

Or, worse, before she finds out that he isn't there, or that he's with someone else . . .

For all she knows, he could be married by now, to Francesca or someone else. Married and living happily ever after here in Queens.

Or he could be alone, still thinking about her the way she's still thinking about him.

There's only one way to find out.

You came this far, she tells herself as she hesitates at the corner of the boulevard. *You can't go back now.*

She covers the distance to Big Pizza Pie in a hurry, before she can change her mind.

There it is, just up ahead . . .

Dark.

Her heart sinks as she covers the last few steps and reads the sign stuck on the door.

CLOSED FOR THE HOLIDAY. HAPPY NEW YEAR.

Okay.

She tried.

It isn't the end of the world, just the end of a short-lived dream.

A dream she had no business imagining could ever come true, especially after all this time.

She must have been wrong about Nino Chickalini's message. He wasn't trying to tell her that Ralphie was in a better place, and that she should go find him there. That was just her own wishful thinking.

As she turns away from the glass door, she sees something flicker out of the corner of her eye.

Spinning back toward the restaurant, she sees that the neon sign in the window—the one that reads Big Pizza Pie—is suddenly glowing red, as if somebody just flipped a switch.

What the . . . ?

Suddenly, the interior lights come on as well, spilling out into the night like a beacon.

Daria takes a slow step closer, and then another . . .

Ralphie.

Her heart explodes like Times Square at midnight.

Ralphie is there, inside the pizzeria, turning on the lights, with . . .

Is that a baby in his arms?

Yes.

A baby.

Watching Ralphie press a tender kiss on the child's soft head, Daria can't help but smile through tears.

He's a father now.

A good one, she knows.

Ralphie's living happily ever after, with a family of his own.

Maybe that's why she's here.

Maybe that's all she needed to know.

What about you? a small voice asks. Did he forget about you?

Probably.

And she should start trying to do the same.

Slowly, she returns to the subway.

It's going to be a long, cold wait for the train to return to the end of the line.

"Stupid, stupid, stupid," Ralphie tells himself back at home, as he finishes tucking his niece into the porta-crib for the second time in as many hours.

Stupid, and selfish, dragging a poor little baby out of bed in the middle of the night, and out into the cold.

This is real life, not a movie.

He and Daria aren't Meg Ryan and Tom Hanks meeting on the top of the Empire State Building.

They're real human beings living in the real world, where not everyone gets to live happily ever after.

Stupid, stupid, stupid.

Passing his bedroom, he sees that he carelessly left the light on earlier, and the iPod lying right out on top of his dresser.

To think he actually convinced himself that his father was here, sending him some ghostly message about Daria from beyond the grave.

It's an electronic device, not a supernatural portal. Just because it happens to still work after a year in a drawer . . . and just because it played a song that happened to fit his situation . . . and all right, just because the damned thing appeared on Ralphie's kitchen table somehow . . .

None of that means a thing, when it comes to him and Daria.

For a little while there, though, he honestly believed it.

That they're somehow cosmically linked; that she would know to meet him at the pizzeria at midnight on New Year's Eve.

Same time, next year.

It would have been so easy . . .

Much, much too easy.

Nothing is easy. Hasn't he spent a year learning that lesson? Hell, a lifetime learning it?

He opens the carved top of the box, about to deposit the iPod inside again. Something catches his eye.

Madame Tamar's business card.

He pulls it out thoughtfully. This time last year, he was planning to get rid of it, certain she was full of—

But she's not.

Regardless of what just happened, his father was here, the other day.

He knows that for certain.

Madame Tamar sees things other people can't possibly see.

Hears things other people can't possibly hear.

Five foot two . . . eyes of blue . . .

Ralphie turns the card over and over in his hands, thoughtfully.

March 31
Manhattan

"You know, I've moved a lot in my life," Daria tells Tammy, squashed right up next to her in the back seat of a yellow cab, thanks to a heap of Daria's belongings taking up the rest of the seat, "but I've never done it in a taxi."

"Welcome to New York, honey." Tammy's reply is muffled by the large duffel bag on her lap. "The fare from my place to yours should be about eight bucks, so it's a lot cheaper than renting a moving van."

"Yeah, and one more trip should do it . . . although I'm surprised I had accumulated this much stuff at your place. I honestly thought I could throw some things into a suitcase, take the subway down to the Village, and be done with it at last."

"At last? It takes some people weeks to move!"

"No, I don't mean the move itself . . . I mean the whole thing. It took me forever—not that I believe in forever, mind you—to just find a place."

"Do you always have to say that?"

"Say what?"

"That you don't believe in forever."

"Well, yes," she says, "I always do."

"Listen, a couple of months is not forever, and you've gotta admit, the place is exactly what you were looking for."

"You're right about that." Daria's new apartment, a one bedroom on East Seventh Street, is on the third floor of a charming old building. It has hardwood floors, tall windows, and a sunny southern exposure . . . well, it will be when the sun actually shines, anyway.

It'll have to pop out sooner or later, after the longest stretch of dreary gray weather Daria can recall ever enduring. Or maybe it just seems that way with George calling so much lately to rub in the year-round Arizona sunshine.

His business got off to a flying start, and he's looking to hire a couple of new designers. Preferably, eclectic ones.

"Are you sure you haven't changed your mind, Daria?"

All right, she did waver just a little before answering, "I'm positive. I'm about to sign a year-long lease in New York."

"Well, if it doesn't work out, I'll be here. Maybe we can rethink your plan same time next year."

Same time next year.

"I'm sure it'll work out here," she told George with a confidence she didn't feel.

It's just that seeing Ralphie on New Year's Eve threw her for a loop.

And all right, maybe that, more than George's calls from Phoenix, has made the world seem impossibly dreary this winter.

Daria didn't tell Tammy what had happened on New Year's Eve, knowing her sister would say she shouldn't still be hung up on him a year later. That, or she'd say that seeing Ralphie settled down with a baby should have brought closure.

She'd be right about that . . . it should have brought closure.

But it didn't.

Maybe this move will help. Maybe once Daria's settled into a place of her own, she'll be back on the road to putting down permanent roots here in New York.

And if not . . .

You can always move on, she tells herself wearily. *After all, it's what you do best.*

* * *

Astoria, Queens

"Careful with that, guys," Nina says worriedly from the doorway as two of Timmy's firefighter friends carry the big wooden hutch down the front steps. "It's got glass in the doors."

Standing beside her, Ralphie watches furniture leave Pop's house forever: down the walk, along Thirty-Third Street a few paces, and up the walk next door to Nina's house.

That's where it will remain . . . for the immediate future, anyway.

"I really hope you and Joey find a big place when you start looking at houses on Long Island next fall," Dom tells his sister, coming up behind them. "You're going to need it with all of this extra stuff."

"Anything is bigger than what we've got now," Nina says ruefully.

"Not Ralphie's new place." That comes from Rosalee, emerging from the living room with a lamp in her hand.

"Hey . . . you can't compare a Manhattan studio apartment to a whole house," Ralphie protests. "And anyway, I've got four hundred square feet to my name, and it's all mine."

Funny how the one thing he always expected to dread now fills him with pride. All his.

For the first time in his life, he's entirely in charge of his surroundings, and it feels good. Not frightening, or lonely, or any of the things he expected to feel when he spent his first night there, last night.

Of course, it's still new. Maybe once the novelty has worn off, he'll be a little homesick.

Or a lot homesick.

But even if that happens, he can get through it.

He's certainly been through worse.

"Four hundred square feet is a lot more than I've got, at this point," Dominic informs them. "Do you know how much stuff babies require? One little kid, and she's taking over the planet."

"Poor Dommy. His life is a living hell," Ro comments, shaking her head in mock sympathy.

Ralphie finds himself relishing the familiar banter among his siblings on this, their last official day as owners of the house.

Tomorrow morning at the closing, they'll turn it over to a young couple who are expecting their first child around Memorial Day. They fell in love with the house the moment they first saw it, according to John Fusilli. That was on January second.

Ralphie's siblings were startled to get an offer so quickly after the New Year.

"It's almost like magic," Ro said. "Come on, own up . . . one of you buried Saint Joseph in the yard, right?"

"It was me," Ralphie confessed, after exchanging a little nod with Mia.

"I knew it! It works like a charm, just like Bebe said. Make sure you bury Saint Joseph in your yard when the time comes, Nina."

Yes, Nina and Joey are planning to trade Queens for the Long Island suburbs sometime after the current school year ends. Joey is going to keep running the pizzeria for the time being, but Nina said he's been thinking about going back to work on Wall Street. They figure the commute to lower Manhattan on the Long Island Railroad wouldn't be as big a headache as getting to Astoria from wherever they wind up living.

Ralphie wonders what will become of Big Pizza Pie if Joey moves on . . . but he doesn't need to worry about it in advance. There are enough changes in the works right now.

"Anyone want this lamp?" Ro holds it up. "It's the one Dominic broke throwing a baseball at my head that time I told Donna DiLorenzo he stunk up the bathroom."

Nina leans in to look. "I superglued it back together. See? Here's the crack."

"Nina and her superglue," Ralphie says fondly. "You pretty much superglued everything in the house at one point or another."

They all look at the lamp, lost in memories.

"So can I keep this, then?" Rosalee asks after a moment.

"All yours," Nina tells her. "Maybe we should take one last walk through to see what's left."

There isn't much. This morning, an antiques dealer Ralphie found in the Yellow Pages came and carted away the kitschy kitchen items which—as Daria said—turned out to be worth something.

Ralphie kept the blender, though. Just in case . . .

You never know when you might want a strawberry shake.

Or chocolate.

As he trails his sisters and brother up the stairs, Ralphie wonders if they're thinking of all the times they slid down the banisters, or raced down the steps on Christmas mornings in their pajamas.

"I wonder which room the new people will give to their

baby when it's born," Nina muses as they walk along the hall, their footsteps echoing strangely on the bare floor.

"Probably our old room," Rosalee says. "It's bigger."

"Yeah, but ours is better," Dom says. "Right, Ralphie?"

He nods. "Brighter, too. Wow, it looks huge without the furniture, doesn't it?" His and Dominic's old bedroom set has been loaded onto a rented U-Haul parked out front; it's being transplanted to T. J. and Adam's room on Long Island.

"I wouldn't say it looks huge," Nina tells Ralphie on a laugh.

"Or bright," Rosalee says, and Ralphie has to admit that the March gloom beyond the window does seem to permeate the room.

Still . . .

"On a summer morning, with the sun shining in, it's a lot different," he says, remembering. "At least, it always seemed that way."

"Do you think the new people will take care of the roses?" Rosalee asks wistfully, gazing out the window. "Maybe one of us should dig them up and take them."

"Are you crazy?" Dom heads back for the hall, with Nina close behind. "In March?"

Ro follows them. "I'm just saying . . ."

The three of them move on down the stairs, but Ralphie hovers in the doorway of his boyhood room. He looks from the open closet to the wall where his bed once stood to the window, where the branches of Pop's tree are just starting to bud—memorizing every detail, just as he tried to do with Daria's face so long ago, knowing he would never see it again.

At last he turns away, brushing tears from his eyes as he walks down the hall, telling himself not to look back.

It's probably easier that way.

But just before he reaches the stairs, he casts one last, long, loving glance over his shoulder.

"Goodbye," he says softly. "I won't be coming back here, but I'll never forget you."

As he walks down the stairs, he opens his wallet, just to make sure the card is still there.

Yup.

Madame Tamar, Psychic and Spiritualist.

"Really, Tammy, you don't have to come back downtown with me this time," Daria tells her sister, back in Tammy's midtown apartment after depositing the taxi load into her own.

"I don't mind, and you need help."

"Not really." Daria carries an armload of garments on hangers from the closet over to the bed. "I'm going to toss all this stuff into that empty duffel, lug it downstairs, hail another cab, and be out of your hair once and for all this time."

"You're not in my hair," Tammy replies, watching somewhat wistfully.

"Sure I am. I've been in your hair for about a year and a half now. Admit it. You'll be glad to have this place to yourself again."

"I don't know . . . I might actually miss you."

"Miss what? My finding your hidden chocolate stash and eating it? My snoring self taking up the whole couch at night when you want to stay up late and watch a movie?

Yeah, I'm sure you'll miss those things, but you'll get over it," Daria assures her with a smile.

"I don't know. It might be kind of lonely around here."

"Maybe it's time to go on a date."

"Daria," Tammy says in a warning voice.

"All right, then get a cat. God knows you have enough mice." Ghostly and otherwise.

"Maybe I will. Hey, what are you looking for?" Tammy asks, watching her hunt among the hangers and garments on the bed.

"The belt to my blue dress." Before Daria can ask her sister if she's seen it, the building intercom buzzes loudly.

"Must be a walk-in appointment." Tammy goes into the living room to answer it.

"See? You have other things to do," Daria calls. "I'll head downtown by myself, and you stay here and deal with the lonely hearts club."

Tammy says something in reply, but Daria can't hear it from the depths of the closet as she sticks her head way down inside to find the missing belt.

As Ralphie arrives at the second floor and walks toward Madame Tamar's apartment, he tells himself that if this doesn't work, he's exhausted his last option.

It seems pretty far-fetched, but you never know. The police use psychics to track down missing persons, don't they?

He's even brought along Daria's iPod, in case it gives off some kind of vibe that Madame Tamar can use to zero in on Daria, wherever she is.

Talk about a long shot . . .

Okay, so admit it. You probably shouldn't have come.

Especially not today, of all days, when he's closing the door on his old life and beginning a new one. He should probably have thrown the card into the Dumpster back in Queens and put Daria out of his head once and for all.

But his new apartment is right here on the East Side, and he figures it might be foolish not to at least give Madame Tamar a try.

Somehow, it seems important to do that—today, of all days.

He raises his hand to knock on her door, but it's already opening.

Not, he reminds himself, because she's a psychic, but because she answered the buzzer when he rang from downstairs.

"It's Ralph Chickalini, and I have a favor to ask," is what he said over the intercom, and she hesitated for a second before telling him to come right up.

Standing in the doorway of her apartment wearing jeans and a sweatshirt, she doesn't seem the least bit mysteriously powerful.

She looks so ordinary, in fact, that he has to remind himself that she did, indeed, channel his father's spirit just a few months ago.

"Well, this is a surprise." She's eying him with a strange expression.

Maybe she thinks he wants her to bring Pop through again.

"I, ah, guess I should have called first, but I was in the neighborhood, and your sign says walk-ins welcome, so I gave it a shot."

"Good. What's the favor you need?"

"I'm trying to find someone, and . . . I'm kind of desperate."

"Someone on the Other Side?"

Uh-oh. He never thought of that. What if she doesn't do missing persons, only dead ones?

"Someone on this side, actually," he tells her. "She's . . ."

He trails off, overcome by uncertainty.

This isn't a good idea. He shouldn't be here. He was doing so well with his new life. He should have just left well enough alone.

"Is she a friend?" Madame Tamar nudges gently.

"Kind of, but more . . ."

"An ex-girlfriend?"

"Not really. She's just . . . someone I feel like I can't live without."

Madame Tamar raises an eyebrow.

"You've got to help me find her," he says in a rush, "because I need another chance with her, and I never should have let her go, because she's the only person I've ever—"

"Ralphie?"

He breaks off, startled.

Whoa.

He could have sworn Daria's voice just came out of Madame Tamar, and she wasn't even moving her lips.

"That's amazing," he tells her, his heart pounding in excitement. "I can't believe you just—"

When Daria herself steps out from behind Madame Tamar, Ralphie gasps and grasps the door jamb to keep from keeling over.

"How the heck did you do that?" he murmurs to Madame Tamar in wonder, instinctively reaching toward Daria to see if she's real, or just some kind of psychic vision.

His hand closes over her arm, and it's warm and solid.

She's real, all right. She's real, and she's here, and it's all he can do not to pull her into an embrace.

He probably would, if he weren't positively reeling by this unexpectedly dazzling turn of events. He came here hoping to get a lead on Daria's whereabouts, not thinking Madame Tamar was capable of conjuring the real thing right on the spot.

"By any chance," Madame Tamar asks, wearing a faint, and slightly smug, smile, "is *she* the person you were looking for?"

He can only nod, trying to absorb the enormity of what just happened here.

Talk about impossible!

"So that means I'm the person—" Daria breaks off, clears her throat, finishes in barely a whisper, "I'm the person you feel like you can't live without?"

Gone is the wonder of seeing her again, replaced with a fervent prayer that she won't slip away from him this time. "Yes."

"Listen, you need to come inside," Madame Tamar says, and he's barely conscious of her propelling him over the threshold.

"Did you do this?" he hears Daria ask the psychic.

"Me? Are you kidding? No cosmic matchmaking, remember? A promise is a promise."

Madame Tamar closes the door behind him, and looks

from him to Daria, still grinning, before she discreetly disappears.

Not disappears as in *Poof!*—the way she made Daria appear. No, she simply goes into the next room and closes a door behind her, leaving Ralphie alone with Daria, who looks as bewildered as he feels.

"So how, uh . . . does this work?" he asks incredulously. "Were you just sitting there in Arizona or somewhere and suddenly—"

"Arizona? I never went to Arizona."

"Why not?"

She answers the question with one of her own. "What about your baby? And the baby's mother?"

Ralphie blinks. "Camille?"

"Who's Camille?"

"She's—wait, are you talking about Nino?"

"I'm talking about your baby."

"Nino."

"No . . . your daughter." Sounding impatient, she clarifies, "The little baby in the pink snowsuit, on New Year's Eve. I saw you, and—"

"My niece! She's my niece, and . . ." He hesitates, watching the light dawn in Daria's blue eyes.

"Your niece?"

"Yes. You saw me with her?"

"Through the window at the pizzeria," she tells him, and her eyes are sparkling clear again. "I went there just before midnight because I thought maybe you would remember—"

"Same time, next year," he cuts in. "I did remember. Only you didn't come."

"But . . . I did."

"I didn't know. If I had known . . ." He shakes his head, trying to clear it. "And now . . . I'm sorry, but it's still so amazing to me that you're here. I never believed in this stuff at all . . ."

"Fate," she says, shaking her head. "I never believed in it, either."

"No, I believe in fate. I meant . . . this magical psychic supernatural stuff. I mean, even now that I'm seeing it with my own eyes, I still can't believe it."

"Oh!" With a sudden gleam in her eye, Daria asks, "What, exactly, can't you believe?"

"That this ordinary-looking woman just made you appear out of nowhere."

Daria seems to be fighting back a smile. "Actually," she says, "it wasn't out of nowhere. I was in the next room, and when I heard your voice—"

"You mean . . . you were already here, in the apartment?"

Daria nods.

"Madame Tamar didn't just pop you in by magic?"

"No." Now she's laughing. "I'm sorry," she says, "I can't help it. Ralphie—Tammy's my sister."

"Tammy?"

"Madame Tamar."

It takes a moment for that to sink in.

Then she hits him with another shock. "Ralphie, my sister's . . . uh, she's not the only psychic in the family."

"*What?*"

"I've got the same ability."

"You mean . . . you can see the future?"

"I mean, I can see things others can't see."

"What kinds of things?" he asks slowly, somehow sensing what she's about to say, impossible as it seems.

Nothing, he now knows, is impossible.

"Mostly, I see people." She hesitates. "People who have passed on."

Ralphie's breath catches in his throat. "Like . . . whom?" he asks, both hoping—and knowing.

"Like your father. I've been seeing your father. He's been with you, right beside you, from the first time I saw you."

A sob escapes him and he presses a trembling fist against his mouth.

"He was so worried about you, Ralphie. He wanted to see you through the pain, help you heal."

"He did. He healed me."

"No, Ralphie. You did it yourself. You found so much strength—strength you didn't even know you had. I don't think your father knew, either. Not for sure."

"But . . . he knows now?"

"He does know," she tells him, gently taking his hands in her own. "He knows everything. He's finally found peace, just like you have. *Because* you have. And he's so proud of you, Ralphie."

He wipes hot tears from his eyes. Incredulous, he's still unable to get his head around what she's telling him. Yet, somehow, he doesn't doubt any of it, doesn't doubt her, not even for a second. "Why didn't you tell me any of this, Daria?"

"I was afraid to. I didn't want you to think that she—that I—was any more crazy than you already seemed to think."

"I don't think you're crazy at all. I think you're . . ."

He shakes his head, knowing words can't possibly convey what's in his heart, and hoping she sees it in his face, feels it coming from his heart.

"So . . . you've been here all along?" he asks, when he finds his voice again. "In New York, I mean?"

"I've been here all along. I was in the next room, packing, when I heard your voice in here and I thought I had to be imagining it."

Dread seeps in. He should have known, even now, that some things are too good to be true. "You were . . . packing?"

"I'm moving . . . all the way downtown."

"What?" He holds his breath, not daring to believe it. "Downtown. You mean here . . . in New York?"

She nods, sending a jolt of elation through him. "I decided to stay."

"Forever?"

She opens her mouth. Hesitates. Then she smiles.

"Yes," she says softly. "Forever."

It's too much.

Five minutes ago, finding her at all was a shot in the dark, too much to hope for. Now she's here, forever, and it's just too much to absorb.

Ralphie can't think of a thing to say . . . so he doesn't talk at all. There will be plenty of time for that later.

Right now, he takes Daria into his arms, and as his lips meet hers, he could swear he hears someone whistling a familiar tune.

Five foot two . . . eyes of blue . . .

"I've missed you, Ralphie," she says, and he smiles.

"I've missed you, too," he tells his gal, at last.

Epilogue

Maybe it's not appropriate today, of all days, but Ralphie couldn't help it. He had to stop off for a slice of pizza on the way, buying it from a new place that just opened on Thirty-First Street, near the bottom of the steps from the elevated subway platform.

Of all the things he's learned to live without, a regular supply of hot, cheesy pie fresh from the brick oven is perhaps the most unexpected.

This is pretty good, he acknowledges, walking along Ditmars Boulevard munching a pepperoni slice. But it isn't Big Pizza Pie.

Struck by a bittersweet memory of his father with a wooden pizza paddle in his hand, Ralphie reminds himself that it gets easier every day. But even now, more than two years after Pop's passing, Ralphie misses him.

He always will.

And now he can't even stop in at the pizzeria when he's feeling nostalgic . . . or even just hungry for a slice.

Big Pizza Pie is no more.

When Joey and Nina announced—as Ralphie anticipated—that they were moving to Long Island and Joey was going back into finance, they all tried to figure out a way to keep Pop's business alive.

In the end, though, there was just no way. They all have lives, jobs, families, and homes that aren't right around the corner from the old pizzeria on Ditmars Boulevard.

Sometimes, you just have to let go. Ralphie knows that better than anyone.

Come January, after the new owner finishes his renovations, a Chinese restaurant will open on the site.

Ralphie was dismayed when he found out. "Couldn't someone have just put a new pizzeria in there? What a waste of a brick oven."

But maybe it's better this way. No other pizzeria could ever hold a candle to Big Pizza Pie. No pizza will ever taste as good as Pop's.

Ralphie dumps the last bit of crust and the white fluted paper plate, stained with orange grease, into a garbage can.

It's all right. There are other things in life besides pizza. Far more important things. Things you really can't live without.

Ralphie checks his watch.

Thirty-five minutes to go.

He quickens his pace, hurrying across the intersection at Thirty-Third Street, allowing himself just one fleeting glance down the block.

For all those years, it was home.

Not anymore. The house on Thirty-Third Street is occupied by a new family, and Nina and Joey no longer live next door. Now home is a one-bedroom apartment in Manhattan, a recent upgrade from the little studio.

But home could be anywhere. He knows that, now. Anywhere Daria is.

Today his destination in Astoria isn't Thirty-Third Street. It's Most Precious Mother, the old church where so many Chickalini milestones have come to pass. Christenings . . . communions . . . funerals . . .

Weddings.

Having reached the church, Ralphie sees that the big double wooden doors—decked in tremendous evergreen wreaths for the holiday season—are still closed. There is no white satin runner stretched down the concrete steps of the old brick church. There are no dressed-up guests hurrying to get an aisle seat, and there's no black limo parked out front, bearing a nervous and radiant bride.

Not yet, anyway.

Ralphie checks his watch again. Half hour and counting, and he's arrived right on the nose.

But when he steps into the rectory, he finds them all pacing around like a bunch of agitated penguins: Dominic, Pete, Joey, Timmy . . . and Nino, the best man.

The sight of them in their tuxedos brings an unexpected lump of emotion to Ralphie's throat.

Pop should be here, too.

That thought, however, is immediately tempered by another.

Maybe he is here.

Ralphie smiles.

A year spent with Daria has taught him well.

"Good, you made it." Dominic spots him, looking relieved.

"What, you thought I wasn't going to show up for my own wedding?"

"No, we *knew* you'd show," Joey claps him on the back, "we were just worried you might get stuck on the subway or something."

"You should have let us get you a limo, like we wanted to," Timmy tells him.

"I never take a limo to Queens. I take the subway," Ralphie says reasonably.

"Uncle Ralphie doesn't like change, remember?" That's Nino, cracking on the last word, his voice on its way to becoming an octave lower.

"Yeah, but the thing is, some things have to change," Ralphie says with a smile. "Like your voice. And my being single."

"Yeah, and speaking of change, it's time for you to do that." Pete thrusts a garment bag at him. "Here's your tux. I'll help you with the tie if you want."

Ralphie smiles. "I think I can do it on my own."

"You sure?" Dom asks. "Because maybe you should let us—"

"Guys, I'm positive."

No, Ralphie doesn't need his big brothers—or even his sisters, for that matter—the way he used to. He's perfectly capable of tying a tie on his own. Even living on his own.

But he won't be, after today.

Daria is the one person he really needs in this world. With her beside him—for the rest of his life—he'll be okay. Very okay.

More than okay.

Ralphie checks his watch again, ready to get this show on the road.

Twenty-five minutes later, he finds himself standing with his groomsmen beside the altar.

Daria's friend George was here until late last night arranging dozens of white poinsettias, white candles, and thousands of tiny white lights. Live pine boughs fill the air with the fresh evergreen scent of Christmases past, and Auld Lang Syne.

Another milestone, and as always, joy brings with it a bittersweet longing for what once was, and for what might have been. Ralphie swallows hard, gazing out at the familiar faces before him, thinking longingly of the two beloved ones that are missing.

One by one, his sisters and sisters-in-law make their way down the aisle, trailed by maid of honor Tammy. Ralphie sees her slip a glance toward the pews, seeking—and finding—Jim, a kindly new neighbor in her new Upper West Side apartment building.

Watching them smile at each other, Ralphie wonders fleetingly if there might not be another family wedding in the not-so-distant future.

Then Millicent Millagros shifts organ chords dramatically, heralding the start of the Bridal March. With a creaking and rustling, the congregation stands and turns expectantly toward the back of the church.

Ralphie straightens and takes a deep breath.

It's time.

At last.

Time to forget about what once was, and what might have been.

Time to focus only on what will be, from this day forward.

Time to marry the woman he loves, and begin a new journey together.

Daria appears, all in white, a bouquet of roses shaking hard in her hands. On her father's arm, she makes her way toward Ralphie, her shiny eyes fastened on him alone.

Only when she's almost reached the altar does her gaze waver, but only for a moment as she darts an anxious look at the front pew, just to be sure.

Yes. Her mother made it here on time.

So Ralphie's future mother-in-law isn't the most reliable person in the world. So she isn't anything like his own mother would have been, and maybe she hasn't entirely been the mother Daria deserved.

But Aurora Rivers does love her daughters—that much is clear. Both she and Daria's father managed to get themselves here, to Queens, for the most important day of their daughter's life. That means the world to Daria, so it means the world to Ralphie, as well.

Still, he can't help but glance longingly at the front pew on the opposite side of the aisle.

It's not empty by any means.

The pew is occupied by Aunt Carm, Uncle Cheech, his grandmother, all the nieces and nephews.

And, seeing their exultant smiles, Ralphie knows that whatever he has lost in the course of his life, he has always been well-loved.

He will always be well-loved.

And really, when you come right down to it—what more could a man ask for?

What more does a man need?

Daria has reached his side, more beautiful than he has ever seen her. Her father places her hand in Ralphie's, then steps away.

Giving his fingers a reassuring squeeze as they walk the final steps toward the altar, Daria whispers over the ongoing organ music, "Are you okay?"

"*Now* I am." Ralphie squeezes her fingers back, never wanting to let go, grateful he doesn't have to.

He sees Daria's blue eyes shift from him to the family pew over his shoulder, where his parents would have been—should have been—sitting. Following her gaze, he senses that she knows what he was thinking earlier.

"I just wish—" he begins in a whisper.

"I know. But they are, sweetheart," she says softly, smiling at something—someone—only she can see. "Believe me. They are. They're here."

And for the briefest moment, Ralphie glimpses them there, together: his mother and his father, hand in hand, smiling at him. Of course. This is the wedding of their youngest child, and they wouldn't miss it for the world.

Ralphie blinks away a tear, and the spot is empty again.

Maybe the vision was a mere figment of his imagination.

Maybe it wasn't.

Anything is possible.

Anything at all.

Clasping Daria's hand firmly in his own, Ralphie feels his heart soar to the heavens as Father Tom begins the age-old ceremony, "Dearly beloved, we gather here today to witness the union of this man and this woman . . ."

About the Author

"Wendy Markham" is a pseudonym for *New York Times* bestselling author Wendy Corsi Staub, who has published more than seventy novels under her own name and various pseudonyms. She has won several awards, including two Washington Irving Fiction prizes, two RWA "Ritas," and an RWA-NYC Lifetime Achievement Golden Apple. Wendy was raised in a large, loving Italian-American family in small-town western New York, with both sets of grandparents and dozens of aunts, uncles, and cousins within blocks of her family's cozy Victorian. Upon moving to New York City at twenty-one, she settled for several years in the Astoria neighborhood in Queens, where she felt right at home. Now a happily married mother of two, she lives in a cozy old suburban house filled with framed vintage family photos. In keeping with family tradition, Wendy makes spaghetti with homemade sauce almost every Sunday.

THE DISH

Where authors give you the inside scoop!

♥ ♥ ♥ ♥ ♥ ♥ ♥ ♥ ♥ ♥ ♥ ♥ ♥ ♥ ♥

From the desk of Larissa Ione

Dear Reader,

Growing up, I wanted to be both an author and a doctor. Too bad I suffered from an unfortunate tendency to pass out at the sight of blood. For some reason, doctors fainting in emergency situations is frowned upon. Go figure.

So I concentrated on my first love, writing, but I never got over my fascination with emergency medicine. A few years ago, I swallowed my squeamishness and earned an Emergency Medical Technician certification in order to help me accurately portray the medical heroes and heroines I love so much.

Something else I love is the paranormal, so when I decided to follow my heart and write dark supernatural tales, I still couldn't let go of those hot doctors and paramedics. I wanted them to play a large role in my paranormal novels, but how? How could I combine medicine and the paranormal?

The answer came to me while watching an episode of *Angel*, when my favorite broody vamp got hurt. My poor baby! He needed medical attention, stat. But really, where could demons, vampires, and werewolves go for help?

To a demon ER, of course!

PLEASURE UNBOUND (on sale now), the first in a series of novels set in and around an underworld hospital, is the result of both my interests and my addiction to TV shows such as *ER*, *Grey's Anatomy*, and *Buffy the Vampire Slayer* (and okay, maybe my fangirl crushes on George Clooney, Patrick Dempsey, James Marsters, and Joss Whedon).

In PLEASURE UNBOUND, you'll meet Tayla, a tough, street-savvy demon slayer who lands in a demon hospital under the care of a sexy incubus surgeon named Eidolon. When a sinister plot forces them to work together in order to learn the truth behind a rash of killings that threatens both demons and slayers, Tayla and Eidolon find that the biggest danger of all is to their hearts.

I hope your visit to Underworld General proves to be the most pleasant trip to a hospital you've ever experienced. Happy reading!

Sincerely,

Larissa Ione

www.LarissaIone.com

♥ ♥ ♥ ♥ ♥ ♥ ♥ ♥ ♥ ♥ ♥ ♥ ♥ ♥ ♥ ♥ ♥

From the desk of Wendy Markham

Dear Reader,

When I wrote THE NINE MONTH PLAN five years ago, I never dreamed the book would kick off a series. Then I began hearing from readers who could relate to the loud, loving, laughing Chickalini family and wanted to know whether Nina's siblings would find their own happy endings.

In my latest novel, THAT'S AMORE (on sale now), Ralphie—now a newly orphaned adult in the wake of his father's passing—must come to terms with a broken engagement, the upcoming sale of the only home he's ever known, and an unwanted attraction to a woman who's all wrong for him. What he doesn't know is that Daria Marshall's presence in his life may not be entirely accidental. Daria can see dead people—including a sad-eyed spirit who seems to have led her right to the Chickalini doorstep.

Writing this latest installment was like coming home . . . and not just because I'm so familiar with these characters and their cozy, more-shabby-than-chic Queens rowhouse. The thing is, now that I'm a married mom living in the New York City suburbs, I frequently find myself nostalgic for my own small-town youth almost five hundred miles away—and for the loving extended family that is never far from my thoughts.

Simply put, writing about the Chickalini family brings me back home again.

Raised in the heart of western New York's snow-belt, I had parents who were married at twenty-one, had me at twenty-two, and strolled hand in hand through four-plus decades of marriage. Our sprawling Italian/Sicilian family—dozens of aunts, uncles, and cousins, plus all four grandparents—lived within a few treelined blocks of our Queen Anne Victorian. Family and friends dropped in at all hours and were greeted with coffee and cookies or wine and cheese. We celebrated milestones at Holy Trinity Roman Catholic Church and holidays around noisy, crowded dining room tables laden with food.

There were times when all that togetherness got on my nerves, as it does on Ralphie's. But like Ralphie, Nina, and their siblings, I learned the hard way about the importance of family, and tradition, and holding on—and letting go.

My beautiful young mom was tragically taken from us, much too soon, a few years back. Gone, too, are two of my grandpas, a grandma, cousins, and countless old friends. But they all live on in my heart, and every now and then, they are captured in a fictional glimmer right here, in the pages of the Chickalini family books.

Cent'anni!

Wendy Markham

www.wendymarkham.com

♥ ♥ ♥ ♥ ♥ ♥ ♥ ♥ ♥ ♥ ♥ ♥ ♥ ♥ ♥

From the desk of Shari Anton

Dear Reader,

There's a moment during the writing of a book when an author knows she's telling the story she's supposed to tell. For some authors, this sublime moment of serendipity occurs in the initial stages of plotting. For me, these pleasant, priceless discoveries tend to happen when I'm writing the first draft of my books.

Each time that moment happens, I'm relieved at my good fortune and thankful for a cooperative muse who always seems to know I'm headed in the right direction even when I'm doubtful.

Such a moment happened while I wrote MAGIC IN HIS KISS (on sale now). I knew all along that Rhodri ap Dafydd, the hero of my story, was a talented Welsh bard. But I didn't realize the importance and significance of his music until I wrote the scene where Rhodri is composing a new song on his harp. I knew then what course his life was meant to take, and why he was the perfect hero for Nicole de Leon.

Of course, at that point in the story, Rhodri doesn't realize how important his music will be to Nicole's life work, and Nicole has no idea that because of the magic in his music Rhodri is destined to be her life's partner. At that point in the story, they aren't even sure they like each other! But, of course, they are bound together by the music, by destiny, and by love.

It's always fun to watch a story unfold. An author sometimes blindly follows the lives of the characters to discover where they're going and why, just as a reader keeps turning the pages of a good story to learn what happens next. The experience for both of us can be (dare I say it) magical!

Enjoy!

Shari Anton

www.sharianton.com

Want to know more about romances at Grand Central Publishing and Forever? Get the scoop online!

GRAND CENTRAL PUBLISHING'S ROMANCE HOMEPAGE

Visit us at www.hachettebookgroupusa.com/romance for all the latest news, reviews, and chapter excerpts!

NEW AND UPCOMING TITLES

Each month we feature our new titles and reader favorites.

CONTESTS AND GIVEAWAYS

We give away galleys, autographed copies, and all kinds of fun stuff.

AUTHOR INFO

You'll find bios, articles, and links to personal websites for all your favorite authors—and so much more!

THE BUZZ

Sign up for our monthly romance newsletter, and be the first to read all about it!